# ONCE UPON A BRIDE

# ONCE UPON A BRIDE

## JEAN STONE

BANTAM BOOKS

ONCE UPON A BRIDE
A Bantam Book

Published by
Bantam Dell
A Division of Random House, Inc.
New York, New York

Bantam Books and the rooster colophon are registered trademarks of
Random House, Inc.

ISBN  0-7394-5079-4

Printed in the United States of America

To my sister, Joan,
who taught me the magic
of make-believe.

# Once Upon a Bride

# PROLOGUE

How well do you think you understand women?" John Benson asked the question as if it had an easy answer.

Andrew Kennedy laughed. He sipped his martini and leveled his eyes on his long-ago mentor, now the hard-driving editor of *Buzz* magazine, the sexy male counterpart to *Cosmo* and *Elle*, the *GQ* with soul, the *Playboy* with intellect.

"About as well as any forty-two-year-old, unattached male," he replied.

John raised his gray-white eyebrows. "Perfect," he said. "I'd do it myself, but my wife might object." It was rumored—had been rumored for years—that John's marriage was, at best, shaky, his string of "other women" as long as the female queue at a Springsteen concert.

Andrew's gaze fell to the provocative covers of the

latest *Buzz* issues splayed across the large glass cocktail table. He supposed he was being set up, that he was being recruited for something to which he'd have to say no.

With a slow, cautious smile, he let his eyes wander the spacious, thirty-fourth-floor office, out the window past Rockefeller Plaza and the NBC headquarters ("30 Rock" the media called it), over the treetops of Central Park. He did not miss the city. After a startling divorce that left him with the baffling chore of raising his then five-, now eleven-year-old daughter, he'd found solace in the Berkshire Hills of Massachusetts, trading his subway tokens for an old Volvo, his 73rd Street apartment for a cottage with a yard, and high-pressure journalism for an assistant professorship at Winston College.

He was not unhappy.

And yet, when John had called and asked Andrew to come to New York and check out his new office and his new job, Andrew had not hesitated.

He sipped his drink. The gin was deliciously reminiscent of late nights and warm sheets and Patty. He shifted on the art deco, black leather chair. "Okay, John," he said. "What's this about?"

The older man cleared his throat. He circled the rim of his glass with a large, manicured fingertip. "*Buzz* is in trouble. They hired me to give it a quick boost."

Andrew listened because John was his friend, had been his friend, despite the fact he was twenty years older and actually thrived on the lifestyle that Andrew had grown to detest.

"Women's magazines feature columns about men," John continued, "how we think, what we want, that kind of crap. I think *Buzz* could shake things up with a high-voltage column about women. Written, of course, by a man."

"Which would increase circulation."

"And much needed ad dollars."

Andrew laughed again. "I'm a journalist, John. Not Ann Landers. Or that *Sex and the City* girl, Carrie What's-Her-Name." He did not want to admit that his recent track record hardly qualified him. John, after all, did not know that Andrew was now a content bachelor father, that too many misshaped relationships had turned him off from even joining a singles club or enrolling in *lovemates.com*.

"I'll double your teaching salary," John said.

"If I wanted money I'd have kept my job at *The Edge*." It had been entertainment television disguised as broadcast journalism, and Andrew had been relieved when he'd finally quit. "Besides, the magazine can't afford me if it's in trouble."

"You'd be an investment, Andrew. A sure thing."

Andrew toyed with his drink. "What's the catch?" he asked, because there always was one.

"I need the first installment fast. The September issue goes on the stands in five weeks."

"I'm sort of busy right now."

"It's summer. School's out."

"I'll be teaching three courses in the fall. And I'm the faculty advisor for the college newspaper."

"I can arrange a sabbatical. You can lie. Say you've decided to work on your doctorate."

Andrew studied the olive swimming in his glass. He had to admit that lately there had been moments when he wondered if his life had become too academic, if he spent

too many hours in the quiet of libraries with too many
dusty old books. But did he want the life he'd once had?
Shaking his head, Andrew said, "There are plenty of writ-
ers in the city, John. I can't move back. Cassie loves the
Berkshires."

"I don't want you here. I want you out there, in the
trenches. *Buzz* is for men who live in Kansas and Idaho
and even the Berkshires. The women you write about
should be from there, too. Not city-slick women that
men can't relate to."

Andrew swirled the gin. Not city-slick women like
Patty, who had so slickly broken his heart.

"I want to title the column 'Real Women.' "

"And you're convinced I can do it?"

"You're a hell of a writer, Andrew. My guess is that
women think you're not bad to look at. You should have
no trouble going under cover, so to speak. Getting to the
core of their hearts and their minds."

"And then telling all?"

John raised his glass. "Precisely," he said.

If the idea had come from anyone but John Benson,
Andrew would not have believed it could work. "How do
you propose I find these 'real women'?"

"The Andrew David I knew was always inventive."

Andrew sighed. "It's Andrew David *Kennedy* again."
He had reattached his last name after he'd stepped out of
the limelight.

"It doesn't matter," John said. "For this assignment
you'll be incognito. Sign on with *Buzz* for a year?" He
had more class than to mention that Andrew owed him,
that it had been John who'd secured Andrew the post at
Winston College, the man's alma mater, the place where

he'd endowed a chair back in the late eighties before the media world splintered into shards of financial competition. It had been John who had saved Andrew's sanity, if not his life.

Besides, Andrew thought, closing his eyes, Cassie's riding lessons had become expensive. He could use a new car and a new roof on the cottage. And more money would mean he could take Cassie to Australia to visit her mother. He opened his eyes. "How about six months?"

John reached over and shook Andrew's hand. And Andrew could not help but wonder what he had agreed to, and where in God's name he should start.

# 1

That's the ugliest wedding gown I've ever seen," Sarah said. She leaned back in her chair, her long black hair swaying with her movement, her dark eyes blinking with acerbity. "I can't wait to see what she's picked out for us."

Jo wanted to agree, but didn't dare. Elaine was only in the ladies' room and could return any moment. Sarah was right, however, the gown was horrible.

Lily shook her head, her short blond curls bouncing like little clouds of milkweed puffs against her pink cheeks. "We can't let her do it," she whispered in horror as she plucked the bridal magazine from the table at Le Fusion, the latest boutique restaurant in the small New England town that had once been quaint but was now tourist-choked. "She never had great taste in college. I guess that hasn't changed in all these years." She turned to Jo. "Josephine?" she asked as if awaiting confirmation.

Reaching for her wineglass, Jo glanced over at the picture of white satin bouffant with pink and blue organza roses set into excessive ruffles of tulle. The gown looked foolish, even on the angelic, eighteen-year-old model. On over-forty Elaine, it would look asinine.

Across the restaurant, Elaine emerged from the ladies' room. Her lavender polyester pants were too short, her eighties-style hair was dyed too brown and was too big. Yet Elaine marched along with happy steps, nodding and smiling as she passed the other luncheoning ladies who wore golf skorts and straw hats and had shopping bags from Ann Taylor and Lladró and Ralph Lauren. When Elaine reached her former college roommates, the women she'd selected as her bridesmaids for her "second-time around," she dropped onto her chair with relief.

"Mercy," she said, fanning herself lightly. "I'm not used to drinking in the middle of the day." She smoothed the front of the pink-and-lavender-flowered big shirt, then adjusted her double-strand necklace of red and pink beads and the large dangle earrings that matched. Sort of.

Jo's eyes moved from flighty, elflike Lily to pensive, statuesque Sarah, extremes in looks and personalities, right and left wing, while Jo kept to the middle, with Elaine a few feet behind. Now Lily and Sarah expected Jo to break the news to Elaine. As the leader in the middle, it had always been Jo's role to be the obligatory mediator, the one with the most sense. Two decades apparently hadn't changed that, either. She sipped her wine. "Elaine, honey," she said gently, "have you thought about getting professional help?"

Sarah nearly spit her wine across the table.

Lily's pink lips peeled back in a grimace, revealing professionally whitened, perfectly straight teeth.

Jo smiled. "For the wedding," she continued. "Someone like a wedding planner."

She might have said that one of Elaine's three kids had been arrested on drug-trafficking charges, given the bewildered look Elaine wore on her face. Then Elaine's eyes fell to the magazine that Lily still clutched. A wide grin appeared. "It's the white, isn't it? You think I shouldn't wear white!" She laughed a jovial laugh, then drank more of the wine she wasn't used to drinking in the middle of the day. "Well, this might surprise you, but I read that white no longer is a symbol of virginity. It now stands for 'joy.' I guess they had to change it because there are no virgins left in the world."

She drank again. No one laughed.

Jo leaned forward. "It's not the white, Elaine. It's the flowers. And the ruffles. And the, well, the *little girl* look. I know it's not fair. But even though there are tons of second and even third weddings, it still seems that all the books and magazines—and most of the fashions—are geared to twenty-year-olds." She hoped she'd made her point without hurting Elaine's feelings.

Elaine's wine-pinkened cheeks slowly darkened to red. Even her Miss Clairol-ed hair seemed to deepen a shade. She snatched the magazine from Lily's hands. "I'm not entitled to the wedding of my dreams just because I'm over forty?" She didn't have to mention that she'd been cheated out of a wedding when she'd married Lloyd because they'd still been in college and Elaine had been pregnant, so they'd married in haste at the town hall. The redness abated and fat tears slid down her cheeks.

Lily produced a clean lace hankie from her Asprey purse.

Elaine waved it away, then reached into her crocheted tote bag and located a travel pack of Kleenex. She blew her nose loudly.

The waitress appeared bearing three oriental chicken salads with dressing on the side, and a veggie platter for Sarah.

"Maybe we can help," Jo suggested once the waitress had left. "After all, as your bridesmaids, we have a vested interest." She grinned and patted Elaine's hand. "It's a little more than three months until the wedding, right?"

"I didn't want to wait," she said apologetically.

"Three months is acceptable," Lily interjected. "Only first-time brides need a year or more to plan."

Lily, of course, would know.

"Then we will do it in three months," Jo said. "Lainey, let us be your wedding planners."

Elaine blinked. "My 'wedding planners'? But you live in Boston."

Jo cleared her throat. "Actually, I've been thinking I might come back for a while. My mother's getting older . . . I want to be sure she can still live on her own." She tried to sound casual and hoped the others didn't notice the tremor that had sneaked into her voice.

"You might come back to West Hope?" Elaine asked. "But what about your business? What about your career?"

Despite a degree in elementary education, Elaine had only taught fourth grade between her second and third kids, then gave up on working altogether. For the past several years she volunteered part-time at the library and served on countless town boards, but as far as Jo knew, Elaine had no interest in business or careers, certainly not Jo's.

Folding her hands, Jo forced her best smile. "I've been thinking about branching out. The Berkshires could use a strong public relations firm. Attractions have grown. Tourism has escalated. We'll soon outpace any New England venue except the Cape and islands." All of which had little to do with Jo's recent debate with herself about moving back. The truth was, her life was no longer the same, and "home" was what now seemed safe. The others, however, did not need to know that. "But I haven't decided. In the meantime," she added quickly, "planning your wedding would be fun." She turned to Sarah. "You're so creative, Sarah. If I organize the wedding, maybe you can make it magical. Elaine's dream come true."

"I design jewelry," Sarah protested. "Not wedding dresses and reception halls."

Elaine lowered her eyes.

Sarah shifted on her chair. "Well," she added, "I suppose I could try."

Lily clapped her hands. "And I'll pay!" she exclaimed.

All eyes turned to Lily. Elaine broke the stunned silence. "But you live in New York."

"Don't be silly," Lily said, dismissing Elaine's comment. "It's a three-hour train ride from Manhattan. It isn't Timbuktu. Besides, it would be such a hoot to be together again! And how better to squander a chunk of Reginald's money if not with my friends?" Lily had recently become a widow when her much older, wickedly wealthy husband had sadly succumbed, leaving his beloved wife, Lily, (and his "beastly old sister, Antonia") a portfolio that probably bulged with more stocks and bonds than Lily could count. She laughed and said, "Think of it as a loan you won't have to repay. Think of it as your second chance." She raised her glass in toast to poor, dead Reginald.

Elaine gasped. "You mean it."

Sarah nodded. "She means it."

Jo held up her glass. "To second chances," she said, and they *clink*ed all around. Jo had little idea what had just happened. But for the first time in months, her spirits had lifted and she thought that maybe her life wasn't over after all.


She had been named "Most Likely to Succeed" by her high-school class. Josephine "Jo" Lyons had also been the captain of the debating team, the president of the student council, and the editor of the yearbook. She had been those things once. Now she was just a middle-aged woman sitting on the edge of the bed in her childhood home, wondering how it had happened that life had come full circle, with Elaine getting married while Jo was not, nor was Lily (perhaps to her chagrin), nor was Sarah, who no doubt preferred it that way.

They had always been different, the Winston College roommates. Lily said they were friends because of that, because they never were attracted to the same types of men, so there was no competition.

Jo had been the studious townie who had saved her

money from waitressing during tourist season so she could live on campus and feel she'd left town, as if at last her life could begin. Jo had been attracted only to one man, Brian Forbes, who was tall and handsome, gregarious and a bit of a bad boy. He had been like her father, she supposed.

Elaine had been the domestic diva wanna-be (despite her dubious taste) long before such a label had been coined by a questionable marketing guru who might have had close ties to Martha Stewart or Pottery Barn. Though Elaine had come from Upstate New York, she and Lloyd had settled in West Hope because his family was there and she'd been embarrassed by the "premature" baby and all. Although Lloyd had gone to law school, Jo had thought of him as rough around the West Hope edges, a small-town boy without the polish, destined for a mediocre life.

Lily had been the orphan raised by a wildly eccentric, rich aunt. A fun-loving, cheerful city girl, Lily knew all the latest fads—like shawls and boots and the resurgence of miniskirts—long before West Hope got wind of them. Lily had been attracted to lots of men, mostly older, mostly wealthy, mostly those who doted on her with great sincerity.

Sarah had been the exotic roommate, having traveled from the West, a Native American with a mysterious ancestry that she'd turned her back on. She'd remained in the Berkshires, in a town even smaller than West Hope, deep in the woods. She never shared much about the men she dated in college, or about the now-famous musician with whom she'd shared her life for many years. He, too, kept their private life private.

Jo's mother used to say she could tell the difference between the roommates by the way they walked. Marion said that even with her eyes closed, she knew that Lily had the light steps of a ballerina; Sarah, the long strides of a slow yet deliberate woman; and Elaine, the short, clipped gait of a majorette. Marion knew Jo's steps, of course, because she was her daughter. She often described them to the others as steady and sincere, if not always heading in the right direction.

Throughout the years, it had been Elaine who had kept the friends together. It had been her idea to meet in New York City each year in the fall for a weekend of girl stuff. New York, after all, was the best place to shop and to eat and to go to the theater. And to laugh. Despite all their differences, they always loved to laugh.

"Third weekend in September," Elaine announced every year, first by mail, then by phone calls, now by e-mail, though Jo suspected none of them needed a reminder.

Other than that, their meetings had been few. Lily's weddings. The birth of Sarah's son. The death of Elaine's mother. An occasional lunch or a quick "Hello" when Jo was in West Hope visiting her mother.

And now, another wedding, a second for Elaine, while Jo had not yet had a first. She'd been too busy being mature, responsible, dependable. Never a carefree kid.

Jo lay back on her bed now and stared up at the ceiling.

"Josephine!" she could almost hear her mother call. "Get a move on. Time's a-wastin'."

Time was always "a-wastin'" according to Marion Lyons, whether it was a school day or a Saturday or time for church.

"As pretty as your mother," Ted, the butcher, said on Thursdays when Jo stopped by to pick up hamburg and flank steak and pounded veal chops for the week while her mother was at work as the clerk at the town hall.

"Such a smart girl," Mrs. Kingsley at the bookstore always commented with a knowing nod when Jo bought one of many books.

"A wonderful sermon," the congregation said, one after another, each month when Jo delivered the "children's" message from the purple-draped pulpit.

How Jo had hated West Hope.

She turned onto her side now and picked at the chenille dots that covered the twin bedspread, the same bedspread that had been there since the sixties and seventies, yet, unlike her, did not seem to have aged. How many nights had she picked at these same dots, dreaming of the day she'd escape the claustrophobic town and its smothering people for a real life of her own?

She had escaped, of course. The "Most Likely to Succeed" had succeeded for a time, in the big city, Boston, where she had a fancy condominium and a to-die-for wardrobe and men, so many men, who loved her, but Jo Lyons was too busy succeeding to bother to love them back.

She had succeeded, and then she lost everything, though she hadn't yet admitted that to her mother, to her friends, or, most of all, to West Hope.

And now Jo had a choice.

The closing on her fancy condo was next week; her movers awaited word as to where her worldly possessions should be shipped; the brass nameplate had been removed from the Back Bay office door: *JOSEPHINE LYONS*

*AND ASSOCIATES, PUBLIC RELATIONS SPECIALISTS.* The "associates" were gone, the office was, too.

She could stay in the city, in a crowded apartment like the one where she'd started out, in a dark office building with no windows and no clients, and now with a reputation to repair and a bruised heart to mend.

Or she could go home. She could move back to West Hope, open a new office, and capitalize on the Berkshires' tourism as she had suggested. She could help plan Elaine's wedding; she could stay a year, maybe two, until her pain had subsided, until her strength had returned.

"Josephine!" her mother called up the narrow, steep stairs. This time the voice was not a memory. It belonged to the robust woman who was just past seventy and who hardly needed Jo's help to get through her busy days and her bingo-playing nights.

# 2

It's a two-bedroom apartment on Shannon Drive," Jo said aloud as she read the Sunday classifieds. She acted as if she'd made the decision to return to West Hope, which she had not. She was merely trying it out to see how it felt.

"There's plenty of room for you right here," Marion Lyons said. They were seated at the kitchen table with hot tea and fresh strawberry muffins made with berries picked yesterday at the Peases' old farm. "Your room is exactly as you left it."

"I'm not, though, Mother. I am twenty years older. I need my space. I have things that need space."

"You won't need anything that's not right here."

Jo laughed. "Mother, one-tenth of my clothes would not fit inside that old bedroom closet."

"You won't need that many clothes. You won't be in Boston anymore."

The words shouldn't have stung, yet they did. Jo folded the paper. Her gaze drifted out the window to three birdfeeders and an indoor/outdoor thermometer that hadn't worked in years. "If I decide to move back, I'd like to know what's available."

"That apartment is in one of those brick buildings where secretaries live." Her mother hissed the word "secretaries" through teeth that she often announced were her own, not plastic.

"You were a secretary, Mother."

"And I worked hard to be sure you didn't have to live in one of those places. To be sure you'd live in a house like a respectable girl."

Jo smiled at her mother who was in her Sunday best, as if there still were such a thing. She wondered if Ted the Butcher still thought Marion was pretty, and if, someday, Jo would have the same white hair that now gently cupped her mother's face, the same wide, full lips that had not, as yet, turned pencil-thin, the same green eyes that had not, as yet, faded with the light of too many summers and too many winters and too much of everything in between. "I am respectable, Mother. You certainly saw to that."

"Then if you insist on your own place, why not buy one of those new condominiums out by Tanglewood? Lorna McCarthy's son and wife moved out there. He's in insurance. He does quite well, too."

Jo set down the paper. "I told you, Mother, I don't want another big place. The condo in Boston was too much upkeep for me." She stood up. "I think I'll get dressed and drive over to look at the apartment."

"No church this morning?" Marion called after her.

"I'll leave that to you," Jo replied. "Say a prayer that the secretaries' building has lots of closet space."

There was no Jacuzzi in the master (and only) bath. There was no fireplace in the living room, no wide glass terrace that framed the skyline of the city. There was only a small balcony next to an identical one, where a neighbor sat on a white plastic chair smoking a cigarette, and a partial view of the hills that were dressed in summer green. Jo nodded at the neighbor, then went back inside.

"There's a stackable washer and dryer here," the agent said, opening what looked like a closet door.

Jo had not thought about that. She had been sending her laundry out for so many years, it had not occurred to her that now she'd be doing her own laundry and cleaning and shopping and God-knew-what again.

"Does the apartment come with a garage?" she asked.

"There's a garage in the basement. Each resident is assigned a space."

Jo nodded and moved back into the kitchen. It was small but sufficient, with old-fashioned oak cabinets and an enamel sink. The step down into the living room reminded Jo of the old *Dick Van Dyke Show*, when he'd trip over the ottoman and sprawl on the floor. But there wouldn't be much room to sprawl: no more than half of Jo's furniture would fit in the room. She supposed she could store the rest.

Biting her lower lip, she thought about the expense.

She'd sold her BMW and bought a Honda; the cash that was left over would support her for a while. Until she regained her balance and rebuilt her life. Until she could breathe again.

Jo told the woman she'd have to think about the apartment. Then, with a long, deep sigh, she returned to her car, wishing she could fast-forward a year, when surely she'd have made it from point A to point B, when surely she'd know if home was Boston or West Hope, when surely she'd know what she was going to do for the rest of her life.

When surely she'd no longer flinch when she heard Brian's name.

Lily called later that afternoon.

"I thought you'd be back in Manhattan by now," Jo said.

"No," Lily replied. "I couldn't resist renting a car and spending the night at the Route 7." She meant the Route 7 Motor Lodge. It was where the Winston College underclasses had partied, the underage drinkers; it was where they had dabbled with sex and with pot.

"Dear God," Jo said. "Is that place still standing?"

"Still with the same orange shag rug on the floor. Still with the smell of stale beer."

"Well," Jo replied, "I'm sure it's a refreshing change from your Park Avenue penthouse."

Lily giggled. "Oh, quite! And it helped me come up with a fabulous idea."

"The Route 7 inspired you? Why does that frighten me?"

"Stop it, stop it! I'm serious!" She was excited, almost breathless. "At first I thought I should use some of Reginald's money as a gift to the college. You know, to do something honorable."

Jo realized then how much she'd missed Lily, how much her friend's unjaded view of love and of life had brought unexpected fun to Jo's studious world. She couldn't resist saying, "You hated school, Lily."

Lily filled her small lungs, then let out a sigh. "I know. I had a memory lapse, but that's over now. I have a better idea." A flurry of static told Jo that Lily was on her cell phone. "A business," Jo thought she heard her friend say.

"Did you say 'a business'?"

"I sure did."

"Have you been drinking wine again with Sarah and Elaine?"

"I mean it! I want to open a wedding-planning business. Right here in West Hope."

More static. More short breaths.

Then, "Second weddings!" Lily cried above the noise. "Encore marriages!" She banged her phone against something. The static stopped. "Can you hear me, Jo?"

Yes, Jo could hear her.

"Think about it, Jo. First weddings are for those fanciful starter marriages. No one—*no one*—gets married just once anymore. But what about second-wedding etiquette? Should it be different? The gowns, the ceremonies, the gifts, and—oh, my—the *relatives*? Oh, Jo, don't you see? Second weddings are a market just waiting for someone like us to manage. And West Hope is perfect. You said yourself that the tourism is terrific. We could promote the Berkshires as a destination for weddings, with nearby reception venues like Tanglewood and The Mount . . ."

"Whoa, slow down!" Jo wedged in her words. "Lily," she said, "you don't want a business. You've never even worked."

"Don't be a poop, Josephine. This could be fun. We could get a showroom and everything. We could have lots of respect in this town. We're Winston grads, after all."

Static interrupted again. Or perhaps it was the ghosts of other alumnae cheering Lily on.

Jo ran her fingers through her hair, which was still taupe, not yet white like her mother's. She thought about each of Lily's three whimsical weddings, when the bride had been in her center stage glory, and the groom had looked delighted, if not slightly bewildered. It was hard to imagine Lily with a head for, or an interest in, the sensibilities of business. "Lily," Jo said, "business isn't a game. Besides, I'm not even sure if I want to come . . . back." She purposely said "back" and not "home," because it made West Hope seem more detached, less important. "I think it's great if we help Elaine plan her wedding, but none of us really knows what we're doing. How on earth could we open a business?"

There was a long pause. Then Lily said, "We can learn, Jo. For one thing, I've been to tons of weddings. Elegant, fabulous, outlandish weddings. Here, there, everywhere in the world. I'm sure I've picked up a tidbit or two."

It was Jo's turn to pause. "You really *are* serious."

"Completely." She sounded so matter-of-fact, so un-Lily-like. "Since Reginald died, I've had nothing to do except talk to my attorneys and his beastly old sister. My life was Reginald's. His friends, his parties, his favorite places to travel. I want my own life now." Then her light heart returned and she giggled in the way that only Lily giggled. "At least until I find another man."

*Another man.* Apparently Lily still believed that true love conquered all.

"I'm going to talk to Sarah," Lily continued. "She's so creative, Jo. Imagine the grand ideas she could come up with!"

"Sarah said it herself, Lily. She designs jewelry, not banquets for three hundred."

"Oh, it's all the same. Besides, I think she won't say no to a change. Between you and me, I think her musician-boyfriend is on the road way too often and I think our Sarah gets a little lonely."

Jo shook her head. When it came to Lily, all trials and tribulations came down to a man.

"Elaine's wedding can be our first," Lily continued. "We can build our portfolio with the photos. And it will help us learn about vendors and service people to connect with, that sort of thing. Come on, Jo. Wouldn't it be more fun than dreary old public relations? Wouldn't if be fun to be together again?"

"Oh, Lily, I don't know . . ."

"Please, please? You're so successful, and you know all about business. As long as you're thinking of coming back to West Hope, wouldn't it be perfect? Oh, Jo, wouldn't it be grand?"

Static again crowded the line.

Jo closed her eyes and wondered if Lily's idea might just be the way from point A to point B.

# 3

I am a forty-two-year-old man who knows nothing more—or less—about women than any of you. I have had my share of lust and no-lust relationships, one-night stands, two-year stands, relationships that were too short, and some that were too long. Sometimes I look at my eleven-year-old daughter and realize I don't even understand her: why she now only pretends that she wants to go fishing with her dad when she used to love it. (I wonder how much longer it will be before she simply says, "No thanks.")

And so my mission is for all of us: to root out the essence of this thing called "woman" so that we may learn, if not master, the artful games they play, and unearth our own answers as to why it is, despite our Venus/Mars, yin/yang differences, we still remain attracted, like a moth to flame, a bee to pollen, and, yes, a fly to shit.

Are we really so

*self-centered,*
*shallow, and*
*manipulative,*
*that it's only about sex?*

Andrew leaned back in the old oak chair at the antique Yankee dining-room table in his cozy cottage. He closed the lid of his new silver-blue, shiny laptop and wondered if *Buzz* had circulation in Australia, and if so, would Patty figure out that this column was his?

# 4

♥

While Lily busied herself looking for a shop that would showcase their "business," Jo began making the endless tangle of calls necessary before the final closing of her condo: the phone company, the electric company, cable. And the most difficult, to the elderly president of the condominium association, who had thrown her annual red-and-white Valentine's ball to which Jo and Brian had gone.

"I haven't seen you and that handsome man of yours in some time," the woman said.

"Are you moving to New York?"

"Are you tying the knot?"

"Oh, it's so wonderful to see young people so much in love."

Jo spent the rest of that day lying on the chenille bedspread, tears leaking from the corners of her eyes.

Two days later, when Jo was at the kitchen table trying to decipher all the small print, Lily called. "I've found a to-die-for storefront in the center of town," she squealed. "It even has an adorable apartment upstairs for me, which will be easier than the commute! But we have to act fast, because someone else wants it." Jo recognized a real estate agent's ploy, but was stopped from speaking up when Lily quickly added, "Oh, Jo, this is the best time I've had in years."

"I'll meet you in half an hour," Jo reluctantly agreed, then jotted down the Main Street address. She hung up the phone and looked at the mess of papers on the table. Her attorney had scheduled the closing. Thank God, she'd break even after paying back the first mortgage and the second and the third. She tried not to think about the money she had lost, at how much Brian had cost her. She tried only to focus on moving forward, moving on.

Thank God her mother had been busy at the church that week, setting up for the rummage sale that always brought in big bucks from the Yuppie tourists who thought old New England stuff was somehow something to be treasured. Thank God Marion did not have to witness her daughter's fall from grace, financial and otherwise.

"It just didn't work out, Mom," Jo had explained to Marion the first night she'd come home and the two sat at the same table where they'd shared their troubles as far back as Jo could remember, as far back as when Jo's father had run off with Doris Haines, the science teacher at the junior high, as far back as when Jo had her first date with Brian Forbes, the West Hope football star who was two years ahead of Jo in school, and, her mother warned her, was only looking for "one thing."

He didn't get that thing that year. Not until the next year, when she was a junior and he was working at his father's antiques store and was supposedly making up his mind whether he'd "bother" with college.

"He's not as smart as you are," her mother had warned more than once, as if that should matter. He'd been smart enough to know that Jo was madly in love with him; he'd been smart enough to know that once they'd "done it" on a Sunday night in the back room of the antiques store when everything was locked up tight and the only light was from a lamp that had come from Tiffany's that Brian covered with a thin red lace cloth—well, he'd been smart enough to know that Josephine Lyons would be his forever.

They never did get married, though.

Her mother said that people commented on the pair, saying that Jo kept Brian away from pranks and out of trouble. They said Brian never would have finished college if it weren't for Jo, that he would have killed himself on that motorcycle he rarely drove because Marion had forbidden Jo to ride on the back of it. They said that Brian was a lot like Jo's father, a good-time boy with charm and flash, but not a lot of sense.

Jo hadn't cared what anyone said. Those who talked didn't know how much Brian loved her. How much he needed her; how much she needed him.

At least, it had seemed that way.

When Jo was in her last year of college, Brian and his older brother, Frank, had an argument, something about the family business. Brian announced that he was leaving town. He said he might go up to Montreal to work in a logging camp.

She'd thought it was a joke. But one week later Brian, indeed, was gone, and Jo was left to face final exams alone, and an uncertain future. Her mother said she should be glad he hadn't married her and left her the way Sam Lyons had left them.

*Enough*, she thought now and scooped up the mortgage papers and utility bills from the table. She stuffed them into a brown paper accordion file that she'd lugged around for weeks. Her hand brushed the edge of the large white envelope tucked in the back. She hesitated, then quickly withdrew her hand and snapped the elastic tie around the file. She did not need to look in the white envelope again. She did not need to examine, for the hundredth or the thousandth or the millionth time, copies of the documents she'd filed with the Boston Police, Missing Persons Bureau.

Scrawling a quick note for her mother, the way she'd done in high school, Jo raced out the back door, jumped into her Honda, and headed for town.


None of her old roommates knew that Jo and Brian had gotten back together. They no doubt would remember Brian's name, the boy Jo had known most of her life, the townie like she was.

But they would not remember that he'd gone off to Montreal, that he'd broken her heart, that she'd been devastated and had briefly considered suicide when she'd learned that, on top of everything, she was pregnant with his child. They would not have remembered, because Jo had never told them. She'd simply said they'd broken up and she wanted to move to Boston, anyway. Josephine Lyons, the Most Likely to Succeed, who, by age twenty-two, had succeeded only in having the two men she'd adored abandon her: first, her father, then the father of her baby.

The townsfolk had been right: Brian had been a lot like Jo's father. Maybe Jo had hoped she could hold on to the boy's love because she'd lost the man's. In any case, her love had simply not been enough.

Surely Lily had not remembered the details of Jo's loss, or known the depth of Jo's pain. If Lily had remembered, she never would have chosen a storefront that sat squarely between Sweeties, the town candy shop, and a store with a shingle that read ANTIQUES AND SUCH. FRANK FORBES, PROPRIETOR.

Frank Forbes. Brian's brother.

Jo made a U-turn in the middle of Main Street, and stepped on the accelerator without looking back.


"An abortion?" Marion had barked as the kitchen chair scraped the linoleum and she stood up in anger. "No! I forbid it!"

The sight and the sound and the emotion of it all on that long-ago day were as clear to Jo as if they'd happened yesterday.

She sat on a bench in a small park on the shoreline of Laurel Lake now. She remembered going there as a kid to wade in the cool, crystal water, to sit on the rocks and fish for trout with her grandmother, to languish in the peace. It had been long before the picnic tables and the trash bins and tourist comfort stations were installed, long before the lake was encircled by beautiful resorts and million-dollar homes. It had been long before Jo Lyons would have thought she'd wind up pregnant and unmarried, with nowhere to go.

It had been a mistake to tell Marion.

"Mother," she'd said. "What do you want me to do? Brian is gone and I'm alone."

"You're not alone, Josephine. You have me."

"And you have your friends and your job and your church. You have West Hope, Mother. What will everyone say when your daughter becomes a single mother?"

Marion did not answer. She sat down again.

"Don't you see, Mom? It's the only way. I can't have a baby. If I do, I'll be stuck here in West Hope where everyone will talk about me and about my baby. And they'll talk about Brian, too."

"You could make him come back."

Jo shook her head. "I don't know where he is."

"Then I'll find him myself," Marion said.

And that was the first time Jo remembered getting angry with her mother. "If I thought you'd be such a problem I wouldn't have told you," she shouted. "You will NOT tell Brian and you will NOT tell anyone. If you do, I will never speak to you again."

She couldn't admit—even to herself—that she wouldn't survive being rejected by Brian the way her mother had been rejected by her father.

The next morning Jo left for Boston. She had the abortion the following week in a brightly lit clinic that was as cold as the ice on Laurel Lake in winter. She had been alone, without her mother, without even a friend, in a city that seemed as far from West Hope as if she'd landed on the moon.

And now there she was, sitting by the water, knowing if she left West Hope, this time it would be for good. She'd have to tell Lily she couldn't work with them, that something had come up—business, of course.

She'd have to say, "Sorry," then wish them luck. She'd tell them she'd see them in the fall, the third weekend in September, unless they were so angry with her that they changed their tradition.

She'd have to miss out on the fun. But it would be more rational than working in a shop next to Brian's brother.

Then Jo thought of Elaine, who managed to go on despite that she'd been humiliated by an unfaithful husband in a town that loved to talk. Elaine, like Jo's mother, had held her aching head high.

Did Jo have that kind of courage?

Could she reveal that Brian was missing? Could she bear it if people, like the police—and like herself in her most secret heart—assumed he'd left of his own free will, that he'd simply, boldly, utterly ditched her?

Would Jo have the strength to argue they were wrong, that he must have been kidnapped, killed, or was suffering amnesia? On her best days, even Jo thought those suppositions were absurd. But it hurt less to believe them.

His brother Frank might know.

Did she dare risk finding out?

Jo stood up and took a last look at the lake, a last breath of the cool air. Then she walked back to her car, and wondered why facing the truth was often so much scarier than living with the unknown.

The clapboard shops had been freshly painted, mostly in white with black or deep green shutters, many with window boxes bearing plump red geraniums, some still adorned with the red, white, and blue buntings of last week's Fourth of July. A parking lot behind the string of shops looked newly expanded, no doubt to accommodate the swell of summer people who began their mornings with hearty bed-and-breakfast fare, then went into town to stroll off a few calories and spend more than a few dollars.

Jo parked and got out of her Honda with renewed determination. She told herself it was a good time to start a business in West Hope: The economy there was getting stronger. She told herself she wouldn't obsess about Brian or make a fool of herself in front of Frank, no matter what he told her or how much he knew.

She would hold her head high like her mother, like Elaine. She would not lose her dignity over a mere man.

Averting her eyes from the back door of Antiques and Such, Jo opened the latch on the door next to it. She stepped into a large, dark room that was cluttered with heaps of cardboard boxes and had a strong scent of sandalwood. She sneezed. Then she called out to Lily.

A door across the room opened. "Josephine! Is that you?" Lily stood in the doorway, her small frame silhouetted by the light that seeped in from the street. "Isn't it divine?"

Jo laughed. "No. It's dark. And it stinks in here."

"Oh, stop. Wait until you see."

Jo heard a *snap*, then the room was lit. Amid the boxes was more dust than Jo had ever seen except at her Aunt

Amanda's, who'd been a hermit for thirty years until she died at ninety-eight or ninety-nine.

"God," she said. The room was about a thousand square feet of mess.

"We'll find someone to get rid of this stuff," Lily said, waving her hand as if dismissing little kids from school. "Look beyond it, Jo. It will be our workroom. And our storeroom. Now come see our showroom."

She had labeled every area as if the deal already had been made, as if Jo had agreed and they were indeed in business. Jo stepped through the maze of boxes until she reached the doorway.

Lily was right. The "showroom" had potential to be a lovely shop. On either side of the wood-carved front door were broad, full-length windows shaded by canvas awnings that offered a soft, welcoming light and an allure of privacy. Gently scalloped trim decorated the perimeter of the room; a lingering scent of gardenias or jasmine added to an ambience of femininity. Unlike the back room, it was not at all unpleasant.

"It was an aromatherapy shop," Lily explained. Apparently the aromatherapy business had been cast aside in lieu of changing trends, mainly this one, if Lily had her way, of second weddings that needed to be planned.

"I think the walls should be dark," Lily said. "Navy-blue, maybe. Something to contrast with the whites and pinks of the gowns."

Jo laughed. "I thought Sarah was the creative one."

"Yes," Lily agreed, "but it's my money." Her tone wasn't bitchy but lighthearted. Jo did not doubt that Lily would remember not to challenge Sarah. She'd tried that a few times over the years. It never had worked.

Jo went to one wall that held a dusty, gold-framed mir-ror. She ran her finger around the beveled edge and looked at Lily's reflection. Unlike the tiny lines that al-ready etched the edges of Jo's eyes, Lily's face still seemed porcelain, doll-like, unscathed, as if she'd never frowned or fretted or even cried. Botox, perhaps? They were, after all, over forty. And Reginald had left her all that money . . .

"Do you miss him?" Jo asked suddenly. "Reginald?" As unaccustomed as Jo was to speaking about matters of the heart, Lily had always been open, unashamed of her emo-tions. It had seemed childlike when they were young; now Jo envied her the ability to embrace her humanness.

Lily moved toward the glass. "I cried my tears," she said. "I really did. The poor dear loved me muchly. But he was my third husband, after all, and I've learned that life goes on."

Jo nodded.

"You never married," Lily said. "I found that so odd."

Jo was startled. She turned and looked at Lily, at her gentle, girlish face. "Did you? Well, not everyone is right for marriage."

"But you are so beautiful."

"And what does beauty have to do with marriage?"

Lily laughed and waved her thoughts away. "You could have had your pick of many men, Josephine. You wouldn't have had to work. You know, you wouldn't have had to bother about making a . . . living." She wrinkled her nose and said the word as if it were something foreign and quite distasteful.

Jo didn't point out that if they opened the busi-ness, some people might consider it "work." Instead, Jo laughed and said, "Oh, Lily, don't ever change. I think your job on earth is to remind the rest of us not to take life too seriously." If Lily understood, she gave no indication. "Now show me the upstairs. And the adorable apartment that will save you the commute."

The second floor was small but cheerful, with nooks and cubbyholes tucked here and there and windows in surprising places. From the living room there was a view of the center of West Hope and the white church and the town green and the gazebo where the school band once played on holidays, but which had been converted to a visitors' center that now dispersed maps of walking tours and discount coupons to the shops and restaurants. Jo smiled and wondered if she'd ever looked down on her hometown—no pun intended. She thought about the apartment on Shannon Drive, up on the fourth floor, the highest thing to high-rise that West Hope had allowed to be constructed.

"Come see the kitchen," Lily called out from another room.

Jo followed a hallway maze until she reached a tiny room that had been painted buttery yellow and had white cabinets.

"Isn't it so pretty?" Lily asked, though Jo knew it did not—could not—compare to the penthouse palazzo in Manhattan where Lily had lived with Reginald. She wondered if Lily really would be content there, and for exactly how long.

"It's darling," Jo replied. "It looks like you. Small. Dainty."

Lily laughed. "You're such a goof," she said. "It's a perfect pied-à-terre where I can hang my new chapeau when I'm here and not in town."

Then they laughed together because, well, it was what they did best.

"Hello? Are you upstairs?" It was a man's voice, a deep, distinct man's voice.

Jo's laugh stopped abruptly. She backed against the wall as if sucked there by a magnet.

"Oh!" Lily exclaimed. "That must be our new landlord."

Lily did not have to say to whom the voice belonged. It was Frank Forbes, who sounded so much like Brian that the brothers might have been twins.

Skipping past Jo, Lily headed toward the stairs. "Come and say hi," she called back.

But Jo stood immobile, frozen to the wall. She shook her head. "I'll catch up with you later," she said.

If Lily was surprised she did not show it. But then, Lily always took life at face value; she never showed distress. Perhaps her parents dying when Lily was only seventeen had taught her the art of letting go of tragedies, the big ones and the small. And perhaps she'd learned to differentiate between the two. Maybe that was what accounted for the lack of tiny lines edging Lily's eyes.

Yes, Jo reminded herself, she would do well to follow Lily's lead and not make life so intense.

But did that mean she had to face Frank Forbes that very moment?

Sooner or later, it would be inevitable.

After all, didn't she want to know if Frank knew about Brian?

She walked to the kitchen window that overlooked the parking lot. She closed her eyes and felt the familiar squeeze of the town and its expectations. Then she decided that, yes, seeing Frank Forbes later would be preferable to seeing him sooner.

# 5

From the bleachers at the outdoor training ring, Andrew watched his daughter look ahead, flatten her back, lean forward, lift up from the saddle, then push her weight onto her heels. The horse jumped over two fenceposts, landed safely, trotted on. Andrew resumed his seat, sensing from his taut muscles that he'd gone through Cassie's paces as if he were the one atop Big Bailey, Cassie's favorite horse at the West Hope Stables.

"She's a natural."

Shielding his eyes against the sunlight, Andrew looked at the woman who sat a few feet away. She was dressed in a light denim sundress and wore a baseball cap. He did not recognize her. "She's my daughter," he said. "Cassie."

"I know," the woman said. She looked at him and smiled, her pale peach lips soft against healthy white teeth. She had the smooth edges of a country girl, not sharp angles like Patty.

Andrew returned the smile. He wondered if she were a "Real Woman," someone who would help him get past page one of his first column, which was due in less than two weeks. Clearly, he needed some proper "field work." Clearly, he needed to find a woman.

He slid across the bench, closing the wood-plank gap between them. "Do you know my daughter?" Andrew asked. He supposed it was a thinly veiled pick-up line; "Lame," Cassie would say, but though John Benson thought otherwise, Andrew Kennedy was out of practice.

"I've watched her progress since she's been coming here," the woman replied. "She's a wonderful athlete."

Andrew grinned. He was glad he had shaved that morning, that he'd put on a fresh shirt and relatively clean jeans. "When we moved here from the city, this was all Cassie wanted. 'Can I ride a horse, Daddy? Please. Please?' " He laughed. "For weeks that was all I heard."

He thought he was being quite entertaining.

The woman smiled again. "She doesn't look like a city girl."

"We've been here five years. She's adapted well." The woman nodded and looked at Andrew. She had delicious skin that looked well cared for. "Do you have a daughter who rides here, too?" he asked. *Lame* again, but what the heck.

"My daughters—both of them—used to ride. They've grown up and left West Hope now. But my husband and I have kept their horses here. We enjoy riding, too."

Husband.

Oh.

Andrew cleared his throat. "Well," he said, "that's nice." Then he introduced himself and she introduced herself, and he knew he didn't need to remember the woman's name.

# 6

After Lily had kiss-kissed Jo and flitted away to drop off the rental car and catch the train back to the city, the thought of going home did not appeal to Jo. Marion would have returned from the library trustees meeting and would be going through her mundane tasks of reading mail, watering plants, cooking dinner—the kinds of things Jo had never wanted for herself. She'd wanted excitement, productivity, take-out food grabbed on the run between the office and the theater. She'd wanted life, lived to the max.

She had tried to convince Lily to stay long enough for dinner, but Lily was eager to return to Manhattan and close up her apartment ("For the time being, Josephine, because nothing is forever"). Lily told Jo she'd signed the lease on the storefront, despite the fact that Jo had not yet confirmed she'd be part of the business, that she'd move back to West Hope and be part of the "fun."

"You will, darling," Lily cooed. In the meantime, they'd need people to fix up the shop to look like the booming business it was not. Sarah and Elaine surely would know some local handymen or handywomen, Lily said, and gave Jo both of their addresses, which Jo had among her clothes and her furniture and her *stuff* in Boston, the stuff that sat idle, awaiting Jo's decision as to where it should be shipped.

Lily went off with her trademark butterfly wave, saying, "Remember, darling, think happy second-wedding thoughts," and Jo said, "Oh, sure," because what else could she say? Lily seemed determined—she'd offered to "fund" the business, including salaries, for up to a year. She was so upbeat, so excited, that, as usual, Lily made it hard to say no.

It reminded Jo of when they were freshmen in college, when Lily wanted to recruit the entire gold-medal-winning U.S. Olympic Hockey Team for Winter Weekend. Using the generous allowance provided by her Aunt Elizabeth, who'd been named Lily's legal guardian, Lily paid the way for Jo and Elaine to go with her to Minnesota, where most of the team was from. (Sarah said Lily was crazy and wanted no part of the escapade.) But Lily had insisted they could make it happen. How was she to know the team had other commitments, that their whirlwind tour of nationwide appearances had only just begun, that even if one or two players had been so inclined, chances were Winston College was just too far out of the way?

Lily and Jo and Elaine had a memorable trip, however.

They were stranded in a snowstorm while trying to change planes in Pittsburgh; Elaine had her purse stolen at the bus station in Minneapolis; and Jo came down with a cold that kept her ears blocking and unblocking on the long flight back to Albany.

The trip had cost Lily a couple of thousand dollars and netted absolutely nothing. She did, however, have Aunt Elizabeth, who was always good for more, a fact that Lily tested often in the name of having fun.

But that, Jo mused, had been two decades ago. Lily's aunt, as well as Lily's husband, were gone now, leaving no one for Lily to turn to if she squandered money on another foolhardy idea.

Maybe, Jo thought, she could at least steer her friend in a sensible direction. Jo's experience in business had taught her how to quickly compile research and determine whether or not an idea had merit. She could at least do that for Lily.

With her computer still in Boston, she'd have to resort to old-fashioned techniques. So instead of going home, Jo drove back to the center of town and cruised around the block four times before she found a parking space away from the antiques shop, but close to the bookstore.


The West Hope Bookstore looked the same as when Jo was a young girl, when she frequently went after school and spent her baby-sitting money on Nancy Drew and Agatha Christie stories about Miss Marple. It hadn't mattered how young or old the heroines were, Jo loved books about independent women who were strong and smart and always came out on top.

The bookstore looked as crowded as ever, not with customers, but with familiar stacks of magazines and newspapers and row upon row of colorful, upright spines of books from romance to science fiction, from reference books to self-help tomes. Jo should not have been surprised that the owner was also the same.

"Josephine?" The woman behind the counter had snow-white hair. She had a stocky build and wore a navy cardigan that might have been as ancient as the bookstore and much of its inventory.

"Mrs. Kingsley?" For an instant, Jo felt the familiar suffocation creep around her. That *West Hope* suffocation. Her eyes darted around the store; she fought the urge to flee.

"How are you, dear? I heard you were back in town."

Trapped. How she hated being trapped. She forced a smile. Of course Mrs. Kingsley had heard. In addition to owning the bookstore, the woman attended the same church as Jo's mother.

"You're taking an apartment on Shannon Drive?"

Her eyes traveled the store again. Why had she come here? Didn't she know better? "Well," she replied. "It's not definite yet."

"That's nice, dear," Mrs. Kingsley replied, as if Jo had said, yes, she was taking the apartment. "Well, welcome home. It's always a special time when one of our young returns."

Young? Jo wondered if she should remind the woman that Josephine Lyons had graduated from high school nearly twenty-five years ago, that she was hardly young.

"What can I get you today? Still reading Nancy Drew?"

Jo smiled again and fidgeted with the shoulder strap of her Coach bag. She almost laughed out loud at the prospect of asking Mrs. Kingsley for books on wedding planning. Within half an hour word would scatter through West Hope like tourists on the lawn at Tanglewood during a rainstorm, that "young" Jo Lyons must be getting married, though no one knew to whom. It wouldn't be that boy, Brian Forbes, would it? They had gone together for so many years . . .

"Actually," Jo said, "I'm looking for something to help me decorate the apartment. Some ideas. Color. Style. That sort of thing."

"Books or magazines?"

"Oh, gosh," Jo said, sweeping back her hair and tucking it behind her ears. "Just a magazine or two."

Mrs. Kingsley came from behind the cash register counter and walked toward the magazine rack. Jo followed obediently. She decided acquiescence was the quickest way to a graceful exit.

"Here's a good one," the woman said, and continued talking while she flipped the pages, mentioning the colors of today versus yesterday as if she had her own segment on the Home and Garden channel. "I know those apartments," she said. "My daughter lived there when she was working in the office at St. Alsworth's Trucking. She had a one bedroom. Nice enough place. But then she married Burt Langley. You remember Burt, I'm sure."

How could she not? Burt had dated nearly every high-school girl except Jo, and was famous for his "Russian hands and Roman fingers," and for the fact that his father was the owner of two limestone quarries and the richest man in town. Jo had often wondered why he'd married plain Jane Kingsley, unless it was because she would keep his home fires burning while his hands and fingers continued their life's work.

"They have four children, you know," Mrs. Kingsley prattled while Jo shifted from one foot to the other.

It might have been five minutes, not the five hours that it seemed, but finally Jo was in her car again, having spent forty dollars on magazines about home decorating that she didn't need. She tried not to think about the fact that she should not be so cavalier about spending forty dollars now that money was no longer "easy come, easy go"—easy anything.

Unlike West Hope, the town Sarah lived in wasn't big enough to need a town green. The "center" boasted only a Universalist church, a general store with a single gas pump, and a combination town hall, volunteer fire department, and library. There wasn't even a police station.

It had been a few years since Jo had visited Sarah at Christmas. Hopefully, she could find the house. She wondered if Sarah would suggest they try to talk Lily out of her "business" plan. As flighty as their darling Lily could be, Sarah was sensible; Sarah was sane.

As Jo drove, it occurred to her that anyone who thought summer was cool and shady in the Berkshires had never driven the narrow, winding back roads when the temperature was high and the humidity was higher. Huge cathedral pines and ancient oaks and maples blanketed the air. Not a leaf, not a bird, not a bumblebee stirred; the only sounds were the monotone drones of the cicadas, who were too hot to move, too.

Thank God the Honda had air-conditioning.

Jo finally spotted the mailbox that had been crafted from the outer shell of an old bass guitar. DUGAN, the top name read. DONALDSON, it read underneath.

Turning down the dirt drive, Jo wondered why Sarah and Jason had never married. They'd been together many years: Had their relationship worked because they'd maintained independence?

A large brown dog loped from between a row of pines and what Jo recognized as Sarah's pickup truck. The dog lumbered toward the car. His pink tongue dangled, his jaw dripped wet drips, his sweeping tail swished welcoming swishes. Just as suddenly, Sarah appeared behind him. She wore long khaki jeans and a long-sleeved cotton shirt: in the woods, mosquitoes and tics were abundant. She grabbed the dog's collar and reined him in.

"He thought you were Jason," she shouted, as Jo rolled down her car window. "He always hopes it's Jason when he hears a car." Maybe like Lily, the dog believed Jason was away far too often.

Angling the car between two pine trees, Jo was sad they hadn't been in touch more often, that they hadn't shared more of the grown-up parts of their lives. Where had the years gone? Hadn't Sarah just planted the herb garden on the windowsill in their dorm room, only to have it slip off and crash to the sidewalk, narrowly missing the housemother's car? Hadn't Lily just danced in *Swan Lake* in the costume Elaine made? Hadn't one of the straps torn during the performance, leaving the male lead holding Lily's small, uncovered breast in his embarrassed hand?

Hadn't those things happened only yesterday?

With a small sigh, Jo turned off the ignition and got out of the car.

"Lily found a storefront," she said, following Sarah up toward the house, a shaded log cabin surrounded by lofty yellow and orange lilies, clusters of tall daisies, and water-falls of thick ivy.

"I know," Sarah said. "She called. She wondered if you'd mind that the landlord is Brian's brother."

So, Jo thought, Lily, the eternal romantic, had remem-bered. Jo stopped for a moment, then breathed again. "Oh," she replied. "Well, no, of course not."

Sarah laughed. "That's what I said. I told her that Brian was years ago and we were just kids, for godssake."

*Years ago*, Jo reminded herself. *Not yesterday.* She went up the stairs and into the house.


It was a great house. An enormous stone fireplace stood at one end of a huge room that served as the kitchen, dining and living rooms. The master bedroom, bath, and sitting room were in the back, tucked behind a rustic staircase that led upstairs to two more bedrooms, another bath, and a loft that Sarah had once said was "Burch's domain."

"How old is Burch now?" Jo asked as she trailed her friend to the kitchen area.

Sarah tossed back her long, black hair. She wore it down today. It was shiny and silky and reached her waist. Despite the fact that Jo was a natural light brown, not-quite-blond, she'd always envied Sarah her Native Amer-ican bloodline that had rewarded her friend with such luxurious hair and such Cher-like cheekbones.

Sarah poured an iced drink. "Twelve," she replied. "Can you believe it?"

So Sarah had a twelve-year-old son, yet she'd never married. She'd once said she never felt marriage was necessary, that independence was more important in life.

In college Sarah had often been called a leftover hippie, though she'd been too young to be a leftover anything. But in the early eighties, in New England, her Cherokee roots—her ties to the earth, her innate spirituality and creativity—had been mistaken for West Coast flower power and most of the old Yankees were fed up with that.

"Here," Sarah said, handing Jo a glass, "it's tea from the herbs in my garden."

Jo took the glass, then ambled around the room, her eyes taking in the wall hangings and blankets and accoutrements in shades of grass and berries and cloudless skies. She sat on the plump, moss-colored cushion of a chair that was framed by twisted tree branches. "This is a wonderful house," she said. "It's very much you."

Sarah laughed and tossed back her hair. She sat cross-legged on the floor in front of Jo and set her glass on a rug that Jo suspected had been handwoven, probably by Sarah. Sarah pulled her long hair over her shoulder and began plaiting a braid. "Not exactly a froufrou wedding environment," she said, her eyes indicating a wall on which about two dozen tambourine-size artifacts hung. Each had been painted with a different, primitive design—an eagle, a bear, a wolf. "Tribal drums," Sarah said. "Made of honest-to-goodness buffalo hide."

Jo wrinkled her nose, but smiled. She wondered what it would feel like to have a heritage so strong that it was rooted at one's center, to have a link with something substantial beyond church ladies and a gazebo on a town green.

"So," Sarah said, "you like Lily's idea?"

With a quick shrug, Jo sipped her tea. It was sweet, pure. "I think I'm hoping that you'll talk me out of it," she said. "Or talk Lily out of it."

Sarah nodded, her short-nailed fingers flicking through her hair with practiced expertise.

"It is rather ridiculous," Jo continued, "don't you think? I mean, what does any of us know about planning a wedding? Two out of four of us have never even been married."

"Yes, but Lily's been married three times, so that makes up for us."

Sarah's dry sense of humor was comfortably familiar, like the words to a James Taylor song that Jo had learned long ago but would have thought she'd forgotten. "Your jewelry," Jo said. "I saw some last winter at a shop in Quincy Market."

Sarah nodded. "One of my reps has done real well in Boston."

"I bought a piece."

"You shouldn't wear silver. Your coloring is all wrong." She did not say it to be critical.

Jo didn't tell her the "piece" had been a man's bracelet, that she'd bought it for Brian, and that he'd taken it with him. "You've been so successful," Jo said instead. "I'm surprised you want to be bothered doing something so ordinary as planning weddings."

"Nothing is ordinary if it's one-of-a-kind. I think Lily

has a good idea. I think a second wedding, especially, should be an art form, not a cookie-cutter event that follows some archaic set of rules."

"But aren't rules important? To use as guidelines?"

Sarah shrugged. "Depends on the user," she said with a wink. "And the use-ee."

"Oh, Sarah," Jo groaned, "I'm not sure I can do this."

Pulling a large silver clip from her shirt pocket, Sarah snapped it onto her braid. She picked up her tea. "Hey, it's not exactly my dream-come-true, either, Jo. But for me, it's a wonderful gift. Jason's on the road more than he's not, and Burch is no longer interested in spending time with his mother. If I don't get some sort of change in my life, I'm going to go out of my mind."

Jo looked around the wonderful log cabin with its eclectic art and the richness and fullness of life it depicted. She was reminded that no life was perfect, no matter what, no matter whose. She thought about what it would take to open another public relations business: the long hours, the worry, the struggle. Then the dog trundled over and lapped from her glass. Jo laughed out loud. He looked up at her as if to ask, "What? Is something wrong?" Then he continued to drink, and she continued to laugh.

"He likes you," Sarah said, which was nice, though Jo suspected the dog liked most everyone.

The dog dripped iced tea on her leg as he meandered away. Jo closed her eyes and thought of her friends. "Maybe you're right," she suddenly said. "Maybe this is a wonderful gift."

If she'd had a girl she'd have named her Amanda Josephine, after her eccentric, fun-loving aunt and herself; a boy would have been Emmett Gray, after Jo's maternal grandfather, who'd died in Jo's sophomore year of college, the man who'd taught her to fish and to ride her first two-wheel bicycle and to build a snow fort that lasted from December until the spring thaw.

As it turned out, Jo didn't have to worry about girl or boy names, because she'd had the abortion and never became pregnant again. Despite many lovers, none had been worthy; none had been Brian.

Driving away from Sarah's, Jo hated that she was thinking of all that again, dredging up that old wound that had never quite healed.

While she'd been in the city, while her life had been chaos, it had been easy to ignore those feelings as if they didn't exist, like crumbs between couch cushions or socks under beds.

In West Hope, it was different. And it was why, until now, her visits had been short, quick "touchdowns" to say "Hi," leaving no time to think, no chance to remember that every store was a store she'd gone into with Brian; every restaurant, a place they'd had a hamburger; every dark, woodsy road, one where they'd parked and made love under the old stadium blanket he kept in the station wagon that belonged to his father and brother and their antiques business.

Everywhere were memories of Brian and of what could have been, of what almost was.

The years had passed and then they were miraculously, wonderfully together once again.

"Jo," he'd said as he stood inside her office door, holding a small Christmas tree decorated with tinsel and red bows, wearing a dimpled smile that she hadn't seen for nearly twenty years. "Oh, Jo, can you ever forgive me?"

She did.

He said he never had forgotten her.

She said she hadn't forgotten him.

It wasn't long—days, in fact—when they began to talk of a future at last. He hadn't known about Amanda or Emmett, the baby that could have been theirs but was not. Jo planned to tell him on the night that had turned out to be their last.

She'd worn his favorite dress—the short emerald sheath that he said matched her eyes—as if the dress would help him not hate her when she said what she'd done to the baby, their baby.

And now, memories of Brian were in Boston, as well. It didn't matter where she went, the thoughts would be inside her, lingering, hovering, there.

Jo turned into the driveway of her mother's small house. She knew then that she might as well move back to West Hope, work with her old friends, be with her old friends, and try to rebuild a life of her own.

She wondered if she would still be likely to succeed, and how she would feel if, this time, she did not.

# 7

Ordinarily, Cassie was the light of Andrew's life, the apple of his eye, and every other cliché coined regarding fathers and their daughters.

That night he did not need her to turn into a pain in Andrew's tired ass.

He'd spent the day writing and rewriting his column. He was sick of talking to women, pretending to be casual, trying to root out the basic flaw that he believed was what separated him from them. He'd combed the campus, watching women on the faculty who thought he was on sabbatical to work on his doctoral dissertation, because that had been a more acceptable explanation than writing about foreplay for a pop-culture magazine.

Staring at the screen of his laptop, Andrew had congratulated himself that at least he had figured out this much: that dating, or the art of trying to date, was nothing more than sexual foreplay disguised as *getting to know each other.*

He'd landed on that hook but nothing more when Cassie burst through the French doors that led from the living room into the study and announced, "I'm never going back to school. I don't care what you say."

Andrew closed his eyes. "What?" he asked.

"You heard me!" Cassie screeched and bolted from the study as quickly as she'd come in.

Which meant, of course, that Andrew had to stop what he was doing, go and find his daughter who was pacing in the kitchen, calm her down, and prod her into telling him what happened and why she did not plan to further her education into the sixth grade.

"It's all your fault," she said, which was no surprise. Wasn't it always? "You're dating the school principal! How could you do that, Dad? Ms. Brouillard is a . . . a . . ."

Andrew supposed that at eleven, even *his* daughter's vocabulary was limited when it came to matters of the dating game. "An old battle-ax?" he asked.

Cassie scowled. "A what?"

Andrew laughed. "Honey," he said, "I'm not dating Ms. Brouillard. I had lunch with her yesterday to talk about a project I have to do." He had bought the thirty-seven-year-old battle-ax a grilled chicken sandwich at Friendly's and told her he was doing research about dating over thirty. He had inferred neither that he was working on his dissertation nor on the "Real Women" column. And he certainly had not implied that it had been a date.

Had he?

Or did a woman over thirty automatically think that

when the man picked up the check for $13.95, he fully intended to marry her within the next six months or so?

Andrew sighed. "It's part of my new job, honey," he tried to reassure his daughter. "The column I'm writing for John." Among other things, John Benson was Cassie's godfather, a doting one, who had supplied her with the full contingent of American Girl dolls, though Cassie would have preferred collectible horses, and Junior Miss diamond earrings, though she'd wanted leather chaps.

Nonetheless, Cassie loved John. But that was not the issue now. "You're not dating Ms. Brouillard?"

Andrew shook his head. "No, honey. It will be safe for you to go back to school in September."

She put her hands on her narrow hips, rolled her eyes and sighed. "Geez, Dad, why can't you just get a real job like other people?"

# 8

♥

laine's house was exactly as Jo remembered. A "family" of white ceramic ducks lined one side of the brick front walk; pots of red geraniums stood as sentries on the stoop; above the door hung a green flag decorated with a yellow sun and pink letters that read, SUMMER.

The last time Jo had been there, a flag had read WINTER. It was so like Elaine: She took pleasure in the things that were homey and crafty, even if her choices weren't very stylish or didn't match one another. Jo wondered how difficult it had been for Elaine to be divorced, to no longer belong in the well-defined role of a man's wife and homemaker.

Now that would change, beginning with the wedding that her old friends would plan.

Jo rang the doorbell and Elaine quickly answered, her

smile wide, her hair gelled and blow-dried with its high peak of bangs, her blue plaid cotton shorts and matching shirt neatly pressed. On her feet were white canvas sneakers and short socks with a pink ball at each heel. Behind her stood a short, broad man dressed in khaki pants, a shortsleeved shirt and tie. He was clearly older than Elaine—close to sixty, maybe. What he lacked for in hair, he made up for with a full and generous smile.

"Jo," Elaine said, "Martin was just leaving, but say 'Hi.' " She stepped aside and the man extended his hand. His smile had not faltered.

"Martin Schiffman," he said in a voice that was just a little too loud.

Jo shook his hand. "The groom," she said.

His head nodded with the same beat as his handshake. "The *lucky* groom."

"Martin, stop," Elaine said. "You'll make me blush in front of one of my oldest and dearest friends."

"I've heard a lot about you, Jo," he said.

The amenities continued for another moment, then Martin kissed Elaine on the cheek and went off down the driveway. Elaine led Jo into the living room of the four-bedroom, two-bath colonial house that was about to have a husband again.

"Isn't he great?" Elaine said. "I know he's a little old, but he's crazy about me. Imagine that!"

Jo smiled. "Of course I can imagine that, Lainey. And if you love each other, what difference does it make how old he is?" She cleared her throat, realizing that she sounded an awful lot like Pollyanna Lily.

———

They moved to the screened porch out back, where Elaine offered gin and tonic, but Jo said she'd prefer lemonade. They settled in and Jo took a long, cool drink.

"I thought while Lily was in New York we could start to renovate the shop," she said.

"So you've finally agreed?" Elaine asked.

Jo shrugged. "I've been lured by the prospect of hanging out with you guys."

"There are worse places you could live. And worse things you could do."

*Like staying in Boston and waiting for Brian to come back to her. Again.*

After taking a long drink, Jo tried to smile. "We'll need a Dumpster or a rubbish person who will haul away the trash, then scrub the place from top to bottom. Sarah thought you might know of someone here in town." Unlike Sarah, the artist in the woods, Elaine was active in everything from the PTO to the Fourth of July parade committee, not unlike Marion, not unlike Mrs. Kingsley, not unlike most of the other women of West Hope.

Holding up her hand, Elaine said, "Wait a minute. I'm the bride, not one of the partners."

"You aren't going to work with us?"

"Not now, not after my wedding. I shall be a housewife, and this time I shall not screw it up."

Jo could have replied with any of several uplifting replies, but she didn't feel like listening to Elaine's troubles with men. "Okay," she quickly said, "but surely you know someone . . . a handyman . . . or handywoman?"

Elaine seemed to think a moment. "We could ask Frank," she said at last. "Frank Forbes, you know."

Yes, of course Jo knew. She took another drink and wished she'd taken the gin.

"Well," Elaine continued, "what with the antiques business, I'm sure he's always hiring people to clean out houses when people die or get shipped off to nursing homes or whatever."

Jo studied her ankles, then the patch of indoor/outdoor carpeting spread across the concrete floor, which she bet Elaine scrubbed every day as if her husband had never left her, as if her life had never changed. She wondered how other women managed, how they survived the process of suddenly being alone. Did they all scrub floors?

"Was it hard," Jo heard herself ask, "when Lloyd left?"

The air on the porch seemed to have cooled. "Lloyd didn't leave," Elaine said. "I told him to get out."

Jo supposed that, when faced with a situation as ugly as divorce, the semantics of who really did what and to whom were important. She knew, of course, that Lloyd, an attorney who "should have known better," had been screwing around with a county court judge. She thought he'd even married the woman. "Was it hard?" she repeated, though it seemed an understatement.

Elaine stood up. She went to the screen and faced the backyard, the picnic table, and a badminton net stretched between two trees, symbols of a house in the suburbs where kids grew up like one another and rarely broke from the mold. She plucked a droopy leaf from an African violet that sat on a small white wrought-iron table.

"For a while I thought I would die." Her voice was a whisper.

Jo remained silent. In the few times she'd seen Elaine

since the divorce, Elaine had not shared the details other
than to say "Thank God he is gone."

"I don't think I left the house for three months,"
Elaine continued. "I made the kids do the shopping and
yard work and anything that meant having to face the
world, having to answer a question, or worse, listen to
sympathy. I even made the kids answer the phone." She
laughed and swirled the ice in her glass. "Then one day I
said the hell with it. I got up and showered and dressed
and marched down to the courthouse. I stood on the steps
and told every person who was coming or going that the
judge had stolen my husband, until Lloyd's brother, the
cop, came along and said I was making a spectacle and
asked me to leave. By then I felt a little vindicated."

Elaine laughed again and returned to her white plastic
chair. It was then that Jo realized the chairs were the same
she'd seen at her new neighbor's on Shannon Drive. She
wondered if Arnold's Hardware had featured them on
sale.

"I have three kids, Jo. My oldest is twenty-one. I'd
been married too long to the same man."

"Maybe," Jo replied.

"Oh. Without a doubt."

Jo couldn't imagine doing the same anything for
twenty-one years, let alone be married to the same man.
Unless, of course, it had been Brian.

A bird outside made some kind of noise. Jo knew her
mother would know the type of bird and probably what it
was saying. Things were that simple in West Hope: bird-
songs and badminton and white plastic chairs, with the
pain of living layered somewhere beneath, cushioned by
the grounding of everyday life.

"Well," Elaine said, raising her glass. "Here's to our futures. Your business, my wedding."

Jo smiled. They sipped. "Now tell me about your new man, and how wonderful your new life will be." It was healthier, she was learning, to focus on the potential of tomorrow, than to dwell on the past.

Elaine's husband-to-be was named Martin Schiffman and he owned a Chevy dealership on Route 7 in Pittsfield. In the summers he also acted at the Berkshire Summer Theater, which Elaine found endearing because here was this automotive guy who played a great MacBeth. They had both served on the chamber of commerce board of directors for many years, and not long after Lloyd left, Martin's wife died of stomach cancer, and so there they were.

And now there was Jo. With a future of her own, for better or for worse, it was all up to her.

After two glasses of lemonade and half a plateful of sugar cookies, Elaine invited Jo to stay for dinner with Martin and see her kids—Kandie, Kory, and Karen ("You won't believe how grown-up they are!")—but Jo said she'd promised her mother she'd be home tonight, thanks, another time. Before leaving, however, Jo made one phone call to the leasing office on Shannon Drive.

Yes, the apartment was still available. It required signing a six-month lease.

Yes, it could be ready by the end of the week.

She gave a verbal agreement and asked if they needed a credit card number as a deposit to hold it.

No, they did not. This was West Hope, not the city.

She then called the moving company in Boston that was scheduled to pick up her things on Friday. "I don't want my furniture put into storage," Jo said. "I need it delivered to West Hope instead." She had to explain that West Hope was in Western Massachusetts between Stockbridge and Lenox . . . had they heard of it?

"It might take a couple of days for your things to get there," the woman on the other end of the line said. "Until we have a full load headed west." It was as if anything past Exit 14 on the turnpike was uncharted frontier.

"No problem," Jo said with relief. It would take her that long to figure out what pieces would fit and what would have to go in her mother's garage.

"Done," she said as she hung up the phone. "Looks like I'm in business."

Elaine gave her a high five. "Sure you won't stay for dinner? Or how about that drink?"

Jo declined, said thanks again, and decided she'd stop at the IGA: She'd surprise her mother with pasta primavera for dinner and strawberries for dessert. Because even though Jo would be living in the secretaries' building, her mother would be delighted that she'd come back to West Hope to stay, at least for the moment, at least for right now.


Juggling two paper (not plastic) grocery bags, Jo fumbled with the doorknob, then let herself in. Marion was seated at the table, studying what appeared to be the mail.

"Mother," Jo said, "didn't you hear me?" She turned from Marion and set the bags on the counter. The late afternoon had grown oppressive again: time to bring out the fans. One thing that Jo had forgotten about "home" was that few people had air-conditioning, as if it would be a sacrilege to their Old New England ancestors who had suffered so much for them.

She'd forgotten to ask if Shannon Drive had central air.

She opened the refrigerator door, inhaled the coolness, and began to unload the shopping bags. She realized then that her mother had not replied.

"Mother?" she asked, turning back to the woman who rarely looked her age except in times of stress. Jo noticed that the lines around her mouth and the furrows of her brow were exceptionally deep now.

Marion set down the paper she was examining and peered at her daughter. She no longer needed glasses, thanks to her cataract surgery and the miracle lens implants she'd had last year. Still, her eyes looked tired, old. "Jo," she said, "I've been waiting for you to come home."

Jo closed the refrigerator door. She supposed she should ask, "What's wrong?" but Jo figured she'd know soon enough. "I was with Lily and Sarah and Elaine," she said. "Lily wants us to open a wedding-planning business, Mom. I've decided to move back to West Hope after all."

Instead of nodding and smiling and saying, "Oh, Jo, that's wonderful," Marion stayed in her seat and tightened her lips.

"Mother?" Jo repeated, because Marion just sat there.

Then her mother *cluck-cluck*ed and quietly said, "I've asked myself a thousand times where I went wrong with you, Josephine. Over the years, I've asked myself a thousand times."

Jo felt her insides buckle. She fought the urge to say

she'd suddenly changed her mind, that perhaps staying in Boston would be a better idea.

But then there was the loneliness,

and the memories,

and the fact that she had now made a commitment to her friends.

Resigned, Jo sat down and waited to learn how her mother had gone wrong.

"When you first left home, I went into some sort of shock."

Jo nearly groaned out loud. All these years later, couldn't her mother let it go? Couldn't her mother forgive her for her trespasses, the way Jo had forgiven Marion for hers?

"You may or may not believe this, but the hardest part for me to accept was that, so many years ago, though you trusted me enough with your secret, you didn't trust my advice. That you did not trust your own mother to take care of you and your child, to protect you from what the world would say and do."

Jo watched the lines around her mother's mouth multiply. She knew better than to speak. She tried to stop the tears from welling in her eyes. On some level she had always known that the abortion had not been easy for either of them, that Jo had not been the only one to carry the suffering and the guilt and the sadness it had wrought.

"And then this morning you had a phone call and I've been sitting here just waiting for you to decide to come home."

Jo knew what was coming next. She did not know how her mother had found out; she did not know how much she knew. But she knew her latest pain was about to be exposed. She held her hand across her stomach and asked, "Who called me, Mother?"

"The call was from the Boston Police. The Missing Persons Bureau. Josephine, what's going on?"

They hadn't found him. But another case had turned up a photo from South America in which someone looked suspiciously like Brian Forbes.

Did Jo want them to e-mail her the picture?

She wound the old-fashioned telephone cord around her fingers, aware that, though she sat at the telephone table in the front hall, her mother was in the kitchen and her mother was not deaf.

Besides, her computer was still in Boston. She'd have to go to the library to access her e-mail. She'd have to open the image there, with others all around.

A thin line of perspiration formed on her upper lip. "That won't be necessary," she said. "I'll be in the city later this week. I'll stop by and look at it then." She tried to sound calm, tried not to sound urgent. But when Jo hung up the phone and returned to the kitchen, one look at her mother unraveled her composure.

"I guess," she said, "you should know the truth."

Marion did not say a word; she just pulled out a chair for Jo to sit down.

# 9

♥

Placing her hands on her mother's kitchen table, Jo began to share select parts of the story.

"He had come back to me," she said slowly. "We'd been talking about our future. But Brian had been having a hard time getting his investment business off the ground. I believed in him, though. I thought that was important if we were going to get married." Then she told her mother she'd decided to tell Brian about the abortion. If he could forgive her, their relationship might work. "I suggested we meet at McNally's after work. It was our favorite pub."

She pressed her fingertips together; she did not look at Marion as she continued. She said they'd ordered beer and popcorn shrimp, that Brian had looked tired, but that things had seemed all right. Just as Jo mustered her courage to bring up the abortion, he held a finger to her lips. "Hold that thought," he said. "I need to use the men's room."

Jo sat back and sipped her beer and waited for his return.

She chatted with the waitress, who knew them both by now.

She said, "Hi, how are you?" to at least half a dozen regulars at McNally's, too.

She played out her words over and over in her mind. "I was so scared," she would say. "I was so hurt that you'd left me."

She finished her beer, but did not order another.

Then she saw Charlie, a man Brian played squash with. He invited himself to sit down.

"Brian will be right back," Jo explained with a smile. "But we're having a private discussion." She did not want Charlie to intrude. But Charlie sat anyway and began talking about things that did not interest Jo.

She began to wonder if Brian was sick. She glanced at her watch: He'd been gone twenty minutes.

"Excuse me," she interrupted Brian's squash-playing companion, "would you do me a favor and check the men's room? I can't imagine what's taking Brian so long."

At that point in her story, Jo paused a long and quiet pause. Marion let out a sigh as if she knew what happened next. And then Jo raised her gaze to meet her mother's eyes. "Oh, Mom," she said, "it was horrible."

Marion reached across the table and took hold of Jo's cold hands.

Jo closed her eyes. "He wasn't there," she said. "Charlie came back and said, 'I think he flushed himself down the toilet.' He laughed, because I guess he thought it was a joke."

Charlie had then resumed his seat and taken a swig of Brian's beer. He started telling Jo about a woman he had dated the night before, but then Jo snapped at him. "For godssake, Charlie, where is Brian?"

He flinched. "How do I know? Maybe he got a call. Maybe he went outside to use his phone." It was noisy at McNally's, but no more than usual. And Brian had a good cell phone . . . Jo had paid for it.

And then Jo knew Brian wasn't coming back.

Sitting in her mother's kitchen now, in the home where she'd been raised, the place where she'd been protected, Jo could still feel the nausea that had rolled through her, the cold, slow wave of bile that said she'd been abandoned. Again.

She had tried to sort out her senses. She had tried to be logical.

Perhaps Brian had been lured outside, then robbed of his wallet.

Perhaps he'd been abducted by the jealous husband of a former lover.

Perhaps he'd been shot through the temple by an unhappy client.

Perhaps . . . a million and one things could have happened. But the hollowness inside her felt oddly familiar. She recognized it for what it was: abandonment.

She told her mother how at that moment she remembered a news story about an ordinary couple who had traveled to Atlantic City to celebrate their anniversary. While at the blackjack table, the husband excused himself.

He left his money and his cigarettes on the felt top next to his wife. It was three years before the wife heard of him again. He had run off with another woman, in an act he had planned for several months.

Jo said that was when she stood up at the table and rushed out the front door, that her rational mind kept insisting there would be a simple explanation.

Brian would not have been mugged, abducted, shot.

Which meant he must have left of his own free will.

But he wouldn't do that, not again.

They had waited too many years to be together.

Brian, however, was not outside.

Jo had gone back into the pub and headed for the men's room. She threw open the door and shouted, "Brian?"

When no one answered, she pushed past the line of urinals while a man quickly zipped his fly. She slammed open the doors of two stalls, both of which were empty.

She returned to the table. Charlie had moved to the bar, apparently just Brian's squash-buddy not Brian's friend. She sat down again, her heart thumping bold thumps of fear.

An hour passed, and then another. She asked the bartender to call the police.

The police came. They wrote a few ambivalent notes. They told Jo if she didn't hear from Brian in forty-eight hours she should call Missing Persons.

Jo ended her story there. She did not tell Marion that she had invested all her assets in Brian's business. There was no point in sharing that.

When she signed the lease on the Shannon Drive apartment, Jo persuaded herself she was not ruling out the fantasy that Brian still might return. She rationalized that she was merely trying to rebuild her finances, her sanity, her life.

Two days later, when Lily was back in West Hope, eager to oversee the renovations to the shop, Jo steered her Honda up the ramp onto the turnpike. She followed the signs east toward Springfield, Worcester, Boston.

"We should have a trademark," Sarah said from the passenger seat. "Something that will be distinctive to our business." She had insisted on making the trip with Jo; she would visit wedding consultants and boutiques while Jo dealt with her movers; she would steal some ideas. Well, not steal, exactly. Just find out what was current, what was urban-hip. Jo had hesitated at first: She was so accustomed to doing everything alone, and she worried that somehow Sarah might learn the details of what had happened with Brian. But Sarah had persisted, and Lily urged her to go, and Jo couldn't think of a good enough excuse. She wished there was a convincing way to prepare Sarah for what she'd see, to explain the remnants of Jo's indulgent lifestyle and why they were no longer hers.

"What kind of trademark?" Jo asked.

Sarah flipped through the pages of a bridal magazine. "I don't know. A diamond baked into a wedding cake . . . custom silver earrings woven into the bridal bouquet for the lucky girl who catches it . . . something everyone will get excited about when they learn that we'll be the wedding planners."

Jo smiled. "A diamond in a wedding cake. I like that."

Sarah flipped another page. "Of course, we'd have to

do it so it wouldn't be a liability issue. The last thing we'd need is to have to perform the Heimlich on the mother of the bride."

"Or on the kids," Jo added. "Remember that these will be second weddings. There might be lots of kids. Which reminds me, we should come up with a standard list of dos and don'ts."

"Such as . . . Don't lick the frosting from the wedding cake? Don't play your Game Boy during the ceremony?"

"Very funny, but no. More like specific things for second weddings. Like, Do wear white if you want, and Don't wear a veil, wear a headpiece or ring of flowers instead."

" 'Don't wear a veil'?"

Jo shrugged. "I read it in a magazine. I think some guidelines would be good. Etiquette stuff." She did not mention that she'd read it months earlier, when she'd thought she might be planning a wedding of her own—a first wedding.

From Stockbridge to Natick, they kicked around ideas. Too soon they passed through the last exit; the skyline came into view. Jo's fingers tensed on the small steering wheel, the skin across her knuckles grew taut and pale, her jawline more pronounced.

"Well," she said. "Here we are."

If Sarah noted the change in Jo's demeanor, she did not comment. Instead, Sarah turned her face out the window and quietly said, "I never thought I'd be back here again."

Jo could have asked what Sarah meant, but decided both of them were entitled to their secrets.

———

It was summer. The city should have been throbbing with kids darting up and down hot, steamy pavement. It should have been vibrating with roller blades that cruised along the bike path by the river, and been dotted by tourist groups and their guides giving brief oral histories along the Freedom Trail. John Hancock lived there. Paul Revere's blacksmith shop was there. The Old North Church still had the same bell.

Who could argue?

But Boston was shrouded in the eerie stillness that happened when humidity drizzled from a gray, friendless sky and sent even the duck boats heading for cover, in case the heavens cracked and thunder shook the ground above the tunnels now mazed beneath the city like Pavlov's labyrinth.

Jo stopped the car along the curb in front of Copley Plaza.

"I can't talk you into coming with me?" Sarah asked.

Jo shook her head. "You'll have to find the perfect wedding ingredients without me. I have too much to do."

They decided they'd meet later at the Holiday Inn in Brookline—a little on the outskirts, but cheaper than the Ritz. If Jo had been alone, she might have slept amid the cartons at her former condo, but with Sarah there . . . well, the fewer white lies needed, the better.

Jo wished Sarah luck, then stole away, not in the direction of the condo, but toward the Boston Police Station Annex, Missing Persons Bureau.

It was not one of those buildings one might expect, of crumbling redbrick and dusty, arched windows that had been there a hundred years or more. It did not have a cobblestone walk that lead into a dark foyer where a crusty old sergeant sat behind a long wood desk that was elevated three steps to intimidate visitors.

Instead, the Missing Persons Bureau of the Boston Police Department was housed in a pristine new building with well-lit corridors and user-friendly directions.

Lieutenant Williams would be happy to see her, a young woman in a long cotton dress said to Jo. She gestured to a comfortable-looking chair by the wall, but Jo declined. She was not relaxed enough to sit. She tried to turn her attention to several notices tacked onto a wall, photocopies of faces, mostly of children who had been missing since July 1999, April 2003, October 1996. She scanned the information as if she were perusing ads at the market for housekeeping or lawn-mowing or gutter-cleaning services for which she had no need.

"Ms. Lyons?"

Lieutenant Williams was tall and good-looking, with a regal posture that spoke of hard work and respect. She wondered if he'd grown up in a black neighborhood in Roxbury, and, if so, what he'd had to do to make it to the top.

"Lieutenant Williams," she said, extending her hand. His hand was large, but his handshake gentle, for a cop.

He ushered her into his office, a glass-walled room with tasteful furniture.

"Have a seat," he offered, and this time, she sat.

He plucked a manila file folder from his desk. He sat beside her, not behind his desk. "As I told you on the phone," he said, "we have someone working on a case in

South America. A picture he sent back includes a man whom we think resembles Brian Forbes."

Jo nodded. She thought about the photo she'd given the police. It had been taken at Mrs. Dotson's Valentine's Day party. It was of the two of them, Jo and Brian, reunited; Jo and Brian, all dressed up, in love. When Brian disappeared, she'd been so upset she forgot to tell the police it was the only copy of the photo that she had.

Her gaze fell from the lieutenant to the closed manila file folder on his lap. She remembered the red dress she'd worn, she remembered Brian's happy smile.

"The case we're working on is in Argentina," Lieutenant Williams said.

She wasn't sure if he expected a reaction, a link she might know connecting Brian to South America. But she knew none. Not now, nor in the past months they'd been together. Before that, who knew? It had often occurred to Jo that in their twenty years of separation, she knew little of Brian's whereabouts, other than he'd stayed in Montreal for several years, then moved down to the Adirondacks in Upstate New York, where he'd worked at a hunting lodge. He'd become a local hero when he rescued a group of Wall Street investment brokers stranded in a snowstorm. Over scotch and venison, they convinced him to try his hand at a more lucrative business.

"Investments," Brian often quoted one of them as saying. "It's where the money is."

They'd laughed about those words, each time Jo wrote another check to help get Brian's business started. They had not laughed when she agreed to invest in a fund he believed in, because it was serious money then, the deal that would surely make both Jo and Brian rich.

The lieutenant opened the file folder. Jo's vision blurred; she blinked to focus.

"As I explained on the phone," Lieutenant Williams said, "this was taken for another case. A man whose wife went missing with a bundle of his cash."

He hesitated long enough for Jo to understand his meaning. A man. A wife. Brian in a photo. Brian in a photo with another man's wife.

Oh.

She sat up straight, unsure if she had moaned out loud.

She cleared her throat. "Let me see the photo, please," she said in a voice that did not sound like hers, but was smaller, quieter, a voice lacking confidence.

He handed her an eight-by-ten black-and-white glossy print. In the picture was a long-haired, half-naked woman, laughing. She held a bowl-shaped glass that had a straw and a tiny, paper umbrella. Bending to the glass, taking a drink, was a shirtless man. The man had dark hair and flashing eyes.

But he did not have Brian's dimple deep in his left cheek.

# 10

♥

The deadline clock was ticking.

Andrew roamed the halls of the administrative building of Winston College, wondering if it was too late to tell John Benson to forget it, to admit that Andrew Kennedy, alas, no longer had the stuff that it took to charm the opposite sex.

He had, after all, been in too much trouble with his daughter to risk being seen with any of her elementary-school teachers. Which left only a few obvious choices.

But the coeds were too young.

The professors were off-limits, unless he wanted gossip, which he did not.

The wives of the summer people whose husbands joined them for golf on weekends might be candidates, but they'd be gone when the season ended and where would that leave Andrew?

Practically the only women left would be the one who owned the laundromat and the one who cleaned the cottage, both of whom were nice enough, but way past sixty-five.

He strolled the empty halls. He considered that the morning's visit was not to seek out real women after all, but to find out if there was a class or two he could teach come fall. Maybe he should accept that this "sabbatical" ruse wasn't going to work, that he was no more capable of writing about women than about the mating habits of earthworms, if they even had mating habits. (Were they the insects who fornicated with themselves and produced squirmy offspring sans the aid—or pleasure—of a male/female bond?)

He thought about Patty and how, if he gave up the column, he'd have to forfeit the trip to Australia.

Outside the Graduate Office, contemplating that thought, Andrew grabbed the latest edition of *Winston Words*, the college newspaper. It was a scant four pages, due to the slack of summer. Still, Andrew felt guilty for having bailed out on his duties as faculty advisor in order to concentrate on his new career, which was quickly turning to shit.

He opened the sheet and his eyes fell to a large ad at the bottom of the page. The format didn't resemble that of any regular advertisers: It was bordered by illustrations of tall calla lilies.

**RECEPTIONIST WANTED,** the ad read in bold type.

*Wedding consultants need mature, well-rounded individual to meet and greet prospective brides-to-be. Full-time position. No experience required.*

A frilly logo at the bottom of the ad read:

*SECOND CHANCES*
*Specializing in magical marriages*
*for the second-time around.*

Another symbol then caught Andrew's eye:

*An equal opportunity employer.*

He folded the newspaper and stuffed it into his backpack. At least the paper was getting new advertisers, something that would surely help in these shaky economic times.

It was not until he'd left the administration building and was walking across campus that the idea of Second Chances lit up like a cartoon lightbulb high over his head.

*Wedding consultants . . . mature individual . . . no experience required.*

And then . . . *an equal opportunity employer.*

# 11

♥

"Video wishes," Sarah said that night over dinner.

Jo knew she should be grateful for Sarah and her exuberance, and for the distraction they afforded from the rest of her lousy day. She tasted her sole français and asked, "What are video wishes?"

"We'll set up a small booth in a corner of the reception hall. Every guest is invited to step inside and record their best wishes to the bride and groom. It's great fun. Everyone is dressed up and looks their best. They're in a party mood, and it becomes part of the wedding memories. We have it burned onto a CD and voilà, they can pop it into their TV or computer and watch it time after time."

"That's great," Jo said. "What else?"

It was easy to feign interest, because Sarah was so animated, so energized by the city and by new ideas. But while Jo listened to such thoughts as "posy pocketbooks for bridesmaids," and "confetti" of wildflower seeds and buds of dried lavender, she was very much aware of the shroud of anticipation looming ahead tomorrow, of the gruesome task of dismembering what had taken nearly twenty years to build and only five months to dismantle in the name of love.

"The most important thing we can do is hook up with certain vendors, caterers, florists, DJs," Sarah continued. "That's where we'll make our real money, from a percentage of their fees." Then Sarah smiled. "But the business side of things is your department, not mine."

Jo nodded. She had already intended to seek out businesses with which they could have "partnering" arrangements.

"Tomorrow I want to go to Chestnut Hill," Sarah added. "I understand there is a terrific bridal shop there. Are you sure you won't join me?"

Jo supposed the movers were perfectly capable of packing her belongings. They would not get caught up in the emotion of remembering where each item came from and who she'd been with and what fun she had or hadn't had. Yet to have her memories wrapped and sealed without one last look . . .

"No," she said. "I really need to be at the condo. I won't have room for everything in my new apartment— I'll have to mark the things I'm going to store at my mother's." It seemed a credible excuse. "Who knows how long I'll take. Don't wait for me for dinner."

They finished their meal amid amiable chatter about Lily ("Can you believe that she goes on year after year living in another world?") and Elaine ("I guess it's good that she's found another man") and their impending business

("It's nice that we're all at an age and place that we can risk some things for the greater good, like the possibility that we won't have money to pay the rent or dump into our 401Ks"). That last comment had come from Sarah, surprising Jo that her free-spirited friend knew about 401Ks. Still, Sarah must have some business savvy to have designed and sold her own jewelry all these years. She did not comment that Sarah assuredly had more in her retirement than Jo, who now had none.

It was beginning to seem that the other roommates had been more likely to succeed than Jo had, after all.

She ignored the waiter who flirted with them, passed on dessert, and tried to quell the gnawing ache in her stomach that warned her the next day would be more difficult than she might imagine.


Limbo.

Jo remembered being fascinated by her second-grade best friend's story of the Catholic belief of limbo—the place where dead babies went because God didn't know what to do with them. It was not a bad place, just a place where nothing happened, good or bad.

That was how Jo felt the next morning as she watched one man and three women wrap and pack and seal her life in corrugated cartons called book boxes and wardrobes and dish packs. She had worn old jeans and a denim shirt as if she were going to be the one who dug in and got her hands dirty.

*Crinkle, crinkle* went the plain, brown paper as it cushioned Jo's crystal and pottery from Crate and Barrel and her gleaming silver cookware from Williams-Sonoma.

*Rrrrrrrrip* went the tape from the dispenser.

*Thump, thump* went one carton as it was stacked on top of another.

By ten-thirty she escaped across the street to Starbucks, where she ordered lattes for the packers and a double espresso for herself. Caffeine, perhaps, would distract her nervous system so she wouldn't feel the pain.

On the way back to the condo, she ran into George, the doorman. She had hoped that wouldn't happen: Jo no longer could afford the ten- or twenty-dollar tip she gave to George when he'd done something special like carry up her packages or give her clothes to the pick-up-and-delivery man from the dry cleaner's.

Tweaking the long sides of his gray mustache, George said, "Are you leaving us, Ms. Lyons?"

"Yes, George. Time to move on."

"Heading from the city?"

She gripped the tray of coffee cups. She thought of Brian. "George," she said, "remember Mr. Forbes? The man who stayed here for a few months?"

George nodded. Naturally, he saw, heard, and knew it all.

She handed him the tray of coffees, which he accepted without hesitation, while she dug into the pocket of her jeans. She withdrew a wrinkled twenty, two ones, and a bit of change. "If Mr. Forbes comes by looking for me," she said, extending the cash, "would you please tell him I've gone home to West Hope?"

George looked at the cash, then pushed the tray back toward her. "Put away your money, Ms. Lyons. If the gentleman comes by, I'll be sure he gets the message."

Jo smiled at the grim irony that while the man who had supposedly loved her hadn't hesitated to take hundreds of thousands of her hand-earned dollars, her doorman wouldn't accept a mere twenty-two. She returned the money to her pocket, took the coffee tray, nodded, and went into the lobby and up the elevator.

Back inside the condo, the sounds continued.

*Crinkle, crinkle, rrrrrrrrrip, thump, thump.*

Jo stood by the window, looking out across the city, sipping her espresso, wishing she'd gone with Sarah.

The next day Sarah had insisted on going to the condo.

"It will make it easier if you don't have to stand there all alone," she'd said over breakfast of coffee and croissants. "We can leave right after the truck is loaded, and save the cost of another night in the hotel."

Because she'd barely slept, because she didn't have the strength to argue, Jo merely said, "Only if you promise not to say how beautiful the condo is, or ask how I could give up something so perfect for, of all things, West Hope."

Sarah had smiled and said, "Cherokees believe that only God is perfect."

But that had been in the morning, and now Sarah was the one who stood at the window looking out across the city. True to their agreement, Sarah did not even say, "Wow, what a great view this is."

By one o'clock the truck was loaded with boxes and furniture: pink stickers indicated Shannon Drive, yellow for Marion's garage, basement, or attic.

"See you out west," the driver said with a chuckle.

And then Sarah and Jo stood alone in the gorgeous, empty condo.

"I'll meet you at the car," Sarah said, "if you want to lock up first."

She went out the door before Jo had the chance to say, "No, wait! Don't leave me with these memories!" But Sarah was gone, leaving Jo to lock the front door and the back door and, most of all, the past.

The rooms echoed with change: the guest room with its private bath; the library with the mahogany walls, the built-in bookcases, the fireplace; the living room, the dining room, the gourmet kitchen. The master suite, where she had spent so many lonely nights until Brian found her again. The Jacuzzi, where they'd made love so many times among the bubbles, with champagne.

She ran her hand around the white marble of the Jacuzzi, wishing she could hear Brian's voice again, his laughter, his whispers to her in the night, of love and lust and where he wanted to touch her.

And then her tears spilled down her cheeks, onto the white marble. She held her arms around her waist the way Brian once had done, and finally Jo cried for all she'd had and all she'd lost and all she'd never need again if only Brian would come back.

Somewhere between Palmer and West Springfield, Jo told Sarah that she and Brian had gotten back together, that he had disappeared, and that was the real reason she was going back to West Hope.

She did not tell Sarah that her money had gone, too. Of all the roommates, though, Sarah would be the one she could trust with any secret. Unlike Elaine, Sarah was not easily scandalized. Unlike Lily, Sarah was realistic. Still, Jo was only able to reveal so much, as if the older she became, the harder it was to admit her mistakes, her weaknesses, her character flaws.

When Jo had finished, Sarah merely patted Jo on the knee. "Shit," she said. "We're intelligent women. Savvy. Talented. Why is it we still let ourselves get so screwed up by men?"

Apparently life in the log cabin was not idyllic after all. "Jason?" Jo asked.

Sarah shrugged. "Jason, Brian, are any of them different?" She looked out the window of the car and said, "I love my son with all my heart, but sometimes I wish I hadn't brought a boy into this world."

"Maybe Burch will be different," Jo said, and Sarah laughed and Jo laughed, too, at the absurdities of men. Then they quit the subject over which they had no control, and spent the rest of the trip talking about weddings and how, even if women were foolish enough to tempt fate again, at least they could make the second wedding extra special.

An hour later, they parked the car and went into the storefront.

"I won't go into shock if you won't," Sarah said to Jo as the two of them stood in the doorway, staring at the changes that had happened in their absence.

Where once there had been rubble, now the room was sparkling clean, with shiny navy walls and a rich walnut desk. Behind the desk, oddly enough, sat a man.

"Welcome to Second Chances," the man said. He

stood to all of nearly six feet. His hair was blond with a few streaks of white along the sides. His eyes were slate, perhaps made darker by the deep blue shades around him. "My name is Andrew," he said with a broad smile. "How may we help you ladies today?"

# 12

♥

---

*I* *have no idea where the inspiration came from,* Andrew typed into his laptop, which he'd offered to use in the shop until the women ordered a computer system.

*One look at that newspaper ad and I realized that the common route of trying to get to know a woman, of taking her to the movies or to lunch, of talking on the phone, of sitting in a bar over well-olived martinis, was way too artificial. The women would, without a doubt, say the things they thought I wanted to hear. I knew that because I knew I'd do the same.*

*"What do you do for a living?"*

*"Where did you go to college?"*

*"What's your sign?"* (Do they still use that one? he wondered, but kept typing anyway.)

*What an awful way to meet a woman,* he typed with a smile. *How long would it take to learn if she was being herself or a persona who'd been packaged by her girlfriends or her mother, who had told her what to say and how, because they had been so much more successful (?) at the game of love?*

He raised his fingertips above the keyboard and eavesdropped on the voices in the other room.

"Good grief, Lily," one of them said. "Do we honestly need a receptionist? We don't even have a business yet."

"Oh, hush. I decided a receptionist would give us credibility. Then, when a man walked in—oh, darlings, don't you see? It's perfect! Women will adore having a man greet them at the door, help them with their coats, fetch them coffee if they want."

"Lily, you're insane." That came from the other one who'd walked in the door, the one, Andrew suspected, with the long, dark, Native American–looking hair. "These women are getting married. They're not coming to a singles bar."

Andrew smiled. How could he not smile?

"But darlings, don't you get it?" Lily's voice asked with a giggle that sounded like little bubbles dancing on the taut strings of a harp. "Andrew isn't here to woo them from their bridegrooms. No, on the contrary, Andrew is quite gay. And every woman needs the attention of a gay man to make her feel extra, extra special."

Andrew sank his teeth into the knuckle of his forefinger to avoid laughing out loud. He turned back to his work.

*And so I've found the perfect ruse to let us go behind the scenes, the perfect twist to help us see inside the real thoughts and real lives of women. As a bonus for my daughter,* Andrew added, *this might be considered something close to a real job.*

"You told them *what*?" Cassie rolled her eyes and flopped on the vintage 1920's overstuffed chair that had come with the furnished cottage. Andrew might know squat about women, but he had known that his leather and chrome furniture was too *New York* for the Berkshires.

"I told them I'm gay," he repeated. "It's not a crime, Cassie."

"Maybe not, but it's a lie. What kind of example does that set for me?"

He studied his freckle-faced daughter, whose huge turquoise eyes, thick, dark lashes, and shiny, coal-black ponytail predicted that she'd be as gorgeous as her mother was. He needed Cassie's help, because chances were good the women would learn of her existence, and what would happen then?

He laughed. "Think of it as undercover work. Pretend I'm a famous detective. Like that Nora Roberts character you love, or that *Crossing Jordan* girl."

The huge turquoise eyes rolled again, then closed. "Eve is from the future, Dad," she said. "And Jordan is a medical examiner, not a detective. You're a college professor who's trying to make a buck writing something you don't know anything about, by way of doing something you know even less about."

"Ouch," he said, clutching his heart. "You really know how to hurt a guy."

Cassie sighed.

Andrew picked up a fringed, square pillow and tossed it at her. It knocked off her baseball cap. She tried not to laugh. "Good shot," she finally said.

"At least I'm not washed up at everything," he said.

She bent her head in resignation. "No, Dad. You're not washed up at everything. But this is weird."

"Weirder than if I dated Ms. Brouillard?"

She threw the pillow back at him. "Don't you dare!" she shrieked.

"Then help me! Be my cover!"

She groaned, then looked back at him with Patty's woeful eyes. "What do you want me to do?"

"I thought we might say you are my sister's daughter and that my sister was killed in a car accident, so I adopted you."

She stared at him. "You really *are* weird, you know that?"

"Well, it's not as if we'll have to make a big deal out of it. But just in case, you know?"

"And in the meantime," Cassie said, "how are you going to pretend to be gay?"

He scowled. "I was counting on your help there, too."

"My help? What do I know about gay men? Geez, Dad, I'm only eleven."

"Yeah, well, you know, I thought you might know what gay boys do. They like show tunes, don't they? And singers like Liza Minelli and Julie Andrews?" He supposed it was an odd conversation to be having with his daughter, but what else was he to do?

"Have you ever even had a gay friend, Dad?"

He thought for a moment. "Hap Little."

"Who?"

"Hap Little. He was a photographer assigned to me at *The Edge*."

"Can't he help you?"

"I doubt it. The last I heard he'd moved to South Beach and opened a camera shop."

"Oh, God," Cassie moaned. "Face it, Dad. Your little scheme is never going to work."


She had been on the cover of every major women's magazine by the time she was twenty-two. Patty O'Shay was more than beautiful: She had a wide, wide smile; perfect, flawless teeth; and a mane of thick hair that dared most red-blooded males to bury their face and hands and other body parts into.

From the first moment Andrew saw her, he had been a hopeless mess.

It was at a cocktail party, a kickoff for the advertising campaign of O'S cosmetics, the line of ultraexpensive creams and lotions and foundations and concealers that, if used, could offer other ladies the same silken complexion as Patty O'Shay herself.

*Yes, O'S*, the campaign slogan read and featured a photo of a barely-clad Patty on the deserted beach of a desert island, looking to the horizon for her ship to come in. Andrew had no idea what the hell the slogan had to do with selling cosmetics, but one look at the erotic ad that had been enlarged to a mural and hung from the ceiling of the Waldorf banquet room, and Andrew knew his life would never be the same.

It was three months before he found the nerve to ask her on a date. She said yes, which he realized too late was because he was with the media and she needed exposure to help jump-start disappointing cosmetic sales. He slept with her that night and the next. Two months later, they

were married. It hadn't occurred to Andrew that he'd become just another desperate strategy in what turned out
to be a flagging career: first, the cosmetic line that offered
nothing extraordinary beyond the packaging, then marriage to a journalist, then—the final publicity-seeking
stunt—a baby, Cassandra O'Shay Kennedy.

But by then the magazine covers were graced with
younger, fresher faces. At twenty-nine, Patty was a has-
been, her husband and daughter not enough. So she
joined a rock band and went on a world tour. By the time
the divorce was final, she had landed in Australia and was
living with a cowboy in the outback. When she remembered, Patty sent a card to Cassie on her birthday.

Andrew went to bed that night wondering what the
girls at Second Chances would say if they found out the
truth.

# 13

J o stayed at her mother's house until the movers had deposited the yellow-stickered furniture and boxes and she decided what went where. Over and over, she told herself that everything would be fine.

And it would be fine. She asked Lily and Sarah to wait for her until she was settled; then she would devote all her time to the business. They offered to help her move in, but Jo declined, saying it would go more quickly if she did it herself. The truth was, she didn't trust herself to unseal a carton—any carton—and not burst into tears. She would not, would not, would not, burden the others with her teenage-like emotions.

On the first night Jo was going to sleep at Shannon Drive, she surveyed the remaining cartons in the living room. She was considering getting a take-out salad from McDonald's when there was a knock on the door. The sound startled her: Jo was accustomed to a doorman announcing visitors.

"Who is it?" she asked.

"Jo? I know you don't want any help, but can we talk for a minute?"

It was Elaine, the perfect homemaker, who'd brought homemade bread, a small pan of lasagna, and a plastic container of romaine salad. "If you've already eaten, it will keep until tomorrow," Elaine said as she handed the things to Jo.

Jo could say that yes, she'd eaten, and Elaine might take a quick tour and be gone. But her eyes seemed quite red, as if she'd been crying, and Jo couldn't turn her friend away. "Actually, I'm starving," she said with a smile. "Come in and join me."

They wove around cartons and went into the kitchen. Elaine dug a plate, napkins, a knife, fork, and butter from her oversized purse. From her pocket she retrieved two bottles of water and handed Jo the one that had not yet been opened.

"I thought your dishes might still be packed," she said. "Please, serve yourself. I ate with the kids."

"You are wonderful," Jo said and kissed Elaine's cheek.

While she put food on the plate, Elaine moved from the kitchen and found a seat in the living room on the white sofa. "Your furniture is gorgeous."

"Thanks," Jo replied and did not explain that her entire condo had been gorgeous, that the furniture had been bought by a decorator who had created a breathtaking home overlooking the city skyline and the Charles River.

She carried her plate into the living room and sat on the opposite end of the gorgeous sofa.

"Lasagna on a white sofa?" Elaine asked, cocking one eyebrow over a red-rimmed eye.

Jo laughed. "You've had too many kids, Elaine."

After hesitating a second, Elaine laughed. "Right," she said.

Jo took a bite of her dinner and exclaimed how delicious it was. Then she chewed slowly, waiting for Elaine to reveal the real reason she'd come.

"I feel abandoned," Elaine suddenly blurted out.

Oh no, Jo thought with knowing resignation. Another woman dumped by another man. "Oh, Elaine," Jo said, setting her fork down, "I'm so sorry. Martin seemed like a nice man . . ."

Elaine looked at her with a frown. " 'Martin'? Oh, it's not Martin. It's you. And Lily. And Sarah." Tears spilled from her eyes. She picked up her water bottle and quickly took a drink.

"Us?" Jo asked. "Because of our business? But you said you didn't want to join us as a partner. You said you didn't want to work, that your kind of work took place in your house, with a husband, with your kids . . ."

Elaine shook her head. "No, no, no," she said, then swallowed another swig.

Jo wondered if Elaine's bottle contained more than water. "Well," she said quietly. "What, then?"

"You've all been so busy moving into new places and starting up your business that no one's talked about my wedding. Two weeks have gone by, Jo. Which means I'm two weeks closer to my big day and no one but me seems to care."

She was right, of course. Jo set her plate down on an unopened carton marked BOSTON PR CLUB AWARDS that she knew contained seven glass-etched, foot-tall statues that she had once coveted because they'd declared Jo's work Best in Show seven years in a row.

"That's not true, Lainey," she lied, resting her hand on Elaine's shoulder. "When Sarah and I went to Boston, we talked about little else. Sarah has some wonderful ideas."

"Well, when is someone going to talk to me?"

"By next week, I promise."

Elaine seemed somewhat comforted, then Jo asked, "Are you sure you don't want to be part of the business?" She knew Elaine would say no, but asking again might help her feel less left out.

Elaine said no thanks, then hugged Jo and left.

Jo finished her dinner, tasting not pasta but the guilt of letting down a friend. When she was done, she pushed aside the carton of awards and decided that instead of unpacking, she'd go to the shop and see if anyone was around or if she could do anything to start Elaine's wedding plans rolling. If nothing else, she could begin with a checklist for the dos and the don'ts.

The lights were on in the storefront, but the front door was locked. Jo could see the receptionist—what was his name?—busily typing on the keyboard of a laptop computer. She rapped on the glass. His eyes flicked toward the door and he jumped up. He mouthed the words, "Sorry, we're not open for business."

With her hair in a ponytail and not an inkling of makeup on, Jo wasn't surprised he didn't remember her. She shoved her hands into the pockets of her washed-out jeans. "I work here," she shouted. "We met the other day?"

He stood up and moved to the glass. He looked her over a minute, then unlocked the door. "Sorry," he said. "I didn't recognize you."

So much for a gay man making a woman feel very, very special, she thought.

"I'm Jo," she said, stepping inside and surveying again all that had been done. The navy walls were rich, the hardwood floors gleamed. Different lengths and widths of glass shelving were suspended from the ceiling by transparent wire at different heights. They held clusters of flowers, bouquets of tulle, and tiny clear glass balls that looked like bubbles in the air.

"It's Sarah's creation," the man said. "She thinks the glass makes it look as if everything's floating—'ethereal' is the word she used."

Ethereal, yes, Jo thought. It was quite unusual and quite lovely.

Then she remembered why she was there. "Sarah and Lily," she said, "are they around?"

The man shook his head. "Just me, wrapping up a few things for the day." He stepped back toward his laptop and looked at it. Then he reached out and closed the screen onto the keyboard. He folded his arms across his stomach and leaned against the desk.

"I'm sorry," Jo said, "I've forgotten your name."

He smiled. He had a beautiful smile for a man his age. Over forty, *like us*, Jo thought. She wondered if he had a partner to share his life with, or if men were as tough on one another as they were on the opposite sex. "Andrew," he said, revealing a dimple that could have been carved by a sculptor it was so well-defined into his clean-shaven right cheek.

His right cheek, not his left, like Brian's.

She quickly recouped her breath. "Andrew," Jo repeated. She walked around the showroom, truly amazed at all that had been accomplished in so little time. "Sarah went home?"

"Yes," he said. "She said Jason was due in tonight."

Jo nodded. "And Lily? Is she upstairs in the apartment?" She began moving to the back room, toward the steps that led to Lily's new place.

He laughed. "She spent all day arranging and re-arranging furniture up there," he said. "She decorated it like a doll's house. She bought everything yesterday from Madison Kids."

Jo knew the name. Madison Kids was a Fortune 500 company that started kids early to develop designer tastes. "And it's all here so fast?" she asked, but did not need a reply. She supposed Andrew had been around long enough to know, as she did, that money always talked, and often delivered in miraculous time.

"Go ahead up," he said. "Lily is out, but I'm sure she won't mind."

Jo stopped. "Lily's out?"

"Yes."

Elaine was right, Jo thought. They were all so wrapped up in their own lives, they didn't care about the wedding. They didn't care one little bit. "Maybe I can get started on some things down here," she said. "Do you know where the books are that Sarah brought back from Boston?"

On his way to a credenza, Andrew glanced back at his

laptop. "They're all in here," he said. "Lily said we should put them out of sight. We wouldn't want anyone to think all our ideas aren't original."

Jo laughed and followed him to the credenza. "What time will she be back?" she asked. "I'd really like to talk to her tonight."

Andrew shrugged. "Don't know. She's gone out for dinner." He opened a drawer, then handed Jo three books that were the supposed be-all and end-all: *Martha Stewart's Wedding Guide, Another Journey Down the Aisle, The Ultimate Second Wedding.*

Jo scowled. "Did she go out alone?"

"Nope. She went on a date with that guy . . . oh, man, I'm as bad at names as you are, I'm afraid."

" 'Guy'? As in a man?"

"Yeah, you know. The landlord."

Jo looked at the cover of *The Ultimate Second Wedding.* The white gown that swept across the cover slowly blurred. "Frank?" she asked. "Lily has a date with Frank Forbes?"

"Yeah, that's his name. The guy with the antiques."

# 14

The trouble with a woman is you never know when you'll say something wrong, because who knows what goes on in her mind? For now, however, I'm going to pay attention to my mistakes, and share the lessons learned with you. Maybe between us we'll resolve this issue after all.

*Lesson #1: Never mention another man's name in the presence of a woman unless you know whether or not the woman and said man have a past, a present, or the pretense of a future together.*

*In fact,* Andrew continued, while he marveled at his insight, *maybe it's best not to mention any man's name at all. It's been said that we aren't so inclined, that most men have no problem mentioning their conquests.*

*Here's a clue: It does not work both ways. Don't remind a woman of her past. If the relationship was bad, she'll get depressed, probably because she'll think it was her fault. If the relationship was good, she'll get depressed because it ended. Either way, you'll lose.*

Not using their names, he then related what had happened when he told Jo about Lily and the landlord, how her cheerful nature had turned solemn, how she returned the books to the credenza drawer, then announced that she'd see him the next day, that she really didn't feel like working after all.

All because he'd mentioned a woman and a man. All because he'd opened up his mouth before he knew the histories of the people involved.

He ended his first column by adding: *We must, alas, forget that women are different, that they have no penises with which to think. Instead, they use their brain, which is sometimes unfortunate, but most always true.*

He signed the piece *A.K.*, then turned off the laptop and closed up the shop. Tomorrow he'd reread it one more time, then e-mail it to John Benson in the nick of deadline time. And *Buzz* would have its first "Real Women" column, and Andrew would be much closer to having the new car and the new roof and Cassie's riding lessons paid for several months in advance. And, of course, he'd be closer to Australia, closer to Patty.

Jo wondered how many men lived in West Hope and why Lily had to pick him. Because even though it had no doubt been Frank who'd asked Lily out, "Make no mistake about it," Jo said to her windshield, "it was Lily's idea."

Lily the Romantic.

Lily the Man-lover.

Lily the Seducer, who flitted her "poor little me" flits around every man she could and begged them to take care of her.

As if Lily Beckwith needed taking care of.

As if Lily Beckwith, for one minute, didn't know exactly what she was doing.

Driving faster than she knew she should, Jo took the turn into Shannon Drive. She hated that she was exasperated at a friend, hated that she was—what, jealous? Was that what she was? Did she feel somehow violated, as if Frank Forbes were his brother, Brian, as if he were cheating on Jo with one of her best friends?

Or maybe, Jo reasoned, she secretly envied Lily for knowing how to capture one man after another, when Jo had spent her life proving she didn't need one.

Wheeling into the garage, Jo's jaw tightened with annoyance, at Lily, at herself. If her thoughts hadn't been so tense, so *in*tense, her vision so narrowly tunneled, she might have seen the man emerge from his truck and step into her path. She might have seen him before she had to slam on her brakes, the rubber from her tires skidding on concrete, their echo screeching off cinderblock walls, the back end of her small car fishtailing. The man leapt onto the hood of his SUV.

Jo's car came to a stop. Her breath was short, panting. Her mouth had suddenly gone dry. *Oh my God*, she thought. *I almost hit him.*

Her hand trembled so hard she couldn't open her door. She tried to steady her left hand with her right. But just as the door opened, the man slid off the truck hood and waved her away.

"It's okay. I'm okay," he said.

Jo shook her head. "I'm so sorry," she stammered and tried to get out of her car, but her legs were weak and they were shaking, too.

"Don't be," he said. "Honest, I'm okay. See?" He pirouetted in a choppy, masculine kind of pirouette. At another time, Jo might have been attracted to his sense of humor. Instead, she simply sat there, shaking.

He walked over to her car. "What about you? Are you all right?"

Meekly, she nodded. "I'm so sorry," she said again.

"No problem," he said. "Just let me know when you're coming home again, and I'll be sure to be out of town." He smiled and he winked and he walked away. It was another several minutes before Jo could steer her car into her assigned parking spot and regain what was left of her composure.

# 15

♥

**DO**

*Ask your best friend or your daughter or your mother to be your maid of honor, no matter how young or old or how great or lousy they might look in the attendant's gown you've picked. Get over how chic or unchic the wedding photos might look if your attendant isn't Cindy Crawford or Iman.*

Jo set her pen down on the small notebook that was balanced on the armrest of the white sofa where Elaine had chastised her for eating lasagna. By focusing on her list of dos and don'ts for second weddings, Jo would feel like she was moving forward, getting started on her new life, helping Elaine start on hers, as well. Maybe the distraction would also help Jo forget that she'd almost hit the man in the garage, that her unhappy state of "limbo" had nearly hurt another human being.

She stared at the list that she'd begun and decided it would become her antidote to mend her broken heart, her broken life.

"A spa day for the bridesmaids!" Lily proclaimed the next morning. "With manicures and pedicures and facials and massages!"

They sat in overstuffed navy chairs clustered in front of Andrew's desk—Lily, Sarah, Jo, and Elaine, the bride-to-be.

Jo had made early calls to Sarah and Lily.

"We need to meet this morning," she said. "We need to work on Elaine's wedding."

Then she'd called Elaine and there they all were, sipping Green Mountain coffee and nibbling bagels with cream cheese that Andrew had run to the coffee shop and procured for the group. It occurred to Jo that if the stranger had not been so limber, she might have been sipping coffee from a cardboard cup in the hospital emergency room. Or worse.

She forced her thoughts to the present, to Lily, who seemed exceptionally jovial for the morning hour. *Date afterglow,* Jo mused, the touch of cream in her coffee suddenly tasting sour. She cleared her throat. "A spa day is a great idea for first weddings," she said, "but we're not twenty-five. Besides, we should be thinking about Elaine's needs, not ours."

"Oh, pooh, Josephine," Lily teased. "What better way to celebrate Elaine's wedding? And I disagree. Spa days should be for bridesmaids of all ages. Facials. Pedicures. Manicures. We're never too old to be pampered."

Sarah glanced down at her hands. "I'm afraid I have little to manicure," she said. "An artist's hands usually look like crap."

"Precisely my point," Lily said. "We all deserve to look our best for the wedding. Besides, we can have photos of our outing taken for our portfolio." She spun on her chair. "Andrew, do you shoot?"

Perhaps Lily believed that every gay man liked to take pictures, as she believed that every woman craved a gay man for a friend.

"Sometimes," he replied. "I can practice, if you like."

Lily beamed, her tiny pink cheeks radiating excitement, as if he'd just said he'd fly to the moon if she liked. "Oh, Andrew, that would be divine!"

A small knot formed at the base of Jo's neck. She supposed that if group meetings were ever to accomplish anything worthwhile, she, not Lily, would have to be in control. "Yes. Well," Jo continued, rubbing her neck, "we can work on that later. Right now we need to decide if Elaine will still have her reception at home."

It had been Elaine's original plan, complete with tables from Taylor Rental and folding chairs from the funeral home set between the badminton net and the birdfeeders.

"We're only inviting seventy-five people," Elaine said. "Not enough for a hall."

"We can find somewhere else," Sarah said. "Somewhere picturesque, like The Mount. It's short notice, but we might be able to work something out." The home of the once-famous writer, Edith Wharton, had become a museum, honored for its elegance and its restored grounds. "I could make a phone call. One of Jason's friends works there."

"Wow," Elaine said. "That would be terrific. But expensive, I bet."

"Reginald won't mind," Lily said with a smile. "Nothing is too good for our Elaine. And for our business."

Elaine actually giggled as if she were Lily.

"Should it be indoors or out?" Sarah asked.

"We'll need a caterer," Lily commented. Elaine had intended to ask the Women's Club from the church if they would make finger sandwiches and gelatin salad.

"What about music?" Elaine asked. "It might be nicer to have live music than a DJ. Especially at The Mount."

"Maybe a small group from Tanglewood," Lily interjected. "Do they have a traveling quartet or something?"

"The music would have to depend on the theme," Sarah said, "which we haven't yet determined."

Silence, as the women pondered a theme.

"Gee," Elaine finally said, "the theme of my first wedding was 'Justice of the Peace.' "

Sarah laughed.

"Well," Lily said, "today it's different. Everyone simply must have a theme. Victorian. Medieval. Something like that."

Jo leaned back and looked over at Andrew, who was typing notes into his laptop. The knot eased from her neck; she smiled. Maybe, she thought, she wouldn't need to be in control after all. Maybe, for once, she wouldn't need to assume all the burden of responsibility. And maybe Jo could find the way out of her limbo and begin slowly to relax. Even if Lily ended up taking Brian's brother as her devoted husband number four.

Ambers and russets and deep, rich cranberries, the colors of a New England October in soft, subtle tones, accented by gold. Thick gold ribbons for the bouquets, tall gold vases for the altar flowers, twinkling gold tiaras for each of the bridesmaids.

The theme would be Harvest. They would all wear pearl white. Simple, elegant slip dresses for Lily, Sarah, and Jo, precursors to the centerpiece—Elaine's magnificent gown, a vision of three-tiered pearl satin with fitted long sleeves and a wide v-neck accented by a single gold choker set with a seven-carat, pear-shaped Tiffany diamond. The necklace would be Lily's. "Something borrowed," she said with a wink.

By midafternoon Jo had organized the notes Andrew had taken and the women divided up the duties: Sarah, locate and secure a reception site, then design the décor and flowers and reception around it; Elaine, interview caterers with Jo and select the food, determine limos (if wanted), and decide if she wants any of her kids (or Martin's) involved in the ceremony and, if so, how; Lily, select music and look for appropriate gifts for the guests, as no second wedding would be complete without a substantial memory—not merely a token—something depicting the theme or the ambiance of the location. And Jo, handle the business end of it all: organize contracts, make deposits, set up a bank of contacts they would use, if not for Elaine, then for their future brides. Andrew would be her assistant, and everyone else's when he was needed.

They decided to travel to Chestnut Hill Thursday to try on the gowns that Sarah had seen. Andrew promised to hold down the bridal fort.

Then Sarah stood up. "If we're done for now, I'd like to get home to Jason," she said. "He's off again tomorrow night—this time to the Cape and Martha's Vineyard."

Jo wondered if half a man was better than no man at all, then quickly decided she was in no position to judge.

Elaine stood up, too. "And I must get home to my munchkins," she announced.

Whether "munchkins" referred to Martin or her fully-grown kids, Elaine didn't specify, but before Jo could ask, both Sarah and Elaine had gone out the front door, leaving Jo with cheerful Lily. And Andrew, of course.

Lily grinned. "Do you have a few minutes?" she asked, and Jo suspected what was coming next. "I want to show you what I've done with the upstairs."

*No you don't,* Jo wanted to say. *You want to tell me about your wonderful date with Brian's brother.* Instead, she shrugged and said, "Sure," because she figured, like Frank, she'd have to deal with it sooner than later, and this time she might as well get it over and damned done with.

The apartment looked like something from a child's fairy tale: *Alice in Wonderland* or *Eloise at the Plaza.* The bedroom had white painted furniture and white ruffled everything; the kitchen and living room were cotton-candy colors with fabrics in fun stripes and life-size dolls with huge, painted smiles scattered about as if they'd just finished playing and were ready for naps.

"Lily," Jo said in spite of herself, "you really are something."

Lily folded her hands. "After my parents died, my childhood was gone," she said. "Gone in a flash," she said, snapping her fingers. "Imagine that."

It was the first time, ever, that Jo had heard her friend allude to something distressing.

"But that was then," Lily said, quickly recovering. "Then there was college and my first marriage, and I never got to be a kid again." She nodded as if to agree with herself. "Now I can. Now I can do whatever I want." She did not add that her first husband had left her, to return home to his mother; that her second decided he preferred the company of men; and that Reginald, well, Jo already knew what had happened to Reginald. Thank God he'd at least left his hefty portfolio.

"Well," Jo replied, "the apartment is . . . *darling*. Really, it is. Darling."

Lily looked at Jo and giggled. "It's okay, Josephine. I admit that I'm nuts." She swooped her light hand. "Come into the kitchen where we shall have a tea party. I can make little sandwiches for lunch and trim off the crusts!"

Checking her watch, Jo said, "I'll take a rain check, okay? I'd like to get home and finish unpacking." That's when she realized there were no cartons in Lily's apartment, nothing to say she hadn't lived there forever. "I can't believe that you're settled so fast."

"Well, I didn't bring much. I bought mostly new things. And Frank helped me arrange a lot of the pieces."

Frank, again. Jo leaned against the doorjamb between the kitchen and living room. *Sooner or later,* and sooner had come. "I heard you had dinner with him last night."

Lily nodded. "He's a very nice man. I know how much you liked his brother, Jo."

With what she hoped was a smile that looked sincere, not maudlin, Jo said, "That was a long time ago."

"Did you know Frank then? When you were young? Did you know that he was married for ten years, no kids. His wife didn't want any. Then out of the blue—poof!—she up and left him. Said she wanted more excitement than West Hope had to offer. It's sad, isn't it? That such a thing can happen to a man as nice as Frank?"

Jo leaned over and kissed Lily on the cheek. "Don't ever change," she said.

With a small, startled look, Lily said, "So it won't freak you out if I see him again?"

Well, of course that was coming. "I wish you only the best, Lily. Honestly, I mean it."

"It's just . . . it's just that . . ." Lily plunked down on a white wooden chair. "Oh, Jo, I'm so ashamed to admit it, but I utterly despise not having a man in my life. I'm just so much happier . . . so much *healthier* . . . when I'm in love. Do you know what I mean?"

Jo smiled. "Not exactly," she replied, though she remembered perfectly well the inner warmth, the balance, the *peace* that she'd felt when Brian had been with her and she'd been in love. She supposed she should have asked if Lily was already in love with Frank Forbes, but Jo was suddenly tired from her sleepless night.

She made excuses to Lily, then trundled downstairs. On her way out, a young girl brushed past her and entered the shop.

"Uncle Andrew!" the girl cried. "I thought I'd stop by

on the way home from school and check out your new job."

Jo thought she detected a wince on Andrew's handsome face. "I'll see you tomorrow," Jo said, and dashed outside before she was sidetracked by any more people or caught off guard by any more of her unwanted emotions.

# 16

❤

Sheesh, Dad, she's one of your bosses? She looks pretty hot. Why can't you date somebody like her?"

It was ten minutes later and Cassie sipped on an ice-cream soda at the old-fashioned luncheonette/soda fountain two doors down from the shop. Andrew signaled his daughter to keep her voice down. Then he tasted his egg cream and wondered how long it had been since he'd had one. He'd forgotten how good it was.

"You know very well why," he said quietly, then added, "and don't call me 'Dad.'"

Cassie rolled her eyes, which were so much like Patty's, then said, "Whoever you are, we need to work on your wardrobe. You look like a straight city-boy-turned-college-professor."

Andrew surveyed his chinos, his old polo shirt, his sneakers.

"Pastels," Cassie said. "Maybe some jewelry. And you have to lose the Nike's. Now we're talking Birkenstocks. Sandals," Cassie added, before he could ask what Birkenstocks were.

"So now you're an authority?"

"I've been watching TV. Drink your egg cream and later we'll go shopping." She scooped a spoonful of ice cream and shared it with him.

"I take it this means you approve after all?"

"Hardly. But I do feel a responsibility to please my elderly Uncle Andrew."

Andrew tugged her baseball cap down over her eyes, and Cassie laughed her silly laugh and Andrew felt the sweet joy that he knew was unconditional love, and he was glad that sometimes a man and a woman got together if it meant producing such a neat kid.


The fact that Jo was so tired surely would help numb the reality that she was driving back to Shannon Drive, that it now was home. She stopped at Quikees and bought a few staples—water and orange juice, coffee and tea and a Sara Lee cake in case she was awake again tonight. Without a man or even a half, she could at least have the comfort of chocolate.

Pulling into the garage, she noticed the truck of the man that she'd almost hit. She shuddered. Why had the man been so nice? He could have sued her, she supposed, if she had anything left.

After parking her car, Jo decided to leave him a note, another "I'm sorry" to prove that she was, to show that the next day the incident still lingered on her mind.

In the glove box she found an old bank envelope from First Trust in Boston.

*This is your neighbor,* she carefully wrote. *The one who almost hit you last night. I wanted to let you know that I truly am sorry—no excuses, I was merely preoccupied and didn't watch where I was going. Again, I'm sorry. I hope you're okay. I'll try not to let it happen again!* She squeezed her initials, *J.L.,* in the little space that remained between the F.D.I.C. and the D.I.F.M.

Then she got out of her car, juggled her bundles, walked back to the man's truck, and carefully tucked the note under the windshield wiper, where he'd be certain to see it when he went out.

As she continued toward the elevator, it occurred to Jo that she didn't remember what the man looked like: She'd been so self-absorbed by what she had done, or almost done, that she hadn't noticed.


*Well, I'm learning,* Andrew typed later that night after he'd hung up his pastels and he'd removed his silver chime ball that hung from a black cord around his neck and placed his new Birkenstocks on the floor of his now-gay closet. Cassie had finally gone to bed and was, hopefully, asleep, and Andrew at last sat at the laptop, buoyed by a message John Benson had left that afternoon: The column was great; keep up the good work.

Andrew had no idea what had been so great about it. He guessed John figured that the world was ready for a dose of reality, no more fantasies to end in harsh rejection.

He pushed thoughts of Patty from his mind.

*Let's use "my" four women as our examples,* he typed. *I have a feeling that when you put any four together, one will be the leader.* He paused; he frowned. He could not use real names. He could not call them Jo, Lily, Sarah, and Elaine. He could not take the risk. But he must call them something.

He smiled. He typed *Jo.* Next to that, he typed *Jacquelin.*

Then he typed *Lily. Olivia.*

*Sarah. Sadie.*

*Elaine. Eileen.*

He tried not to tell himself that he was a genius.

Instead, Andrew put the new names into his memory. Then he deleted them from the text and resumed his task. *Men do the same thing,* he wrote, *unconsciously agree that one will be in charge. Does that mean the self-appointed "leader" is the most masculine? In my case, hardly.*

He leaned back on his chair and thought about Jo—Jacquelin. Beautiful, no question. Smart, probably the smartest. Sophisticated, absolutely.

So what was she doing in West Hope? And what did it have to do with Frank Forbes and the way she became nervous when his name was mentioned?

Had Frank been a lover?

Was Lily next in line?

Would the act break up what appeared to be a long-standing friendship between Lily and Jo, and would it jeopardize their newly formed business?

He chuckled to himself. *It's a goddamn soap opera,* he thought.

Then another of those lightbulbs lit up over his slow-witted head.

*Of course*, he thought.

*Shit.*

*That's it.*

If John Benson had liked the first column, wait until he saw the rest.

With another good chuckle, Andrew turned back to his computer and resumed typing, comfortable, at last, with the idea that "Real Women" would really be about the soap opera, the gossip, the women of Second Chances: Jacquelin, the independent power; Olivia, the dependent child; Sadie, the freethinker; Eileen, the traditionalist.

If there was any other type of woman in the world, Andrew had not found her yet. He would tell their stories as they unfolded, with their names changed (not that they'd ever know) to protect the innocent and the not-so-innocent. And then he'd win the Pulitzer and he'd buy Cassie her own horse and have the cottage roof fixed and buy a new Mercedes and move to goddamn Australia if that was what he wanted to do.

# 17

*DON'T*
*Invite your former in-laws, no matter how close you still might feel to them. They are part of your former life, and though you might be comfortable having them as guests, your spouse-to-be's family will not.*

On the way to look at the gowns, Jo told them of her plan to create the list.

"Dos and don'ts?" Lily had asked with a frown. "It sounds awfully rigid. Structured."

But Jo explained that the list wasn't meant to structure, just to be used as a guideline. She did not want to explain that developing the list actually gave her focus, a tangible distraction, a welcome game, one small thing about her life that she could control.

The dresses were perfect, not first-wedding flashy or frilly, but elegant and lovely. When Elaine tried on the wedding gown, she sat down and cried.

"It's so beautiful, Sarah," she said. "It's what I've always wanted."

Sarah told her to get out of the dress before she dripped mascara on it and they had to pay for the off-the-rack sample.

They stopped in Sturbridge for a late lunch at the Ugly Duckling, the nestlike, wood-beamed loft at the renowned Whistling Swan.

Elaine cried again during her second glass of wine. "I can't believe you're doing all this for me," she said.

"And for our business," Lily said, raising her glass in a toast.

"Which reminds me, I'll go call Jason's friend," Sarah said and left the table.

"Who is Jason's friend?" Lily asked.

Jo shrugged. "The one who works at The Mount, I guess."

"Oh," Lily replied. Clearly she didn't have the same checklist running through her mind that Jo did, the mental organizer pages that were so necessary when one operated a business.

Perhaps if Lily spent fewer hours decorating her apartment and dining with Frank she might understand. She had yet to contact Tanglewood; she had yet to look for wedding-guest gifts. But Jo drank her wine and reminded herself that without Lily's money or her generosity there would be no business at all. Besides, what did Jo expect? Lily had no experience in the workaday world. Jo supposed it would be up to her to teach their pampered friend. Gently.

"They're booked October ninth," Sarah said when she returned.

"Rats," Jo said.

"Oh," Elaine whined.

But Lily shook her head. "We'll go tomorrow," she said. "All of us. I'm sure they can work us in."

They piled into Sarah's giant Chevy pickup truck again the next day. Lily's rented, matchboxlike Mercedes was too small for the four of them and Jo's Honda would be too crowded. They could have gone in Elaine's minivan, but Lily had promised herself never to be seen in one.

"No offense, darling," Lily said to Elaine as Sarah traversed the back roads toward Lenox, toward The Mount, "but minivans are so *mom*like, and I'm certainly not that."

No, Lily was not momlike any more than she was businesslike. Lily was just Lily, who had no idea that you could not turn up unannounced at a place such as The Mount and demand they change their plans, just because of how much money you possessed.

Could you?

Jo looked out the side of the truck and smiled, realizing that, as kids, she'd never fully appreciated Lily's determination to get her way.

"Has anyone seen the restoration?" Jo asked. The Mount had been constructed in the early nineteen hundreds. Often called "The Renaissance Woman" for her stunning novels (including *The Age of Innocence*, for which she was lauded with a Pulitzer Prize), for her books on decorating to which professionals still referred, and for her progressive attitudes in a post-Victorian world, Edith Wharton lived there with her husband for only ten years before they split up and she retreated to the south of France. Decades later, with the gardens overgrown and the roof leaking like a postmenopausal bladder, a group of preservationists decided to salvage the estate—one of the few National Historic Landmarks that had been designated to honor a woman.

The concept of holding Elaine's second wedding there seemed appropriate: a wedding planned by strong, take-charge kind of women, or at least by women trying to be.

"I've seen it," Sarah said. "It's an awesome French château. The gardens and the fountains and the walking paths are a perfect venue for a wedding reception. Which someone else apparently believes, as well, or they would not have booked it for *their* wedding on the *same day* Elaine's will be." She steered the truck down a road, past an outbuilding, past what had been a stable. "We're wasting our time," she added with a grumble. "We should be back at the shop trying to locate other sites."

Lily didn't speak, which was, of course, unusual.

Elaine sat with her hands folded across her polyestered lap. "It doesn't matter," she said. "My backyard will be fine."

Jo kept her eyes fixed out the window and wondered if Lily's determination was about to turn into a full-blown spat.

They pulled around the circular drive in front of the grand white house. It had been years since Jo had stood before the unpretentious entrance, years since she and Brian sneaked out there for picnics on the lawn and fishing in

Laurel Lake and making love in the thick stands of pines. They had been trespassing, but it had been safe; a lot of kids went there for the same reasons. At that time, the place had been abandoned and the restoration hadn't yet begun.

Jo's breath stumbled somewhere in her throat.

Then Sarah said, "Come on, girls, let's get this over with." She opened her truck door, and the others followed.


Lily rang what appeared to be a bell at the front door in the forecourt. They stood a moment on one foot, then the other, eyes scanning the white stucco wall surrounding them and the tall topiary sentries, ears hearing nothing but quiet and sounds of nearby summer birds.

The wooden door creaked open. "Yes?" asked a woman older than they were, but neatly coiffed and perfectly attired in a Talbot's flowered dress.

"We'd like to speak with the banquet manager," Lily said.

The woman smiled. "Do you have an appointment?"

"No. I'm from out of town and I didn't have time to phone ahead." She somehow had affected an almost-Southern accent, perhaps because Lily deemed that more effective when trying to get her way.

"Follow me," the woman said, and stepped aside to let them in.

Jo wanted to smile but didn't dare.

The grottolike entrance hall was cool and dark and emitted a sense of being underground. Perhaps recognizing the quizzical looks on all their faces, the woman said,

"Edith Wharton wanted her guests to make a slow transition from the outside. Which accounts for the strong depiction of nature portrayed in the décor."

Nature was not the word. The vaulted ceilings, mirrored walls, and gurgling fountain literally brought the outside in.

Jo glanced at Sarah and recognized appreciation for the detailed plasterwork and terra-cotta floor. Lily, however, trotted along behind their greeter, seemingly oblivious to their surroundings, as was Elaine, who just seemed overwhelmed.

They worked their way up a staircase that had intricate iron railings and a boldly patterned carpet.

"Edith Wharton was from the Jones family of New York City," the guide related as if this was a tour and she was paid to speak the facts. "Her habit of spending money lavishly is where the phrase 'keeping up with the Joneses' came from."

Jo had a sense that Sarah wanted to make a comment about Lily and her spending habits, but Sarah checked her words. Jo smiled and kept climbing the wide steps.

Once upstairs, they followed the woman through an enormous gallery, into a lavish dining room, and out a set of French doors to an enormous terrace.

"I'll tell Denise you're here," the woman said. "Please, make yourselves at home."

It was, perhaps, easier for Lily to make herself at home than for the rest of them. From the wide, long terrace the lawn tiered down to the distant lake, every tree and walkway, every summer, sunlit flower and vivid blade of grass manicured for loveliness. Jo separated from the others to take in the view, to allow herself a brief moment of memories.

Sarah came up beside her and rescued Jo from becoming maudlin. "It's not fair to do this to Elaine," Sarah said. "How can her backyard look like anything compared to this?"

Jo smiled and nodded a little, not wanting to agree in case Lily was in earshot and Sarah's words might start a quarrel.

"It's ridiculous," Sarah continued. "If we're going to be in business together, one of us is going to have to stand up to Lily. We need to bring her into reality and out of that airheaded place where she exists."

Jo smiled again, then she heard Lily shout, "Girls! Come and meet Denise."

When they approached, Denise held out her hand. "Winston College, class of eighty-seven," she said.

"Which was part of why Denise was excited about booking Elaine's wedding here." Lily hooked her arm through Denise's, as if they were old friends.

Jo's eyes darted from Lily to Elaine to Sarah to Denise. Other eyes darted, too.

Lily laughed. "Surprise!" she said and clapped her hands. "I'll bet you thought I haven't been doing anything constructive. Well, Denise and I have been planning this for days. Isn't it fun?" She turned to Elaine and swept her arms across the air. "The reception will be out here on the terrace. The guests will mingle in the gardens, which will be decorated naturally by the golden linden leaves of autumn. The waitstaff will be in period costume. They'll serve hors d'oeuvres on silver trays and champagne from crystal flutes. The music will rise up from the little bandstand and float down toward the lake. Oh," she said, holding her delicate hands to her small chest, "it will be so romantic. Won't it, girls?"

The ride back to the shop was animated.

"I can't believe you did this, Lily," Jo said.

"Behind our backs," Elaine added.

Sarah shook her head more than a few times. "I underestimated you, kid," she said.

But Lily smiled and shrugged them off. Her little prank had made them happy, but now she moved on to other things. "I think I'll go to the city tomorrow," she said. "I need ideas for the wedding-guest gifts. I simply cannot get inspired this far from Tiffany's."

*The city*, of course, meant New York City, because, in Lily's world, was there another? "Nothing too costly," Jo cautioned, then laughed. "If we're going to make Elaine's wedding an example of our work, we won't want to scare off potential brides." She was still stunned, however, that Lily was now doing her job.

"Darling, the only way we'll ever make any money is to promote the finest . . . the kind of event they won't get just anywhere. Besides, that's another tidbit for your dos-and-don'ts list. *DO* give your guests quality, second-wedding remembrances. *DON'T* give them favors as if it's a first wedding. First-timers can't afford it; second-timers, well, should."

"As long as you remember that most of Elaine's guests won't be from Paris or Rome," Sarah chimed in.

"More like Pittsfield and North Adams," Elaine

added. "Regular folks who are more familiar with Wal-Mart than Tiffany's."

They all laughed, then Lily shook her head. "Okay, I get the picture," she said. "Reginald, however, would have been disappointed."

"While you're away, would you like me to contact Tanglewood?" Jo asked, at last feeling the sense that they were now working as one. "You might be gone a few days and we should book someone soon."

"Oh yes!" Lily exclaimed. "That would be wonderful. Sometimes I do wonder if I will ever remember more than one thing at a time."

"Oh, something tells me you'll do just fine," Sarah said with a small sigh and the others laughed, because when the clichéd chips were down, it had always been what they did best when they were together.

# 18

After they returned to the shop ("If I'm going to live here, I suppose I must buy a car," Lily had moaned), Jo was filled with the fullness of friends and a glimmer of hope for the future. She decided that evening might be a good time to show her mother the apartment on Shannon Drive. Maybe now that Jo had unpacked most of the boxes, Marion wouldn't feel as if the place was as bleak and unworthy as she had expected. On the way back, they could stop at Second Chances. Not that Marion hadn't been kept up-to-date, minute by minute, by the church ladies who strolled Main Street with little to do except smile and gawk and make detailed mental notes.

*Some sort of children's furniture was delivered upstairs.*

*They've taken a perfectly nice storefront and made it look modern.*

*There's a man inside at a desk—what's he doing there?*

But as was Marion's fashion, she had not pressured Jo. There was never a need to. Jo could tell from one comment how Marion felt about something, from world economics to last week's price of fruit.

Her mother was home, sitting at the kitchen table reading the newspaper, a rotary fan billowing the armholes of her sleeveless shift dress.

"The apartment's air-conditioned," Jo said. "You might want a sweater."

It took Marion only ten minutes to apply fresh lipstick, grab her crafts-fair quilted purse, pick up her white cotton sweater, and head out the door.

Five minutes later Jo regretted inviting her.

"It must be awfully dark in here at night, Josephine," Marion said as they walked across the garage.

There it was, the one single comment that set up disapproval, that left no need to add other thoughts that were certain to be: "It's no place for a woman alone," or, on the elevator, "I've never liked elevators in these kinds of buildings. They seem so unsafe. If it gets stuck, who would you call?" Then in the hall, "It looks like a hotel, doesn't it? I'll bet you can hear everyone who walks past your door."

Marion didn't need to say any of those things. Jo felt their presence by her mother's hesitant walk and grip on her purse and the way her eyes search-lighted to the left then to the right.

By the time Jo unlocked her front door she was exhausted.

But then Marion said, "Well, this is quite lovely."

No doubt the furnishings had won Marion over.

Jo made iced tea and gave Marion a tour. When they sat on the sofa, Marion said, "I think about that Brian Forbes sometimes and I want to scream," she said. "I simply can't believe he ran out on you again."

It was something Jo hadn't expected. "We don't know for sure that's what happened, Mother. Besides, I'd rather not talk about Brian, okay? I'm trying to get on with my life."

"Still," Marion said, "it would be good for you to have a man in your life."

Jo studied the ice cubes floating in her glass. "What an odd thing to say," she commented, but did not add, "coming from you."

Marion sighed. "Josephine," she said, "now that you've moved back here, there's something I'd like you to know."

Despite gossip and opinions, Marion wasn't often given to theatrics.

"I think you should have a man in your life, because I've so enjoyed having a man in mine," she said.

Jo laughed. Marion's sense of humor often took her off guard. In a second, however, Jo realized Marion wasn't laughing. "Mother?" Jo asked. "Are you serious?"

Marion hesitated, then asked, "Do you remember Ted Cappelinni?"

Jo stared at her mother. Surely this was a joke. "Ted?" she asked. "Ted the Butcher?"

Marion nodded. "We've been seeing each other for years."

"The butcher?" Jo repeated, the word hanging in the air like Ted Cappelinni's meat cleaver poised to align a perfect blow that would separate the short ribs from the chops.

"He's a good man," her mother replied. "Kind. Generous. It would do you good to find one of those, too."

Jo slugged down her iced tea, wishing it was wine. "Well, gosh," she said, and realized how absurd she sounded. "This is quite a surprise. You and Ted the Butcher. Why didn't you tell me?"

Suddenly she felt like the parent of an adolescent: happy for Marion, yet wary about a relationship that had blossomed and developed behind Jo's unsuspecting back. Then she had but one thought: *Did they have sex?*

Seventy, after all, was no longer thought to be old.

But Marion?

And the butcher?

"Don't be so shocked, Jo," Marion said. "I didn't tell you because there was no reason. You were in Boston and I was out here, and the few times we got together there were more important things to talk about, like how you were and the things you were doing."

Jo stood up and walked to her bookcase. She scanned the spines of books that she'd read in the last few years when she'd grown to hate dating, because what had been the point when she still loved Brian?

"Well," she said, "it would have mattered to me, Mother. I would have liked to have known what was going on in your life. I'd have liked to have known that you were happy."

"Oh, don't be so dramatic," her mother said. "Did I ever say I wasn't happy? Did I ever act it?"

Jo realized then that she'd never thought much about it, that she'd never considered that her mother had needs just as Jo did. "Wow," she said, "I feel awful that I was so self-centered I never thought about you. About how your life was going. I thought it revolved around your church and your friends." She walked to the window for the view of the balconies and all the white plastic chairs.

"Ted is my friend," Marion said. "It's not as if we're going to get married."

Jo turned around. "Why not?"

Marion laughed. "Because we've each lived alone for too many years. Besides, it's not easy at our age. You young people can just go off and get married and then get divorced if you want. But at seventy . . . well, in my generation we do things for keeps."

Jo did not remind her mother that her mother might have thought she'd married Sam Lyons "for keeps," yet she sure hadn't kept him, and no one had died because of it, had they?

"Well," Jo said, "I don't know what to say. If Ted makes you happy, that's all that matters."

"And anyway," Marion continued, "he has his house; I have mine. How would we decide where to live?"

Jo laughed. "You could both sell your houses and move into this building."

Marion grinned and put on her sweater.


Later that night, Jo lay in bed feeling empty. Empty and alone.

After they'd finished their tea, Jo had driven to Second Chances and showed her mother around, all the while still trying to digest the woman's news.

She wondered if, over the years, Ted had proposed,

and if Marion rejected him because she was still in love with Jo's father, the man who had broken her heart. She wondered if such misplaced loyalty was genetic, and if that was why Jo had made such a mess of her own life.

"It's quite interesting," Marion had said as she scanned through the software that Jo showed her of the "how's" and the "who's" that they already databased on behalf of the clients who'd not yet showed up. "But if Ted and I ever marry—which we won't, I assure you—we'd do it at the town hall. Why would anyone want this kind of stress?"

"Exactly. Which is where *we* would come in. *We'd* handle the stress so you wouldn't have to."

Marion had then moved from the computer to the books of floral arrangements and gowns and reception venues that they'd been compiling with Andrew's help. One four-inch-deep binder was filled with glossy photos of appetizers alone; another with sample "second time" invitations.

Which did not mean she didn't have high hopes for the business, she'd been quick to say.

Which did not mean she didn't doubt for a minute that her daughter would put together another success.

Jo blinked at the darkness now. What would Marion say if she'd known Jo had failed on the epic scale that she'd failed? Would Marion still be so reassuring?

Not that she knew her mother anymore. Marion was right. The time they spent together had all too often been about Jo. Was that what children did? Were they never supposed to get to know their parents as people, not simply as the ones who were supposed to "be there"?

When Jo had thought of her mother, it had often been

with flashes of guilt for the poor, lonely woman whose husband had left her and whose daughter had, too. That poor, lonely woman abandoned in the small house with no one but her church ladies to talk to and nothing to do but fill her birdfeeders.

"Ha!" Jo said into the night as she rolled onto her side and felt a tear slide from her eye onto the pillow.

All that time Marion had loved and been loved. It had been Jo who was the loser. And all she could hope for was that Marion would not marry Ted, so Jo would not be faced with helping her mother decide what to do with the house.

"Why don't you live there, Josephine?" She could almost hear the suggestion from her conscience. "Your mother can move in with Ted and you can live there, in the house you grew up in? Then you can be reminded every minute of every day of how far you went and how fast you fell. You could sleep in the same, slant-ceiling room where you once dreamed of escaping West Hope. You could roam the same halls you once roamed when you first loved Brian, and then when he'd gone and when you'd been left with the baby that you couldn't have.

Amanda.

Or Emmett Gray.

The baby that you didn't think West Hope would let you have.

"Jesus," she said softly into her pillow. It was neither a prelude to a prayer nor a silent curse. It was simply a "Jesus," because Jo did not know what to think about why she was alive or what in the hell she was doing back here in this stifling town.

————

By some not-so-minor miracle, Jo slept through the night. In the morning she summoned enough spirit to get into the shower, find some decent clothes, and go out into the world, her new world, such as it was.

She would rather have stayed in bed, the covers up to her neck. But the Most Likely to Succeed had a new role to play and, like it or not, it was what she did best.

In the garage, she unlocked her car door, tossed in her Coach briefcase that no one this side of the Connecticut River either knew or cared was a Coach, then sat in the driver's seat and turned on the ignition. That's when she noticed a small square of paper tucked under her windshield wiper.

*Oh, great*, she thought. She'd probably done something else wrong, like forgotten to separate her recyclables or parked too close to the secretary on her right or her left.

For a moment she considered ignoring the note, turning on the wipers and swishing it into space.

*Sorry, Mr. Building Superintendent. I don't recall seeing a note.*

With defiance, she flipped on the wiper-blade switch. But the paper did not fly away: It stuck to the rubber and crossed back and forth in her vision, waiting for Jo to pluck it from its place.

Jo uttered some words under her breath that would have turned the ladies at church a fine shade of pale. She opened her door and reached around to the windshield.

The paper was folded neatly in half. She considered throwing it on the concrete garage floor, then decided what the heck. She might as well know what she had done wrong.

*No need to apologize,* the handwriting read.

She scowled. What was this?

*The last time I was run over I was nine.*

Oh, she thought. Then she smiled.

*I was in the soapbox derby. Jimmy Thompson rammed me and I flew out of my car and ran over myself and broke my leg.*

The note was signed: *Jack. Apt. 304.*

Jo laughed. The guy she'd nearly killed had a good sense of humor.

Stuffing the note into her briefcase, she backed out of her parking space and drove from the garage, the clouds of her life having lifted a little, the darkness having lightened. On her way to the shop, Jo was reminded of how she had survived those first years in Boston, those first lonely, scared years alone. She'd done it by looking toward things she could control, not by focusing on those things she could not. She'd done it by looking toward every tomorrow, and the excitement of building a business.

And now, at forty-three, she might not have a man, she might not have a child, but Jo had Second Chances.

As she drove through the winding, shady streets where white porches and boxes of red geraniums and kids' bikes lined the sidewalks, Jo realized she would be okay, she could have success without loneliness, because she was home with her friends. She could build Second Chances into a thriving business. She could expand the concept to include destination weddings. They could bring it to other New England tourist areas that attracted brides:

Newport, Ogunquit, Martha's Vineyard, and Nantucket. They could become the concierge to the second-marriage majority. They could build a name for themselves. The money would follow.

And then Jo would never feel like a loser again.

# 19

♥

He willed his eyelids to stay open and his thoughts to keep flowing. At this rate, Andrew thought, I'll be writing this column only in the darkness of night.

*Lesson #2: Never underestimate the mood swings of a woman.*

Propping his elbows on his desk, he stared at the screen of his laptop. He was tired, so tired, from working twelve hours a day and trying to digest all the things he was learning about planning weddings and trying to determine what morsels he could extract for his column.

He was tired of pretending to act like a gay man when he had no idea how to do that.

He'd finally reached his old friend Hap Little at the store in South Beach. "Dress with panache and simply listen," Hap said after Andrew had explained his mission.

"And act sensitive. Women will talk. They'll tell you everything." Hap also told him not to worry about his "walk," that, despite rumors to the contrary, not every gay man swished.

Andrew said he owed him dinner the next time he was in Miami.

It all, of course, had been good news. But unsure if his pastels and his Birkenstocks were panache-y enough, Andrew added a few pair of jeans that Cassie had seen advertised in the *Sunday Styles* section of *The New York Times*. And he began to wear a copper magnetic bracelet because Cassie saw it in the window of a tourist shop and the salesclerk told her it would keep his chakras in balance.

Andrew didn't know if he was, in fact, balanced. He only knew he was a few dollars poorer and he might look good to a gay guy, but he was tired.

Consequently, the most challenging part was staying awake, alert, and sharp enough to rise to the demands at Second Chances. Because, though Andrew might be there on a ruse, the work he was doing was real. He was beginning to wonder, however, if Jo—Jacquelin—Lyons was a real woman or part-man/part-machine from a sci-fi thriller.

"It's all about using your head," she'd exclaimed that afternoon as she paced the storefront, as she exercised her fingers by ticking off a laundry list of possibilities inspired either by the trip for gowns the day before or by her visit with Elaine to a potential caterer that morning. Whatever the inspiration, Jo's mood certainly had surged. "Think of each opportunity," she instructed crisply, "then think of opportunities that can come from those opportunities, and on and on."

She'd yakked to Andrew as if she'd forgotten he'd been hired only as a receptionist. Maybe it was because no one else was around: Lily was in New York and Sarah with her man and Elaine, after all, was a customer not a boss. Andrew had pretended to listen because that was his job, but the next thing he knew, Jo was firing off instructions and he was making furious notes like the administrative assistant he pretended to be.

*All this for a lousy magazine column,* he'd thought more than once.

Cassie had fixed hot dogs and beans for his supper, and some kind of brown bread that she said came from a can. He would have teased her about bread coming out of a can, but Andrew was too tired for teasing and Cassie seemed tired, too. She sat with him while he ate, then asked to please be excused, that she had a headache and wanted to go to bed early.

Mood swings, he thought. As far as he knew, Cassie hadn't yet started getting her period, and from things that he'd read, Andrew wished she never would, that she'd be frozen forever at age eleven, old enough to be a pal, still young enough to worship her dad.

The computer screen *beep*ed, then went dark. Too many minutes untended, too many minutes without Andrew typing a word.

He shut the thing off. "Forget it," he said. He might as well go to bed, too, and rest up for another day with that crazy, drop-dead gorgeous, sci-fi of a woman.

He climbed the narrow stairs of the cottage, pausing at

the top. Had he heard a sound? He stood still; he listened. It almost sounded as if someone had been crying.

He tiptoed to the doorway of Cassie's room. It was ajar, as always, letting in enough light so she wouldn't be lonely. Or scared.

"Honey?" he asked, but Cassie didn't answer. She wouldn't, of course, because she'd long been asleep.

He stepped inside her room and moved close to her bed. She breathed steadily; she did not cry. Perhaps she'd been dreaming. Because Cassie had nothing to cry about, not at her age. Andrew had done everything possible to see to that.

"How are the appointments coming along?" Jo asked Andrew the next morning, before he'd barely taken a sip of his morning coffee and right after he'd realized he'd forgotten his lunch that Cassie so painstakingly made each day. If she was having bad dreams, it was probably his fault for being such a lousy father.

"Two next week, three the following," Andrew said now, scanning the scheduling software he'd bought for the shop. Among his other duties, he'd been arranging appointments for Jo and Sarah to visit possible locations for weddings and receptions. They wanted unique places that could showcase their talents, not ordinary settings like the Knights of Columbus or the American Legion Hall.

"Good," she said. "Keep going. The more information we have to work with, the greater our chances of success."

She was driven now, almost obsessed.

And so, he couldn't help it. Maybe it was because of

how he was feeling about Cassie, maybe it was because he was a man. Whatever the reason, Andrew couldn't help it. He twisted the copper bracelet on his thick wrist and said, "There's more to life than success, Jo."

As soon as he'd said it, he wished he hadn't. He wished he could pretend those words hadn't been uttered, that she must have been hearing things, because he was immersed in his work and he hadn't spoken.

"Excuse me?" Jo asked.

He shook his head. "Sorry. Just thinking out loud." He turned back to his computer, Mr. Sensitive that he was.

"I heard you. You said there's more to life than success. Maybe you're right, Andrew. But maybe you're not."

She moved to the desk adjacent to Andrew's that she'd insisted on buying because she needed her own space. She yanked open a drawer. She jerked out a file and quickly flipped through it. She shoved it back inside the drawer, then jerked out another.

"Sorry," he repeated and went back to his work, unsure which was worse: Jo's barking commands or the silence that now lingered.

After a few minutes, Jo spoke again. This time, her voice was quiet. "It's important to me, Andrew. Without success, without goals to go after, I'm afraid my life wouldn't have much purpose."

He wanted to write it down. He wanted to log in to the "Real Women" file on his laptop and copy her thoughts word for word. *Lesson #3*, he'd write. *Sometimes women feel as useless as men do.*

Instead he said, "Well, that's pretty much bullshit."

Jo laughed. "You're in rare form today, Andrew."

He shrugged. "Not really. But it's just such a . . ." Did he dare say it? ". . . it's just such a *man* thing to say."

She leaned back in her chair and crossed her legs. It wasn't the first time that Andrew had to force himself not to stare at those legs, those long, lovely legs. "When, Andrew?" she asked. "When did you know you were gay?" She smiled with kindness. "Is that something people always ask?"

He was grateful that Cassie wasn't around. Or John Benson. Or Patty. He wasn't sure which of them would be laughing the hardest.

"Well," he said carefully, "let's say it's something I never thought about very often."

"Do you have a lover?" she asked.

He smiled. "No. Not right now." Well, at least that part was true. He turned back to his work, hoping the questioning was finished for the moment.

Then Jo added, "You're better off without a lover," she said. "Men have a way of screwing up lives."

Andrew could have said he was surprised that the gorgeous Ms. Josephine had problems with a man, but he knew that must be the reason she was so career-minded. Why else would she look so inviting, yet remain so unattached?

This was, of course, a perfect opportunity to glean more information from this very real woman. This very real woman who was willing to talk.

But as he had in fifth grade when the bases were loaded and there were two outs and he was at bat, Andrew, quite simply, choked.

"Strike three," the umpire called, and Andrew had become like Casey at the bat, losing the game for his team.

So instead of seizing the moment, Andrew picked up the phone to make another appointment, hoping that noon would come quickly that day and he could honestly say he had to run home and pick up his lunch. And he could get out of the shop and away from Jo's presence and the stirring he felt when they were alone, breathing the same air in the same room.

Cassie didn't answer when he called out her name. She'd left no note on the kitchen table, of course: She hadn't expected he'd be there in the middle of the day. Andrew would be glad when summer was over and Cassie was back in school and he'd know where she was and that she was okay, especially since she'd declared their neighbor, Mrs. Connor, was no longer needed on a daily basis because Cassie was capable of looking out for herself. Not that she wasn't. She was too capable sometimes, he thought. Most times.

Still, he skipped up the stairs to the bedrooms: He wouldn't mind a hug in the middle of the day.

"Cass?" he called from the doorway of her room, but there was no reply.

He looked inside: The bed was made, because, unlike her father, Cassie always made her bed and straightened her room. He liked to tease her by saying it was such a girlie thing.

As Andrew turned to head back down the stairs, a piece of white paper caught his eye. It was on the floor by her bed. Without a second thought he went in to retrieve it; Cassie would no more want trash on her floor than rumpled sheets on her bed.

But the paper wasn't trash, it was an envelope. Andrew frowned and turned it over. It was addressed to Cassie. The postmark was Australia. Return address: P. O'Shay.

The next breath Andrew tried to take got stuck in his throat, somewhere between *"Holy shit!"* and *"OhMyGod, no."* His hand trembled as he raised it close to check out the date stamp: eight days ago. It wasn't Cassie's birthday. It wasn't Christmas. Not that her mother always remembered when those events were.

The top of the envelope had been torn open: He could see that something was still inside.

He knew that he shouldn't, really he did. With every bone in Andrew's now-middle-aged body, he knew it was wrong to read Cassie's mail. The envelope, after all, had been addressed only to her. The fact that she hadn't told him about it meant that it wasn't for his ears, or his eyes, or what was left of his head.

Then he remembered hearing what he'd thought had been Cassie crying. What if it hadn't been a bad dream? What if Patty wrote something that Cassie had been too upset to share with her father, something that upset her? What could Patty have written, to do that to his daughter, his tough, "I can handle it, Dad" daughter?

Quickly, he ripped the rest of the envelope and pulled out the contents. It was a card, with a picture of the famous amphitheater in Sydney on the front. He opened the card. He ignored another paper that fell to the floor.

*Dear Cassie,* Patty's unmistakable, oversize handwriting had written, *I hope you're okay and that you're having fun living up there in the mountains.*

Mountains? Andrew thought. Did she think he'd taken Cassie to the middle of nowhere?

*You must be getting quite big now. It's been a long time since I've seen you. I bet you're getting ready for another school year—what grade now, is it fourth?*

Of course it's not fourth, you idiot, Andrew wanted to shout. It's sixth grade! Your daughter is entering sixth grade, no thanks to you.

His eyes burned as he read on.

*Don't forget to look for school clothes that the boys will love! Stick with designers and you should be fine.*

Andrew felt a twinge. School clothes. Shit. They'd been so busy shopping for his new image he hadn't thought about that.

*Speaking of boys,* the note continued, *I'm enclosing a picture of your new little brother!*

Someone, at that point, must have stepped on his lungs and squeezed out the last bit of air. He faltered a little, then dropped down on the bed. His eyes fell to what must be the photo that now was positioned upside down on the floor. He didn't have to look at it. He could pick it up, slip it back into the card, and return everything right where he'd found it. He could wait for Cassie to bring up the subject, which sooner or later she would.

He didn't have to look at it.

Did he?

"Dad!"

Oh.

Shit.

He grabbed the photo, shoved it into the card, shoved the card back into the envelope, and tried to place it on the floor where he'd found it.

He sneaked back to the hall. "Up here, honey," he called. "I'll be right down."

He closed his eyes, took a couple of deep breaths, cleared his throat, and descended the stairs, hoping his guilt wasn't spelled out on his face and that he wouldn't blow the lunch he hadn't yet eaten, all over the hardwood floor.

"Andrew?" Jo asked later that afternoon when it seemed that the two of them could use a break. "I just wanted to tell you I think you're doing a great job. And I'm sorry for what I said earlier about men screwing up our lives. I didn't intend to lump you in with the lot of them."

He looked up from his schedule. "No offense taken."

He had such a nice smile. And that wonderful dimple. It was true, Jo had learned, that gay men were often the greatest-looking guys on the planet. And the nicest.

"May I ask you a personal question?" Andrew said suddenly. "What do you know about buying school clothes? For sixth-grade girls?"

Jo grinned. "Your niece," she said, and Andrew seemed to frown for a second before he said, "Yeah, how'd you guess?"

"I've never had kids, Andrew, so I wouldn't be much help. Elaine has three, though. Two of them are girls."

"No offense again, but I can't picture Cassie in stenciled sweatshirts and Dockers and sensible shoes."

Andrew was a smart man. They were lucky to have him, lucky he had chosen to stop teaching while working on his doctoral dissertation, which she thought he'd said had something to do with history and journalism, or something like that. She felt ashamed for a moment that she'd not listened more closely, that, once again, Jo Lyons had been too immersed in her own interests, in trying to find her own route to success to pay attention to others.

*Life is about more than success*, Andrew had said.

Why had he said that? Wasn't he trying to succeed? Wasn't that why he was working full-time plus writing his dissertation?

Jo put down her papers. "Would you like me to take Cassie shopping, Andrew?"

Andrew looked up. He blinked.

"At her age, I'm sure she knows what she likes. If you give me an idea of some of the things you wouldn't want her to buy . . . like low-rise pants or tops that stop short of pierced belly buttons . . ."

Andrew dropped his head onto his desk and moaned. "Sometimes I hate having a girl."

Jo laughed. It would be fun, she thought, to spend time with a young girl. "I'll take her to the outlets, Andrew. Just tell me when. After all, you're the one who controls my schedule now." She smiled at the look of gratitude that crossed Andrew's face, just as a bell chimed and the front door opened. Jo turned, half-expecting to see a salesperson or tourist or maybe even a client, never expecting to see Frank Forbes standing there.

# 20

♥

**DO**
*Invite only the people that YOU want, not the friends of your parents who haven't seen you since you were five, or the neighbors from the block where you were raised.*

Jo had no idea why that thought ran through her mind as she stood and stared at the man who'd been the brother to the man she'd loved.

"Lily isn't here," she managed to say. Then she quickly turned back to Andrew as if Frank might not recognize her. Fat chance of that.

"Jo," Frank said. "How are you?"

If only Andrew was as good at reading minds as he was at securing appointments, he would now understand that her piercing stare and pleading eyes meant, "Help me get out of this."

But Andrew apparently could not read her mind, for all he did was stare back as if wondering why she was being rude to the man in the doorway.

"I'm fine, thank you," she said without looking back. "I'm sorry, but we're very busy right now. Lily is out of town."

"I wasn't looking for Lily. I was looking for you."

So the "later" of the "sooner or" had arrived. She gave Andrew one last, cryptic look, then gave up and faced Frank.

When they had been young they had not resembled each other, Brian with his shock of blond hair that hung over his collar; Frank, two years older, with a crew cut that had been so out of style. Brian had been taller, more athletic; Frank had been quieter, more serious, dependable. The voices, however, had been the same, with the same deep timbre and hint of a Boston accent passed down from their parents who'd been born and bred there.

*Pahk the cahr.*

*Drink the watah.*

*Eat the yellow bananer.*

Jo's heart slowly thumped as she studied Frank. With the passage of time, the brothers looked alike now: same receding hairline, same softened jowl.

"I understand," Frank said, "that my brother is missing."

Jo felt the color leave her face, as if the slow drain of life was being siphoned from her heart.

Andrew quickly stood up and steadied her. He slid his

chair over and made her sit down. "Jo," he said crouching in front of her, "do you want me to get rid of him?"

He acted so brave, it almost made Jo smile. As if Andrew could evict their landlord with a threat or a punch. As if sweet, gentle Andrew could do anything normally spurred by testosterone.

"She needs to answer a few questions," Frank explained in that voice that was Brian's.

"Jo?" Andrew asked. "I don't care who he is. I could call the police."

Then all of West Hope would know.

Jo shook her head. "It's all right, Andrew. Frank is right. He deserves to know what's going on."

Andrew looked toward Frank, then back to Jo. "Do you want me to leave?"

"No," she said. "Please." She touched his hand. "Please. Stay." She supposed she'd have to tell Frank everything now. Did it really matter if Andrew heard, too? She could trust him, couldn't she, not to tell the world?

She closed her eyes. "Yes," she said, "Brian is missing."

For a moment Frank was silent. When Jo opened her eyes she saw him walk to the group of navy chairs, run his hand over the top of his thinning hair, and sit down.

"How?" he asked.

She told him what had happened that night at McNally's. Her words came quickly, which was no surprise—she'd repeated them so often to herself in an effort to believe the unbelievable.

Throughout the story Frank sat, unemotional. When she was finished he asked, "It's that simple?"

"Yes."

"Had you had an argument?"

"No."

He looked at her with the same doubt that the police had in the beginning, as if trying to determine if she were trying to cover up . . . what?

"Was it about money?" Frank asked. "Did Brian try and pull some sort of scam?"

Oh. Money. If she told Frank the truth, she'd be exposing Brian for the rogue he might or might not be, depending on if he were willingly missing, or if he were dead. Dead. She tried to rub the chill from her forearms. "I don't know," she said, which, in part, was true.

"Four months ago?"

Four? Had it been that long already? "Since April. Yes." And then it occurred to Jo that, as far as she knew, there were only two ways Frank could have learned about Brian: either through her mother or through the police. Surely Marion would not have revealed her daughter's humiliation. "Frank?" she asked bravely. "How did you find out?"

Frank stood up and put his hands into his pockets. He walked first one way, then back another. He stopped in front of Jo. There were tears in his eyes. "The Boston Police were here," he said. "They told me Brian is missing. They wanted me to look at a photo and tell them if it was him."

"But I saw the photo," Jo said. "When I was in Boston. It was of a man and woman in South America. The man wasn't Brian."

Frank shook his head. "The picture they showed me wasn't from South America. It was a picture of a guy in

Boston. He'd been pulled out of the river. Jo, the guy was dead."

Andrew was leaning over her. "Jo?" he asked. "Do you want me to call your mother?" He held a glass of water to her lips. "Jo?" he asked again.

She sipped the water. She realized she was sitting in one of the navy chairs. When had she sat down?

"Are you okay?" It was Andrew's voice again.

She blinked. Frank sat beside her, his eyes steady on her, his expression one of concern. Had she ever seen that expression on Brian?

"I'm okay," she answered. "Please, don't call my mother."

A half-smile crept across Frank's face. It reminded Jo that Frank had a mother, too, a mother and a father right there in West Hope. Right there under the magnifier of their lives.

"Brian might still be alive," he said quickly.

Jo sat up straight. Andrew handed her the glass and moved to another chair.

"I couldn't tell if it was him. I'm going to drive down there. I didn't know if you'd like to come."

The gleaming hardwood floor seemed to captivate her attention. She could not pull her gaze from it to look up at Frank. She could not look at *him*. "I just moved back from Boston," she said, as if that had anything to do with what he had asked.

"I know," he said with polite patience. "I also have no idea what my brother did or didn't do this time, but I'm glad the police came to me and did not go directly to my parents."

Jo nodded. She thought of Helen and Jonathan Forbes. Brian had told her they were in their eighties now, that his mother hadn't been well, that his father was deteriorating from his stressful role as her caregiver. They'd been a family once, with a busy antiques business and two robust boys and respectability in West Hope. There had been rumors, of course, when Brian had gone to Montreal, but the speculation had gone the way of old gossip and life had gone on. And now the parents were ailing, and Brian was gone once again. Jo could only imagine how this news would affect them. "I'm sorry, Frank," she said. "I should have told you when it happened. You're his family, after all."

Frank lowered his eyes. "I heard from him last fall, but we haven't seen him in years. Brian wasn't the greatest at staying in touch." Like Jo, Frank was still making excuses for Brian's hurtful flaws. Frank's gaze moved to Jo, then to Andrew, then back to Jo, almost unsure if he should speak in front of a stranger. "Would you like to go somewhere and talk?"

She shook her head. "This is fine," she said. "Andrew is fine. But, no, I don't want to go to Boston. I don't want to go to the morgue." The word slipped out with surprising ease, as if it were a word she said every day.

Frank inhaled a long breath, then slowly let it out. "Jo," he said, "I'd like to help."

She shrugged.

"I didn't even know you and Brian had been in touch again."

"He found me in Boston," she said. "We spent a few

months together. We weren't going to tell anyone until we were sure about our future." She did not add they were not going to tell anyone until Brian's business was up and running, until he could say that he had finally made it, the way Jo had done, the way his father and brother had done. She drank more water. She supposed she was no different than Frank, defending a man who might or might not be worthy of their efforts. But was it so bad to still protect Brian? Especially if he were . . . dead?

Dead.

Brian?

The only man she'd ever loved.

"You don't think it's him?" she asked.

"I . . . I couldn't tell. It was a police photo, taken when they'd found him. There was mud and blood in his hair and on his face . . ." He hesitated, looked back at Andrew, then out the window. "It's been a long time since I've seen him."

With an unsteady fingertip Jo edged the rim of the water glass. "So you want me to go with you."

"It would help. Yes."

"What if I looked at the picture? Would that help?"

Frank twisted on his chair. "I'd rather you didn't see it, Jo. It's not especially nice."

She flashed her eyes at him. "But a body in the morgue would be better?"

"He'd be cleaned up, I'm sure. He'd look . . . better."

The cry she cried was more like a wail, an animal wounded, caught in a trap.

Andrew stood up. "Frank," he said, "I don't think this is a good time for Jo. Why don't you go to Boston and let us know if there's anything she'll really be able to do. After you've checked things out."

Frank stood up. He was grayer now than when he'd walked in; he looked older and sadder and awfully alone.

"I'm sorry," Andrew said. "If it is your brother, I am very sorry."

Frank nodded and headed for the door.

"Wait," Jo said, as she slowly stood, her legs feeling weak, but her will now resolved. "I'll go with you, Frank. If I sit here I won't think of anything else. Let's just get it over with." And then the wondering might be over, she thought but did not say, and maybe I can finally truly grieve, then get on with my life.

# 21

Andrew wondered how long it would be before Cassie told him about the letter from Patty.

Jo left for Boston with Frank right away—she'd said waiting until tomorrow would only guarantee a totally sleepless night.

With no one at the shop, Andrew closed up early. He supposed he should have stayed and worked on his next column: The soap opera around him was getting quite juicy. But Andrew felt too sorry for Jo to expose this latest angle. After all, he now knew why she'd reacted so strongly when she'd learned that Lily had gone out with Frank Forbes. Jo hadn't been jealous, she'd been afraid. Afraid that her vulnerability would be exposed to the world, afraid that she wasn't equipped to withstand any more pain.

For Andrew, writing about dating and the fun of the

man-woman world was one thing. Writing about some-one's fears was another altogether. He had known that kind of fear when Patty had left him, and he wouldn't have wanted anyone announcing it to the mass market, incognito or not.

Besides, he reasoned, as he headed for the stables, he deserved some time off. And it was Wednesday. Cassie would be at her riding lesson. He'd surprise her and show up to watch.

He sat on the bleachers with no sign of Mrs. Whatever-Her-Name-Was. From high atop Big Bailey, Cassie was hard at work, going through her paces around the ring. She did not notice her father; she kept her eyes forward on the next jump.

"Relax!" Andrew heard her instructor call. It was then that he noticed that Cassie, indeed, seemed stiff in the saddle, as if it were the first time she'd been up on a horse.

Bailey went over a small fence and knocked off the post.

"Cassie, relax. You're too tense on the reins."

It wasn't like Cassie to be tense about anything unless her room was a mess and her bed was unmade and one of her friends had called and said she was on her way over. Andrew watched his daughter with concern.

Another jump faced them. But Bailey slowed down. He did not seem to want to go for it.

Cassie veered him from the course and stopped Bailey in front of the instructor. She said something to the woman that Andrew could not hear. Then she got off the horse and began leading him back to the barn.

"Cassie?" Andrew called out as he stood up.

She looked to the bleachers, shielded her eyes against the sun. "Dad?" she said.

He scrambled down the wooden planks and jogged across the packed dirt. "What's up, honey? Quittin' early today?"

Cassie shrugged and resumed walking the horse. "An off day," she said. "For both of us."

He wondered if she meant it was an off day for Bailey and her or for her and her father. Then again, she wouldn't know that Andrew had been having an off day, too, because Cassie didn't know he'd found the card and the picture and had thought of little else all afternoon besides men and women and their tenuous relationships.

And of Jo, of course. And this perplexing new situation of hers.

"Off days happen," he said, falling in step beside his daughter. "Can I help?"

She hesitated a minute, then said, "You can tell me why I have such a turd for a mother."

He laughed. Well, Jesus, how could he help himself? Patty O'Shay, once the world's most desirable model, being referred to as a turd by her own daughter? "Remind me never to go away," he said. "I can't imagine what kind of word you'd come up with for me." Of course, he would have rather agreed with Cassie, would rather have said, "No kidding your mother's a turd," and added a few expletives of his own. But Andrew had vowed to himself to never do or say anything to turn Cassie against her mother. It was a vow that hadn't always been easy to keep.

Cassie stroked the horse's neck as they walked. "She has another kid, Dad," she said. "It's a boy."

Sometimes, Andrew thought, life works out the way it should. The fact that he already knew about the latest Patty-news acted as a shock absorber for Cassie's announcement. If he hadn't already known, he might not have been able to keep himself in check. "Well," he said, putting his hand on Cassie's shoulder. "I'll bet he's not nearly as pretty as you."

Cassie rolled her eyes. "His name is Gilbert. What a stupid name. Like Gilbert Grape."

"Is he purple?" Andrew asked.

She laughed. "Not quite. But he's bald."

A tiny catch came into Andrew's throat. Corral dust, he suspected. What else would it be? He tried not to remember that Cassie had been hairless, too, with the roundest pink face and the hugest blue eyes and the most fetching smile he had ever seen.

"So," he said, "you have a brother."

"A half brother, Dad. It's not the same thing. Besides," she added, "it really doesn't matter. It's not like I'll ever see him. Or her." The *her*, of course, meaning her mother.

He could have said part of the reason he was writing "Real Women" was to gather some money to take Cassie to Australia, that if Mother Mohammed wouldn't come to the Berkshire Mountains, he damn well would see to it that the mountains went there. He could have told Cassie, but he did not want her to get her hopes up. Besides, the not-so-charitable side of him enjoyed the position that Patty had earned of being the bad guy and the turd.

"Come on," Andrew said, "Let's cool down Big Bailey. Then we'll figure out when you'd like to go shopping. Jo wants to take you to buy some new school clothes."

If Cassie made a connection between Patty's letter and this sudden shopping trip, she was bright enough not to bring it up.

# 22

♥

***DON'T***
*Forget that this is his wedding, too! Let your groom be part of the planning and the fun. Not to mention that, as a second wedding, some of his money is most likely paying for it, as well. It's the 21st century girls; we must allow the men to get involved, and even to make decisions.*

It should have been the longest trip on the turnpike Jo had ever taken. They didn't speak much: She told Frank a little about the business she'd had; he told her how antiquing had become a fine art in the Berkshires, competitive, cutthroat sometimes. Mostly they listened to CDs of the Boston Symphony at Tanglewood, and watched the cars whiz past on their way to the Cape, the islands, the beaches, north and south.

Then, suddenly, they were gliding through downtown

traffic, slipping into a parking garage, climbing the cement steps of an old building, moving as if on automatic pilot, destination predirected by an unknown source.

Once inside they were directed to a small waiting room. It had green vinyl chairs and a small coffee table that held an assortment of magazines: *Parents* magazine, *Woman's Day, People, Buzz.*

Jo sighed, almost surprised that she had been able to sigh, that she had not programmed herself to hold her breath until this was over, until they knew.

She studied the magazines. Why would anyone want to sit in the morgue and glance through such pages as if awaiting the next available manicurist?

Against all judgment that might be deemed sane, Jo picked up *People* and flipped to the back.

"I'll go in first," Frank said beside her, as if she expected a different plan. "If I can't be certain, I'll come out and get you. There's no need for you to go in unless . . ."

Unless he can't tell if it's his brother because it's been too many years and his face is too mangled.

She knew what he meant, but was glad he hadn't said it.

She turned to an article on the L.A. scene. She scanned the images of youthful actors whose movies she had not seen, whose names she did not know, a reminder that those likely to succeed were now a generation younger.

She closed the magazine and tossed it back onto the table. She tapped her foot.

"Mr. Forbes?"

A young man in a crisp white coat approached. Anxiety rushed through her like a hot flash.

A hot flash? she wondered. Wasn't she too young for hot flashes?

Frank stood up and straightened his slacks, adjusted his belt, tucked in his shirt. He hesitated. Jo touched his hand. He looked down at her and nodded. Then he followed the young man from the room.

Her pulse paced out the time at the base of her throat. She forced herself not to wring her hands, not to bite her lip. She glanced back at the magazines, looking for a distraction. She picked up *Buzz*.

Leafing through the pages of not-quite-naked women and their lucky escort men, Jo realized they were from the world of Perfect, where she did not belong.

She turned to the editorial, as if she might be capable of reading, of comprehending, or caring about anything beyond this place and the reason she was there.

But the words bled together like an ink spill on the page.

She pitched the magazine.

She folded her arms.

She waited.

# 23

♥

*L*esson #4: *True or False? Though we don't like them to know it, men are as sensitive as women.*

So, *let's talk about Jacquelin, one of the women I work for, the drop-dead gorgeous one. Forgive the cliché, but you know the type. Light blond-beigy hair, feline green eyes, legs that go all the way up to there. But she has some sort of secret and it has to do with a man (of course).*

*She has an old boyfriend who apparently is missing from the world, or at least from her world. One night while they were in a restaurant, the guy went to the men's room and—abra-cadabra!—he was gone.*

*That was four months ago.*

*Now the guy's brother shows up and wants to whisk our woman off to a morgue to check out a body that has turned up with no name. It might be the boyfriend, and he might be dead.*

*So why is Jacquelin reluctant to find out?*

*You might think it's because if he's dead she can no longer fantasize that he'll come back to her, but I don't think that's the reason. She's too smart for that.*

*I think.*

*I tell you this story, not to spread gossip or invoke mystery, but with the hopes that maybe we'll learn, once and for all, if the old adage is true: that a woman—even the brightest, the hottest, the most unlikely—truly does act with her heart, while a man truly acts with his lower parts.*

He was, of course, writing as much about himself as he was writing about Jo Lyons.

# 24

It wasn't Brian.

Frank returned to the waiting room shaking his head and saying, "Thank God, Jo. It's some other man."

They left the building and got into the car.

"I'm sorry to have put you through this," he added.

"It's fine," she whispered as she buckled her seat belt. She was glad, of course, that the dead man wasn't Brian. Yet if it had been, she was ashamed to admit that she might have felt some relief. If Brian were dead, it would have meant his disappearance had not been her fault, that he was not gone because he no longer loved her or never had at all, or because he had found someone better. If Brian were dead, there would have been closure.

But now the unknown would go on.

"Maybe we should talk to a private investigator," Frank said as he drove up the ramp and onto the turnpike.

She'd already done that months ago.

She told Frank about the man in Brookline named R.J. Browne, who had a reputation for getting the job done. He had said he would be candid.

"Unless there's a reason to suspect foul play, I've found that most times adult males disappear because they want to."

Though he had a tough, muscular build, R.J. Browne was soft-spoken. Jo didn't think he realized how deeply his words had cut into her, piercing her soft cushion of well-practiced denial.

She hadn't returned to the detective. She couldn't afford his fees, anyway. Not anymore.

"If you want to hire someone, go ahead," she said to Frank now. "But please leave me out of it. I think it's time for me to move on."

"Jo?" Frank asked. "Is there more to this story?"

She stretched her neck, each muscle and nerve and tendon letting their irritation be known. "Men," she said. "Women. Does it ever really work?" Then she looked out the window. The "T" zipped past them, loaded with people—some men, some women. She wondered if any of them were attached to one another and if any of them were content.

On the rest of the way back to the Berkshires, they rode in silence, without even the symphony to intrude on their private thoughts.

When they got back to West Hope it was nearly dark, but Sarah was in the back room of the shop, working at a design table set up in a corner.

"The linden tree," Sarah said, not looking up from her drawing. "The heart-shaped leaf. It's a perfect symbol for Elaine's wedding. It changes with the seasons of life; it is gentle and velvet-looking; and they're all over the grounds of the Wharton estate. They should be beautifully golden in October."

Jo walked in and sat on a stool beside Sarah. The illustration was alluring: trellises intertwined with a cascade of linden leaves. "I'll make them from gold foil," Sarah went on, "and create their fruits of pearl-colored silk to match the gowns."

The image was exotic and elegantly original. Jo wondered if Sarah had any idea how clever she was. Then she realized it was late and Sarah was there, which probably meant one thing.

"Is Jason gone again?" Jo asked.

Sarah nodded. "Labor Day weekend at the Thousand Lakes."

Labor Day weekend. The summer was over. Jo was amazed that it had slipped away, that she barely remembered its heat.

"Burch is with his grandparents on the Cape," Sarah added. "They said they wanted to kidnap him one more year before he turns into a teenager and loses interest in spending time with them."

Jo smiled. It was nice that Jason's parents seemed to adore Sarah and Jason's son. Sarah had never talked much about her past, only to say that life in New England suited her better than going back to the reservation where she'd been raised. Even Lily hadn't been able to get Sarah to reveal much about her past. And Lily usually had a way of getting everyone to tell her their secrets.

"The real reason I'm still here, though, is to get you to go out for supper with me," Sarah said, setting down her pencil and slipping off her stool.

"It wasn't him, Sarah," Jo said abruptly. "Brian's not dead."

Sarah nodded and picked up her car keys. "Good," she replied. "But we're still going out. Andrew is meeting us at the restaurant, and we're going to listen."

Jo would have preferred to go home and draw a hot bath and lie there and cry in the warmth and the bubbles. But Andrew had told Sarah what had transpired, and Jo was beginning to remember that this was what friends did: They were there for each other; they listened. She had been on her own for so many years she'd forgotten that friendship bore that blessing—and that responsibility.

"Lily called," Sarah said when they were settled into a small vinyl booth at Smokin' LaDonna's on the outskirts of town. It was a new Texas barbecue place that catered to tourists and was not as apt to have neighbors in every booth, their large ears pressed to the backs. "She's coming back tomorrow."

"Great," Jo replied as they ordered Chardonnay. "Did she find the guest gift?"

"What she found, she said, was inspiration. She asked what I thought about a small book by Edith Wharton, tied with gold and ivory ribbon. *Ethan Frome* for the men; it's companion, *Summer*, for the women."

"But those books are so sad! So unromantic in their endings! Hardly wedding-appropriate."

Sarah smiled.

"Our Lily may have graduated from college, but I'm afraid she spent little time reading."

"Now *that's* hard to imagine." The comment came from Andrew. They laughed happy laughs, then he slid in beside Sarah, both facing Jo. *Friends*, she thought again. It had been so long.

"Where is your niece?" Jo asked him. "Did you leave her alone?"

"Nope. We have a great neighbor, Mrs. Connor, who used to baby-sit. Now that Cassie is too old for baby-sitters, according to her, the woman is there when she needs her. By the way, Jo, I added a shopping date into your schedule."

Jo nodded, though she was no longer sure if she had the strength for an eleven-year-old.

"Cassie has been with you a long time?" Sarah asked.

"Well," Andrew replied, "yes." He picked up the menu and said, "I'm starved." The waitress arrived and he ordered ribs and cole slaw. The women ordered salads: Jo's with barbecue chicken strips; Sarah's, without.

"So," Sarah said, once their food had arrived, "it was a tough day for you, Jo."

Here comes the support, Jo thought. She looked at Andrew. "It wasn't Brian," she said. "He isn't dead."

"Are you sure?"

"That it wasn't him, or that he's not dead?"

"Either. Both."

"Well, I didn't see the man, the corpse. But Frank was sure it wasn't his brother. Which didn't surprise me." She was so tired, the tears started to spill unexpectedly. She set down her fork and quickly picked up her napkin.

"Oh, Jo," Sarah said, reaching out her hand and touching her friend's arm.

"It really would help if you could talk about it," Andrew said in a low, comforting voice.

"No," Jo said. Then she looked at both friends, one old and one new, and she knew that if she didn't tell someone soon, she would split wide open and spill all her secrets out on the red-and-white checkered table.

They closed Smokin' LaDonna's. By that time Jo had told Sarah and Andrew the rest of her humiliating story, from her pregnancy and the abortion right up to the present, how Brian had taken all the money she had, one way or another, and how that had been the real reason she had moved back to West Hope—not merely because she was broken, but also because she was broke.

By the time she was finished she was weak, purged, and head-to-toe numb.

"He's an ass," Sarah said.

"A real prick," Andrew added.

"You should tell Frank," Sarah suggested. "About the money."

Jo shook her head. "It doesn't concern him."

"It does if he's worried that his brother is dead. If he hears the rest of the story he might start to think otherwise."

Closing her eyes, Jo said, "He'll think Brian stole all of my money and dumped me, then left the country or something."

Sarah and Andrew were both silent. Jo opened her eyes. "Which I suppose is what happened," she added, finally saying the words that she'd been trying not to admit, even to herself.

Back at the shop, Jo said good-bye to her friends, then decided to walk, to clear her aching thoughts before heading home. She unlocked her car and tossed her bag inside, then went onto Main Street and took a deep breath of the cool, clear, Berkshire air.

The center of West Hope was dark and quiet, the only attraction the American flag that stood in the spotlight beside the gazebo on the town green. The tourist boutiques were all closed: the shop that sold jellies and jams and candles and things; the one that offered hand-knit sweaters and thick, woolly shawls; the one that featured handpainted birdhouses. The only glimmer of light came from the windows of the real estate offices, where Polaroid snapshots of properties for sale hoped to lure in tourists out for an evening stroll.

*Walk to Tanglewood,* one of the notices read.

*Near Rockwell Museum,* read another.

Then a third, headlined: *Lakefront. Winterized cottage, two bedrooms, screen porch, fireplace, private dock. Needs some TLC. $429,900.*

Jo wondered if, for $429,900, she could have enough TLC to put herself back together again—Humpty Dumpty, back on the wall.

She resumed walking, past the new post office and the old redbrick town hall—ERECTED 1879, its plaque read. She wondered if she'd even known the town was that old.

Brian would have known: perhaps because of the family antiques business, history had been his passion.

Did she know, Brian had asked one autumn night as they'd walked through town, with Jo bundled in his high-school letter sweater from football and track, that Nathaniel Hawthorne thought he lived in Lenox, but that the red cottage where he scribed *The House of the Seven Gables* was actually in Stockbridge?

Did she know, he'd instructed on another night, that the southern part of the county was purchased from the Stockbridge Indians for 460 pounds, three barrels of cider, and thirty quarts of rum? Or that the base of the Washington Monument is made of marble from the quarry in Lee, or that the Hancock Shakers were originally called the "Shaking Quakers" because of the crazed way they danced to rid their bodies of evil?

Jo closed her light sweater around her now and tried not to remember those nights, those hours, when they'd walked and he'd talked, extolling fact after fact, while Jo listened with a lover's ears, thinking he was the most interesting man she'd ever known.

She supposed that, back then, he was. She supposed that, since then, she'd shut down her emotions and not left her heart open to meet others who might be more interesting, more interested, less hurtful.

She cut across the street to the town green, walking along the newly restored brick walkway, past the wrought-iron lampposts to the fountain and the granite memorial of war heroes of West Hope.

World War I. World War II. Korea. Vietnam. Twenty-three names in all; twenty-three men who had never returned, never built a life there, never had a chance to build their futures, or to waste them.

Never had a chance to break any more hearts.

"He's an ass," Sarah had said.

"A real prick," Andrew had added.

They had shaken their heads as if to rid Brian's evil spirit.

Jo laughed out loud at the image. *"Enough!"* she said out loud into the night. Enough introspection! Enough self-pity! Brian was gone and Jo knew she'd be better off if he never came back. Finally, *finally*, she no longer needed him, because Jo had friends once again, and this time she would cherish them. This time, she would not let them go.

She walked back to the shop, then cut through to the parking lot. When she got into her car she noticed that half the contents of her purse had spilled onto the seat when she'd tossed it inside. On the top was the note from her neighbor.

She picked up the note and reread it with a smile. Then she dug around for a scrap of paper, this time a toll receipt from the Mass. Pike. She quickly wrote: *Sorry about your leg. Did Jimmy Thompson win the race? Jo. Apt. #411.*

A few minutes later, when she arrived home, Jo got off the elevator on the third floor, slipped the note under the door of apartment 304, then climbed the fire stairs to her place, a grin on her face the whole time.

# 25

**DO**
*Have your wedding "cake" formed out of Krispy Kremes*
*if that's what you want. The second time around, it*
*doesn't matter what your mother (or the neighbors)*
*think!*

I t was horrid in the city," Lily said the next day in the shop, as she fanned herself with great Lily aplomb. She had arrived on the early train from Manhattan with the other "escapees," as she liked to call them: men who'd traded ties for T-shirts with pockets, and women who'd replaced their leather briefcases with woven designer totes.

"It was so hot I thought I'd perish, marching from place to place trying to find the perfect guest gifts. Then I went past a bookstore and suddenly there it was—inspiration!

How was I to know it was such a dumb choice?" She flung her lithe body into a chair, her winsome pink sundress landing with a flutter.

"But your idea triggered a thought," Jo replied. "Instead of guest gifts, why not make a donation to the ongoing restoration at The Mount? We can make it in the guests' names. We could ask that the money be applied to the renovation of Edith's boudoir or her husband's or to the Henry James suite. It will be years before every nook and cranny of the estate is re-created. It's such a worthwhile attraction for the area, don't you think?"

Lily considered Jo's suggestion. "Give money, not gifts? Charity, not trinkets?"

"A grown-up gesture for a second-wedding occasion."

"Well, sure," Lily said. "Why not? We could have place cards hand-calligraphied to notify each guest. That would personalize the gesture, don't you think?"

Jo smiled. Yes, hand-calligraphied cards would add a classy touch. It pleased her that Lily agreed, though not much could have cracked Jo's good mood today. She felt amazingly wonderful. She had slept through the night free from hazy, dark dreams, from unknown thoughts to awaken her with anxious, dreaded fears, her heart racing, her palms sweating, her mind centered on Brian. Not this morning. This morning Jo had opened her eyes, surprised to see the sun, surprised that she had felt such peace, that she had felt so vindicated and no longer alone.

Now all she needed was to summon the courage to tell Brian's brother about the money that once had been hers, but now was not. Sarah and Andrew were right: Frank had a right to know.

"Have you seen Frank?" Lily suddenly asked, the matter of the gifts apparently resolved.

Jo flinched with surprise. Had Lily read her mind? "Not today," she answered quickly. Then added, "Actually, I saw him yesterday. I went to Boston with him. It was about his brother. Nothing that turned out to be important."

Lily's eyebrows raised. Jo remembered that as far as Lily knew, Frank's brother had vanished years ago and Jo hadn't heard from him since.

Jo took a slow breath and said, "It's a long story. Brian's been missing; the police thought an unidentified dead man was him. It wasn't."

Lily's blue eyes grew large, then larger. "My goodness," she said. "Poor Frank must have been devastated."

Poor Frank. Well, Jo thought, of course Lily would think of Frank first. He was the new man in her life, her paramour, at least for now. She had no way of knowing how distraught Jo would have been, because Lily had not known the rest.

Lily checked her watch. "He prefers a late lunch. I'll go next door in a while and suggest a small picnic. Maybe he'll feel better if he talks about the ordeal."

*It must be how Lily always captures the men that she captures,* Jo thought. She was sensitive to their needs; she was sensitive to trying to soothe their stresses, whether she did it consciously or not. Beneath her flighty ways, Lily cared about others. What's more, she was not afraid to let them know it.

*Maybe I should go with Lily,* Jo thought. *Maybe I should*

*tell both of them together, then everyone would know. Everyone but Elaine and Marion and, oh yes, the police.*

"Don't forget the gowns today," came Andrew's voice from across the room. He was armed with a feathered dusting wand, tackling the fragile glass shelves as if he were removing grime from hubcaps.

"Oh," Jo said. "That's right. Lily, we all need to be here at three o'clock. The woman from Chestnut Hill is bringing our gowns out for a fitting. Sarah convinced her to come here so we can show her around and maybe work some kind of partnership with her."

"Three o'clock. Okay, fine," Lily said.

"We can't be late," Jo said. "We want to try and impress her with our professionalism." She wondered if that would leave enough time to tell Lily and Frank. Lily, no doubt, would be so upset that she'd then feel the need to comfort both of them.

Lily smiled wryly. "I'll be here. Though I'm dying to know more about Frank's brother. I've always wondered what makes people just disappear."

Jo stood up. An unexpected nerve spasmed in her neck. She had to force away the urge to defend Brian again. How long would it take before that need would be gone? "Well," she said abruptly, "Brian's disappearance will probably turn out to be inconsequential. What does matter, though, is Elaine's wedding. Wait until you see what Sarah's done. She's going to transform The Mount into a vision drenched in beauty." No, she definitely wouldn't go with Lily to talk to Frank. She didn't want to talk about Brian that day; she didn't want to disturb the peace she'd found. "Come look," she said, and gestured for Lily to follow her into what had once been the back room and now looked like the design studio of a busy, prosperous business, strewn with fabric swatches and color samples and sketches and, somehow, harmony.

The day passed quickly. While Lily was gone, Jo busied herself phoning the caterer ("We've decided on the cheddar and apple slices to complement the cranberry crème," she informed them about the appetizers). She talked about the field kitchen they would need to set up to serve the hot entrées, which Elaine hadn't chosen yet. Next she called the party-supplies rental agency ("We want the linens in oyster, not white"), then the cellist who headed the group that would play during dinner ("We've decided a harpist would be nice for the social hour. Do you know anyone?" Jo asked his message machine).

When at last she hung up, she glanced at the calendar. Only a few weeks remained until Elaine's wedding; only a few weeks to prove that they could act together and create a second wedding that would be worthy of the Berkshires and live up to their sales pitch.

With Jo still at work and Sarah in the studio, at three o'clock on the dot Lily pranced through the door. Jo couldn't tell from her expression if Frank was still upset, if he'd told her more than he'd told Jo, if he planned to do anything next to find his long-lost brother, the ass, the prick, the man she'd loved.

*Stop it*, she commanded herself. She would not think about Brian. She would not, would not, would not.

Before Jo could ask, the door opened again and in came Dorothy Dixon, an older, square-shaped woman with a stern look on her equally square jaw. Ms. Dixon was from the Chestnut Hill store and gave the impression she was not inclined to dawdle. Which was fine, except that the bride had not yet arrived.

"We'll start with the bridesmaids, then," Ms. Dixon announced.

Andrew dropped his dusting wand and headed to Ms. Dixon's van to retrieve the gowns. "Man's work," he said with a wink, and Jo laughed.

They moved into the back room, where Andrew hauled the goods. Then the rustle of plastic and zippers and tissue paper and clattering hangers played an enthusiastic symphony.

"Andrew won't mind if we change right here, will you, dear?" Lily exclaimed, and Jo noticed that he blushed.

"I'll cover the phones," he said, and Lily shrugged, and Andrew darted back into the showroom as if the ghosts of Princess Di and Jackie O and Grace Kelly had all arrived.

By four o'clock Lily and Sarah and Jo had been nipped and tucked and pinned, when Elaine finally waltzed through the doorway.

"Sorry I'm late," she said. "I had to take Kory to the dentist and there was a wait and it took the Novocain forever to take and . . . oh, God, what a day." Her face was flush; she blinked rapidly as if she wore ill-fitting contact lenses. Certainly it wasn't the first time she'd taken a child to the dentist, never mind that Kory . . . wasn't he almost twenty?

"Get undressed," Ms. Dixon commanded.

Elaine blinked again. She looked to Lily, Sarah, and Jo. Then she did as she was told.

The gown was exquisite. Gone was the housewife-mom of West Hope, transformed into a radiant, silken goddess. Jo had never realized that Elaine actually had a good figure: It usually was masked by sexless cotton skirts or Bermuda shorts and tailored cotton shirts.

"Wonderful," Jo said.

"Beautiful," Lily said. "It's not fluffy like all that first-wedding sugar. But it's a long way from second-wedding suits of the past. I love it," she exclaimed as she clapped her hands, then ran upstairs. She returned a moment later with a small velvet box. She opened it and extracted the enormous diamond necklace. She placed it around Elaine's neck. Sarah nodded approval.

"Perfect," Sarah said and studied the look. "Let me make a quick sketch so I can design the headpiece."

It was six o'clock before the work was finished and the women had discussed possible ways they could partner with Dorothy Dixon and her outstanding firm.

"We don't want to be in the business of selling gowns," Jo explained, "but we want to help a bride and her attendants find the perfect attire to complement every moment and every aspect of the event and its theme. For second weddings, we must always focus on quality and memorability, not sequins and splash."

They settled on percentages of retail costs, which were higher on accessories than on gowns because the margins of the "add-ons" were much fatter and the profits often upward of seventy percent. At last they said good-bye to Ms. Dixon, and Sarah left, as well, saying Burch was home now and she had to get him ready for school.

Elaine stayed in the studio, poking through Sarah's sketches.

"Well," Lily said, "I suppose I should go, too."

Jo followed her into the showroom. She had an idea where Lily was headed. "How is Frank?" she asked.

Lily smiled a small smile. "Upset, I think. I don't know him well enough yet. I can only imagine how it must feel to think your brother's dead. Even though he hasn't seen him in so long, to actually have to go to a morgue . . ."

Jo looked over at Andrew. He winked at her, the kind of wink that reinforced a friend's support. "Are you going to see him now?"

"Yes. He didn't feel like lunch, but maybe I can interest him in dinner."

Jo looked at Andrew again and drew in a long breath. "Could I come with you, Lily? Maybe there are a few things I can say that might help Frank feel better."

She followed Lily out the door and wondered where on earth she would possibly begin.


"Elaine?" Andrew asked as he went to shut the lights off in the back.

The bride sat at Sarah's drawing table, staring at the sketches.

"Everyone's gone. I was about to lock up. Are you planning to stay?"

She sat motionless. Andrew waited for an answer. Then he noticed a tear drop from her eye and land on Sarah's table. "No," she said, shaking her head. "No. I'll go home."

He felt a kind of trepidation that he would rather not have felt. With a hesitant step, he crossed the room. "Elaine, are you all right?"

That's when her shoulders began to shake, when a low moan rose up from her toes, and when the tears burst out, as if someone's underground sprinkler system had just been activated.

And all Andrew could think of was, *Oh shit, why me?*

# 26

♥

I cannot marry Martin," Elaine said after she'd composed herself and Andrew had slumped onto the chair beside the table.

He patted Elaine's hand because he figured that a gay guy would. Hap Little would be proud.

"What could possibly be so terrible?" he asked, not really wanting to hear the details, but knowing he was past having a choice. *Do it for the column*, he tried to tell himself. But her tears flowed once again and he felt like a schmuck.

"I just can't," she said between spasmodic sniffs.

She just can't? *Oh, man*, Andrew thought, *I really suck at this.* He thought for a moment. If Elaine just couldn't tell him, it must be the one reason for which men were so renowned.

Martin had probably said he'd be working late, that he

had to deliver a new Lumina to someone in Egremont or something like that. Then Elaine must have caught him. She must have seen his silhouette in a restaurant, heard him laugh with his furtive female companion, seen them bend their heads close, maybe even kiss.

Or worse, she might have seen Martin's vehicle parked in a motel lot, somewhere seedy and dank, like the Route 7 Motor Lodge.

Suddenly Elaine jerked her head and looked him in the eyes. "Andrew," she barked. "You must tell the others."

"*Me?*" he asked. "Me?"

"They'll be so upset."

Upset? Andrew wondered. What about *her*?

*Men*, he thought, hating his gender, *we can be such scum.*

He patted her hand again. "I'll tell them, if you want. But are you sure about this? Sometimes men do some real stupid things . . ."

She looked at him oddly. "Martin didn't do anything," she said. "It's my fault, not his."

"*You* cheated on *him*?" The words shot from Andrew's mouth like an unexpected bit of spit.

Elaine frowned. "No one cheated on anyone, Andrew. I just can't marry Martin. Being with my friends—Lily, Jo, and Sarah—well, it made me realize I need to be free. I've spent most of my adult life being married to someone. I need to find out who I am."

"And Martin?"

She did not hesitate in her answer. "Martin deserves someone who's devoted to him."

Andrew didn't add, "Good God, Elaine, don't we all?"

# 27

♥

---

**DON'T**
*Invite your boss with the assumption you'll receive a*
*wonderful gift. Ditto goes for wealthy relatives who are*
*retired and live in Florida. We never, after all, really*
*know those we think we know, and at a second wedding,*
*gifts should not matter, anyway.*

Jo was weary: weary from working, weary from talking, weary from thinking about things that had been
and things that never would be.

She wanted only solace now, she thought, as she let
herself into her apartment. She wanted quiet. Darkness.
Solace.

Then a small piece of paper caught her eye on the
foyer floor. She stooped down and picked it up. Some-

thing must have fallen from her purse, a store receipt, perhaps.

It was not a store receipt. As she placed the paper on the counter she saw the handwriting. Clear, distinct handwriting.

*If you want to have dinner one of these nights*, the writing read, *I'll tell you the whole story of the soapbox derby and what happened to that bully Jimmy Thompson.*

The note was signed only with a *"J."*

Jo smiled. Of course, there was no way she'd go. She didn't even know the man. Just because she'd almost run him over, did that mean she owed him dinner? All she knew about him was that he lived in the secretaries' building, which must mean he was no more prosperous than she was, and that was the last thing she needed now, another man without a dime.

She tossed the note into the wastebasket, turned on the small light over the stove, fired up the teakettle, then kicked off her shoes. She stepped down into the living room then went to the windows and looked out at the silhouette of the mountains etched onto the sky in the light from the stars and the half-moon.

No, she didn't need another man who obviously hadn't found his dream as yet, or, if he had, then his dream wasn't very lofty and wouldn't rise to hers. Because she still could dream, couldn't she? She still could dream that once again she'd move up in the world, maybe to those condos over by Tanglewood, after all. *Someday*, she thought. *Soon.* But another pauper of a man would not get in her way. And no one would ever again take away what she had worked so hard for.

Frank had not been surprised. Lily had sat through

dinner, her small mouth parted open, her eyes wide, her heart aching, no doubt, with question after question.

"He took *all* your money?"

"How could he do that?"

"Oh, Josephine, why didn't you tell us before?"

Jo made certain that she blamed herself as much as she blamed Brian. He had been the rogue, but she had been the fool. "One can't scam another person unless they have a willing victim. I should have seen the signs that his business wasn't 'taking off.' I should have been smart enough to stop giving him money, to stop taking loans against my business collateral. Good God, any businessperson knows better."

"But you loved him," Lily said.

Jo sat in silence. A pair of unexpected tears slid down her cheeks. "Yes," she replied. "And for a little while, my money bought his devotion."

Frank hung his head as if he should be the one to feel embarrassment and shame.

"Didn't you try to get your money back?" Lily asked. "Didn't you try to trace it or something?"

Jo shook her head. "He deposited everything into his own account, then withdrew it in cash, a few thousand at a time. He left the receipts in the drawer of the bureau, as if he wanted me to find them, as if he wanted me to know there was no way to trace what he had done."

"You can be sure it's gone," Frank said. "Spent on the high life to which Brian always felt entitled. I have no idea why he was that way. My mother said he had been too good-looking, that things came too easily to Brian because of his looks. It made him think he deserved to have things handed to him. It made him think he was better than the rest of us."

Jo couldn't disagree. "But still," she said. "I should have seen the signs. I just didn't want to. I wanted the fantasy. I let it cloud my head."

Frank had picked at his steak. "That's what I told myself when he tapped our till," Frank said. "He was young and he had big dreams. My father and Brian never saw eye-to-eye. Dad was always holding me up as an example, I'm afraid. 'Why can't you be more like Frank?' he would say time and time again, sometimes with a whack across his butt, a punch in the arm, or a slap on the face. I wasn't surprised when the money started disappearing. Fifty here, a hundred dollars there. Never enough money to make a big deal out of it. I always covered up for him. Until that last night."

Jo had been uncomfortable. She'd never known that Brian had lived in the shadow of his brother. She'd never known that Mr. Forbes had been mean to him.

"Anyway," Frank shrugged, "then they had the big battle. In the morning, three thousand dollars was gone, and so was Brian."

Jo closed her eyes. She couldn't believe what Frank said next.

"He always said he was going to marry you, Jo. When I realized the money was gone and that Brian was, too, I thought that's what he had done. I thought he used the money to take off with you."

She'd pushed aside her plate and taken a long drink of wine. "He said he was going to marry me?" she asked. Her thoughts flashed back twenty years. To the pain of having been abandoned. To the ache about the baby that never had been born.

"I thought you and Brian had planned it together," Frank continued. "But on the day you graduated from college, I went into the butcher shop. Ted wasn't there. 'Gone to watch Marion Lyons' girl graduate from Winston,' the clerk told me. That's when I knew Brian had taken off alone."

Yes, Jo acknowledged, he had taken off alone.

And now she was tired. Tired of thinking and talking of him. It would take time, she knew, to shed Brian's skin from her life. Eventually, she'd do it. But not by having dinner with a stranger, a neighbor, who had few aspirations of his own.

She changed into her nightgown as if the act would ensure a decent night's sleep.

When the whistle of the teakettle blew, Jo fixed a strong pot, then returned to the living room where she curled up on the sofa and only drank three sips before she fell sound asleep.

Sometime later, a loud knock on the door quickly jerked her awake. She pulled herself up and considered not answering. But what if it was her mother? What if Marion needed her?

Still half-asleep, Jo floundered to the door.

"Yes?" she called, then suddenly feared it might be the neighbor, the one who'd left the note.

"Jo?" a man's voice called. "It's Andrew. Can I come inside? We've got a big problem and we need to talk."

"Elaine wants to call off the wedding." Andrew looked at Jo. Jo rubbed her eyes. This must be a dream.

"What?" she asked.

Andrew stepped past her and walked into the apartment. "May I turn on a light?"

"Sure," she said. "Would you like tea? Or something?" She supposed if she were dreaming about anyone other than Brian that was a good sign. Even if it was Andrew.

Andrew shook his head, snapped on the chandelier over the small table, then sat in a straight chair. "I spent the past couple of hours talking to her," he said. "I got absolutely nowhere."

The longer Jo stood there, the more real this became. The edges of the room, the furniture, and Andrew all came into focus. "Are you serious?" she asked.

He nodded. "After everyone left I found her in the back room. She was crying."

Jo slid onto a chair across the table from him. "Elaine?"

"I took her out for a drink to calm her down. She said she needs time to learn who she really is before becoming someone else's wife. She said she can't go through with it, even for the three of you, even after all the work you've done."

Jo raked her hands through her hair. She knew she must look a mess. Andrew would not, of course, care. It occurred to her that if all men were gay, life would be far more relaxing. Then maybe no one would get married and everyone would be wonderful friends. Life, she thought, could be worse. Then she remembered Elaine. "What should we do?"

"I have no idea," Andrew said. "I never knew weddings were so important to women."

"To some women," Jo said. She did not admit that while they'd been trying on gowns earlier that day, she'd had a moment or two of longing for a day of her own, a special wedding day when she'd be wed to a special man. *Fantasy,* she thought again. *God, why do women, including me, still buy into the myth?* She shook her head. "I thought Elaine was crazy about him. I thought this was a match made in heaven, her second chance at love."

Andrew snorted. "All I know is that she seems pretty definite. And I thought you should know."

"Should I go to her house? Should I try and talk to her tonight?"

"She had a few drinks. My guess is she's dead asleep. If I were you I'd leave her alone for a day or two. Then maybe go to her if she hasn't come around."

"Wow," Jo said. Her robe had fallen to one side, exposing her short silky nightgown and the soft curve of her naked breast. She tied the robe slowly: Thank God it was Andrew and not the neighbor. "I never expected Elaine to back out." She looked back at Andrew. "Are you sure you don't want tea?"

He stood up. "No. Thanks. I need to get home and do some work before bed."

"Oh," Jo said, "that's right. Your dissertation. How's it coming?"

"Well," Andrew replied before he hurried to the door, "it's interesting."

She said good night and that she'd see him in the

morning. Then she closed the door and leaned against it and wondered what would now happen to Second Chances. Without Elaine's wedding, would Lily lose interest in the business? Would Sarah?

And then where would Jo be, alone again?

# 28

*H*oly Mary, Mother of God, Andrew typed. *If my mother ever heard that, she'd wash my mouth out with soap. But my mother would not have been prepared for the women of today.*

*Lesson #5: If they don't think you're interested, they will show you some flesh.*

He squirmed a little in his chair. God, Jo had beautiful breasts. Still high and firm for a woman her age, still luscious-looking and . . . *Shit,* he typed. *Why the hell do I have to pretend that I am gay?*

Wiping his brow, he discovered that a thin line of sweat had formed. Just the thought of Jo made him so goddamn hot. How long had it been since he'd had sex with a real, live woman, with something other than his well-callused hand?

He toyed with a few ideas of how to break the news

that he had lied. He tried to think of plausible excuses: He could say he thought if he pretended to be gay he'd have a better shot of getting the job, that he really needed the money while he was working on his dissertation. He could say he had a lot of respect for what the women were trying to do, and that jobs were scarce in West Hope, and that he'd lost his and would take anything to avoid going back to New York.

He could say he was only trying to give his little girl a good home.

He would never, never admit to what he was really doing.

His eyes epoxied to the keyboard, Andrew stopped typing and leaned back in his chair. He knew all his excuses sucked. All seemed like they were veiled lies, which, of course, they were. Lesson #5, he decided, was a stupid one.

*Concentrate*, Andrew ordered himself. *Forget you're nothing more than a horny man.*

He deleted the words he'd written.

He tried to focus on Elaine and on what had happened that night. He tried to think how he could spin her actions into a revelation that his readers would enjoy, that John Benson would chuckle over, that would help secure Andrew's new career, in case Second Chances went out of business.

He started over. *Lesson #5: Never underestimate the power of a wedding over the female mind.*

# 29

---

*DO*
*Expect the unexpected.*

B ut almost everything is paid for!" Lily shrieked the next morning when Jo broke the news.

"Oh, man," Sarah said, tossing back her hair and uncrossing her long, copper legs, "this is a bummer." Then she stood up and grabbed her shoulder bag. "Call me if anything changes. I'm behind on my jewelry, anyway. I might as well go home and work on that."

Jo had called Andrew early in the morning and suggested he stay home for the day. She said she'd talk to the others; that they'd have to decide what they would do next. Jo didn't know if it was possible, but she had to try to keep the others moving forward with the business, despite Elaine's decision. Jo had to keep moving forward, because if she stopped, she feared she would break, piece by piece, head to heart.

They sat alone now, Jo and Lily, staring at each other with mutual disappointment.

"Hell's bells," Lily said. "Elaine has ruined everything."

"Not necessarily," Jo replied. "We can do this without her, Lily. Without her wedding."

"But it was going to be our showcase. Our jumping-off point. How can we sell the concept of second weddings if we don't have one to flaunt?"

"I don't know yet," Jo said. "But I don't want to quit. I think we have a real chance to make a business out of this."

Lily sighed. "But now it will be so much . . . work. I don't know, Jo. Maybe I shouldn't throw away Reginald's money so carelessly."

*Money*, Jo thought with chagrin. *That chafing noose around the neck of life.* "I don't think it's careless, Lily. But a business takes time to get off the ground." Of course, Lily wouldn't know that. Things had often come too easily to her. It made sense that she would expect them to, and when they didn't . . . well, why not walk away? What was in it for Lily other than a novelty?

For one thing, there was their friendship, and the mismatched kindred spirit they finally had renewed beyond a few rushed visits and infrequent e-mails.

"Lily," Jo continued, "I don't know about you, but I've loved what we're doing, spending time together more than just one weekend a year, working on a project. It's given me new purpose. And I didn't realize how much

I've needed my friends. I didn't realize how much I needed to have fun."

A smile traced Lily's pink lips. "Well, yes. It is fun. I love being with you girls."

"And you love your little apartment. And there is Frank . . ."

"Yes," Lily agreed.

Jo leaned forward. "I think we can do it, Lily. Come on, let's give it a try."

Lily laughed. "And to think you were the one who, in the beginning, wanted no part of this."

"Priorities change," Jo said.


They began working with vigor—even Lily, who kept saying she had no idea what she was doing; even Sarah, who'd decided to keep on making the linden leaves that she'd been making. If nothing else, they could take pictures to show as examples.

At first Lily had wanted to dash over to Elaine's, to learn the details of the breakup, to see if she could help. Elaine was one of them; Elaine must need them now.

Andrew had disagreed. "Let her sort this out herself," he said. "She knows you're here. She knows you love her. The best thing you can do right now is give her privacy."

His advice, as usual, seemed sound.

"And who knows?" he added. "Elaine might change her mind again."

With that speculation, they decided not to return the gowns or cancel the reception or the caterer or the cars. Not for a few days. They'd wait and they would see.

Still, Jo knew they needed a big commercial hook right

now, a clever idea that would catapult their business into the bridal spotlight. Lily was right: How could they claim to be wedding planners, without a wedding to plan?

On Friday afternoon, Jo turned the page of her calendar to Saturday: on it was a surprising notation that read "Take Cassie shopping?" Andrew hadn't mentioned the shopping trip since he had asked. She knew he'd understand if she reneged—she was so tired, there was still so much work to do—but Jo decided that would not be fair. Andrew was turning into a top-notch employee. It wouldn't kill her to do the guy a favor. Besides, she reasoned quietly, it might help take Jo's racing mind off other things now at stake.

"Is Ms. Brouillard still the principal at West Hope Elementary?" Jo asked as they drove toward the stores in Lee.

"Yes," Cassie answered, staring out the window, her small body strapped into the seat belt. She was, Jo suspected, shy, awkward, the way Jo had been with strangers when she'd been Cassie's age. "Did you go to West Hope?" Cassie asked.

"Yes. A long time ago."

"Was Ms. Brouillard the principal back then?"

"No," Jo replied, careful not to smile, for Ellen Brouillard was about five years younger than Jo was. "Mr. Williamson was the principal. He was real strict."

"I don't like principals," Cassie said.

"Good thing they're not teachers."

"Yeah. Good thing."

"Who's your teacher?"

"Miss Carroll. And Mr. Ames. I have two this year. I'm in sixth grade."

" 'Mr. Ames'? Not *the* Mr. Ames? The bald guy who wears bow ties?"

Cassie turned and looked at Jo. "The *old* bald guy. Yeah, that's him."

*Old.* Well, of course he would be now. "I can't believe it," Jo said. "I had him thirty years ago. He had bad breath."

"Still does," Cassie said and they laughed, and by the time Jo parked at the outlet stores, the get-acquainted ice had broken and was well-thawed.


By noon Cassie had perused The Gap and Tommy Hilfilger and Big Dogs as if she'd been—heaven forbid!—born to shop. Thankfully, Andrew had given them a budget, or Jo could easily have helped Cassie fill a closet or maybe two.

"I love this!" Cassie squealed over and over. She especially liked jeans that were embroidered. And anything with a Yankees logo or that Cassie perceived as cool. It reminded Jo of happy times, when clothes that bore designer names were beginning to take hold; when puka necklaces and mood rings were replaced by Dorothy Hamill–hair and T-shirts of The E Street Band.

"How about a break for lunch?" Jo asked. It was after one o'clock, and she was delightfully hungry. Being with Cassie made her feel young again, happy, almost as if she'd never felt choked by the small town of West Hope or felt the push to get away. So, she thought, this is why people have kids, to provide meaning beyond mere self-serving success. She forced away thoughts of the child she never had and steered Cassie to a sandwich shop.

While waiting for a table, they sat on a bench in the front lobby, shopping bags heaped at their feet, a small smile in place on Jo's contented face.

"Thank you, Jo," Cassie said quietly. "This has been one of the neatest days of my life."

Jo laughed. "Mine, too, Cassie. We should do it more often." Then her eyes fell to a wire rack that held free newspapers and flyers. While Cassie poked through her purchases, Jo picked up a flyer and scanned the contents for condos, because she could dream, couldn't she?

That's when she saw the ad that would have jumped off the page if ads could really do that; the ad that would make their business an overwhelming, unequivocal triumph.

So much for unnecessary, "mere" success.

"Oh my God," she said out loud.

Cassie stopped what she was doing and looked at Jo. "Is something wrong?"

Jo shook her head and dug into her purse. She pulled out her cell phone and quickly dialed the office. Just as it began to ring, the hostess returned and said that their table was ready.

"Go ahead, honey," Jo said, "I'll catch up to you."

She watched the girl struggle with bags in either hand, as Andrew answered the phone.

"I've got it!" she shrieked. "Cassie and I are going to have lunch. Then I'll come to the shop. I hope everyone is there—please don't let them leave."

Jo felt a little guilty for cutting the shopping trip short, but Cassie seemed content. She asked to go to the office to show off her new things. As excited as Jo was to share her new idea, she couldn't take that fun away from the girl. So after gulping a hamburger (a salad, she reasoned, would have taken longer to eat), Jo tried to be patient while Cassie modeled one outfit after another, including her greatest new treasure, a pair of red cowboy boots.

"What's the matter?" Andrew asked, "don't they make them with a Yankees logo?"

"Dad," Cassie said, rolling her eyes, and everyone laughed, because it was so cute the way she called her Uncle Andrew "Dad."

When the bags were repacked, Cassie settled down to look through a bridal magazine, and Sarah said, "Okay, Jo, what's your bright idea?"

Jo smiled smugly, because she knew this was great. She looked from Sarah to Lily to Andrew, then said, "A sweepstakes. We're going to hold a sweepstakes."

After a moment Lily said, "What in heavens name do you mean?"

Rubbing her hands, Jo pulled together the thoughts that had swirled in her mind since she'd seen the flyer at the restaurant. "I saw an ad for a sweepstakes. Something about sending in a coupon for a chance to win a vacation. Anyway, it got me to thinking. Why couldn't we have a sweepstakes for Elaine's wedding? Everything is in place . . . it's five weeks from now. Why can't we offer it as an introductory splash?"

"Well," Sarah said, "I believe this certifies that Josephine is crazy."

"I'm serious, Sarah. Think of the attention we'll get. Think of the excitement we'll create!"

Mute. They were mute!

"Look," Jo continued. "For nearly twenty years I had a successful public relations firm. I don't know everything, but I do know how to get people to notice us. Giving away a wedding is certainly one way."

"But how will we let everyone know?" Lily asked. "And who will want it, anyway?"

Jo shrugged. "We'll start with the Internet. It's too late for the bridal magazines, and as we found out, they're geared for the young ones anyway. I still might have a few connections in television. Maybe I could finagle us a slot on a network morning show or one of the surviving news magazines."

"Reality TV," Lily said with a groan. "Hasn't the world had enough of that?"

"But weddings never go out of date. Besides, even if we don't have a ton of responses, no one will be able to take away the exposure. We're creating a whole new market for the second-time-around crowd. We're showing them that it's okay to have the wedding of their new dreams, that though they've been married before, this is the first time that they've had this special person for a partner. It's a new angle, so maybe the media will bite."

Sarah and Lily did not seem convinced. She turned to Andrew. "Andrew, please? I know you don't know anything about television or the media, but it might work, don't you think?"

But Andrew merely shrugged, stood up, and said he really should get Cassie home.

# 30

♥

**DO**
*Allow yourself to get excited, even if you're not twenty-five. This is a monumental day for you, and you're enti-tled to make it as big and as grand as you want, no matter what your age, no matter if this is your second or your third or fourth trip down the aisle.*

The last thing Jo expected when she arrived home that night was to find another note under her door.

*Okay,* it read, *if not dinner, then how about lunch during the week? I'm not an ax murderer and I don't drink more than one beer, and then only if the temperature rises past ninety.*

She could not help but smile. He was clever enough, this neighbor named . . . what was his name? Jack. Yes, that was it.

Tossing the note onto the kitchen counter, she had a quick tug on her heart. The day had been wonderful: shopping with Cassie, the sweepstakes idea despite her coworkers' doubts, and now, a man who was showing an interest. Maybe.

She kicked off her sandals and went into the spare bedroom where stacks of boxes remained unopened. If only she could find the computer disks or the hard copies she needed, the ones with the information, the contact names, the phone numbers of the TV shows that might see the business of planning second weddings as a great gimmick, and might help promote the idea of the sweepstakes.

With the wedding scheduled for only weeks away, she'd have to work fast. Who was the misguided genius who'd said second weddings didn't require as much "lead time" as first ones? Pushing down her doubts, Jo sorted through the cartons, checking each carefully marked label:

ACCOUNTS PAYABLE

ACCOUNTS RECEIVABLE

SAMPLES

MEDIA

That was the one. Hoisting the heavy carton with a groan, Jo set it atop a stack of two others. With a thumbnail that somehow had remained strong for weeks without a manicure, she slit through the tape and pulled back the flaps. Shoebox after shoebox of computer disks were there: *TV* was scrawled across the top of one. She lifted the lid and extracted the disks. *Good Morning*

*America, Today, CBS This Morning, E!, Dateline*, and *The Edge*. She removed each disk, one after another, grateful that she'd resisted dumping them in the Charles River.

Then, despite the fact that it was nearly midnight, Jo put her sandals back on and picked up the shoebox. She was happy and hopeful and filled with adrenaline, which was probably why, on her way through the kitchen, she picked up the note from the neighbor named Jack. She set down the shoebox, turned over the note, then wrote: *Lunch would be fine, but I work during the week.* She hesitated to ask if he had a job. Somehow the question seemed a little mean, and she supposed she'd know soon enough. *No job, no second date*, Jo promised herself.

With a halfhearted shake of her head, she left her apartment and took the stairs down one flight. She slid the note under the door of number 304, then continued to the garage, then on to the office, where she'd work all night if she had to in order to orchestrate the media plan of attack.

It was after midnight on Saturday night. Andrew had climbed into bed long ago, after foregoing work on his column to play Sorry! with Cassie, then watching an animated video that she had picked out. He'd pretended to be a great dad, when, in fact, he'd been totally preoccupied with Jo's latest idea: *Maybe the media will bite*, she'd said. Then: *Andrew, I know you don't know anything about television or the media, but it might work, don't you think?*

He could have agreed. He should have agreed, because, after all, it was a terrific idea. Instead, an image had leapt into his mind of his old boss, Kevin Green, who made Geraldo Rivera look as placid as Pat Sajak, and Jerry Springer as conservative as Alex Trebek.

Kevin Green was now the executive producer of *Sakes Alive!*—one of, as Jo had said, "the surviving news magazines," though it was really tabloid journalism at its most tabloid. Kevin Green was also the arch-rival of John Benson, the two having once competed for a top network slot that neither of them won, and for which each blamed the other. If Kevin showcased Second Chances, he'd probably find out about Andrew. Andrew did not know how, but Kevin was like that, able to unearth dirt under concrete poured by the Romans that might have been in tact for two millenniums. It was a cultural artform that Kevin had perfected, and had moved *Sakes Alive!* up in the ratings race long after the others had fallen off the fad-wagon.

Andrew tossed and he turned, then tossed some more. He tried to focus on the yard work that needed tending to tomorrow; he tried to think about how he and Cassie would survive until the next semester if Second Chances shut down and he lost his jobs both there and at *Buzz*.

*Columnist blew it*, John Benson would write. *He put all his lies in one basket.*

He turned again and tried to think about Patty and when Cassie would hear from her again, and if Andrew should or would care. He tried to play out the surprise visit he and Cassie would make, and how much like crap it would make Patty feel.

But even Patty, or thoughts of Patty, could not eclipse his concern.

The tossing and turning accomplished nothing. His mind kept veering back to the same thing.

If Jo went to the media, it would jeopardize more than Andrew's job at Second Chances or his column at *Buzz*. As the former husband of Patty O'Shay and, in his own right, a man who'd been a major player in the theater of the media, who now needed to pretend that he was gay, he'd find himself a media joke, impeccable fodder for Leno and Letterman, front-page ha-ha's for the *The Enquirer* and *The Star*.

John Benson would be pissed. Cassie would be embarrassed. And there would go the job and the money and the new roof and the riding lessons. And the surprise trip to Australia. Andrew Kennedy would be a college professor once more, albeit with a bit more fame than he would have wanted.

That is, if Winston College didn't see his lies and deceit as a breech of the morals clause in his contract and sever his sabbatical and his job along with it. John Benson, after all, held Andrew's college strings, as well.

It would, however, be great publicity for Second Chances. They would come out the winners; Andrew would be the loser.

Staring into the darkness, Andrew realized it would be his job or theirs; his life or theirs. It was exactly the kind of mental gymnastics he thought he'd escaped when he'd left New York.

With a resigned sigh and no more hesitation, he reached for the phone and called John Benson's cell.

"My hero," Benson said when he learned it was Andrew. "Love the latest entry, my boy." John would have loved the column even if he hadn't read it. The latest issue had resulted in an increase in ad sales, and profits were returning. The "buzz" around *Buzz* was that "Real

Women" was the reason for a good chunk of the turn-around. "Real Women" was the gimmick that no one had but *Buzz.* "You're one of the few people I'd actually talk to on a Saturday night."

"Sorry," Andrew said, sitting up in his bed and turning on the light. "Hope I'm not interrupting anything exciting."

Benson laughed. "You were in the media long enough to know not to believe everything you hear."

"Right. Well, the good news is, I didn't call to test your reputation. I need your help, John. I need you to run defense for me. For us. For *Buzz.*" He quickly gave him the overview of Second Chances, and told him about Jo's sweepstakes idea and the media blitz.

"And you want me to kill it," John said.

"Before it gets off the ground. Before it gets past the assistant's assistant to each and every producer. Including Kevin Green."

"Especially Kevin Green," Benson replied. "He's been looking for a way to make me look like an ass."

"I know."

There was silence a moment, then John said, "I'll take care of it, Andrew. Just get back to your business of being a gay man in a woman's world. I thought you were nuts in the beginning, but I have to admit, it's working for both of us. I'll take care of Kevin. And the rest."

"Let me know if I can do anything from this end," Andrew said, then hung up, turned off the light, crawled back under the covers, and went to sleep as if none of this crap had ever happened.

Marion had invited Jo to have Sunday dinner with Ted, the butcher, and her. Now that their relationship was, in Marion's words, "out of the meat locker," she was eager for her daughter to get to know the man when he was not behind the chrome-and-glass counter or adorned in a bloodstained white apron.

Just before noon Jo left her apartment and began the short drive to her childhood home, the same place where, for the past several years, Ted had apparently been hiding on and off, in and out, concealing his involvement with her mother. She thought of Andrew. As a gay man, he must know a lot about hiding relationships: Had he left a former one hidden in New York, where he was from? Could that account for why he'd been so disturbed about the prospect of a PR campaign in the city?

Like her mother and Ted, was Andrew hiding something?

Jo shook her head. She must be overtired. But by the time she'd finished organizing her contact lists last night and sending teaser e-mails that the media would receive Monday morning and preparing press releases to forward Monday afternoon, the sun had already risen over the Berkshire Hills. She'd driven home in full daylight, felt only slightly rebuffed when she realized there was no note from Jack under her door. She'd collapsed on the sofa where she'd awakened three hours later with little time to shower and find something appropriate to wear.

She settled on a powder-blue sundress and matching canvas sandals and tried not to remember that she'd bought the outfit for a luncheon cruise around Boston Harbor on which she and Brian entertained Jake and Mona Coughlin, because Brian had been trying to lure the software giant and his wife to invest with Brian's start-up firm. Jake had been a client of Jo's for several years and wasted no time in letting Brian know that he did not mix business and business. Jo had been upset for Brian at the time; now she was relieved. The Coughlins were nice people and, no matter how wealthy, would not have deserved to have lost money with Brian . . . first their cash, then the equity in their home, then the accounts receivable of their business, the money owed to them, much of which had been meant to pay printers and suppliers and had not belonged in their pockets at any time.

Of course, that would not have happened to the Coughlins, because they were not in love with Brian. They'd been too smart for that.

"Josephine," Marion said when Jo suddenly found herself at the back door with a pint of blueberries in hand, which she'd thought to pick up at the Randalls' farm stand. "Fresh blueberries," she said, "how thoughtful."

Ted must already be there or Marion would not have been so formal. Perhaps she was nervous, Jo thought, stepping into the kitchen, then realizing that—good grief!—she was suddenly nervous, too. Could she look at the butcher and not think that the hands that spent most of their days trimming and slicing beef spent most of their nights caressing her mother?

"You remember Ted Cappelinni?"

"Of course," Jo said with the expected smile, though she hardly would have recognized the white-haired man who got up from the chair at Marion's kitchen table and took Jo's extended hand. He wore a white shirt, navy tie, and a blue-and-white seersucker sports jacket. His eyebrows seemed bushier than Jo remembered, and his nose seemed bigger. He seemed quite shy. "Ted the Butcher," Jo said with a light laugh. "When I was a little girl I thought 'the butcher' was all one word, and that it was your last name."

He smiled and said hello, it was nice to see her again.

"Who wants lemonade?" Marion asked, and Jo said she'd love some and Ted said he would, too. After a few minutes the three took their glasses and filed out to the porch, where they sat and made small talk until the roast finished roasting and the potatoes were done. And all the while Jo tried not to wonder if love would ever again happen to her and why it should matter when she had a new purpose, new goals that were likely to succeed because Jo Lyons was behind them.

She listened patiently to the trials of being a small-town butcher, and how Ted's parents sailed off to America just before the Nazis became aggressive in Europe. When they disembarked in New York they spoke no English. They asked a street vendor where the Italians lived. "New Haven," the man said, so that's where they spent the Great Depression, and stayed until the early forties when Ted was the newest of, by then, three children.

"Our children need country air," Ted said his father had announced. So they piled their belongings into an old jalopy and drove north until they found a place that reminded Ted's father of his beloved Tuscany. The place was the Berkshires; the town was West Hope. None of the Cappelinnis had ever left, and most were now buried there.

When speaking of his family, Ted wasn't shy at all.

During dinner Jo told them about the progress at

Second Chances and about her concept for a sweepstakes to give away Elaine's wedding.

"Will you go to New York and be on television?" Marion asked with a small wink at Ted as if to say, "See what a successful daughter I have?" and "Won't the church ladies just die?"

But Jo replied, "I'm not sure. But Lily might be the best spokesperson. A lot of people will recognize her from the society pages. She was married to a high-visibility man, you know. That will help business."

"Well," Marion said, "I'd like to see you on TV. I think you'd do a fine job." Well, of course Marion would think that.

"In the old days," Ted said, "we didn't need gimmicks to make our business work. 'Give an honest product, make an honest living,' my father always said. Did I tell you he was a butcher, too?"

No, he hadn't said that.

"Who wants blueberries?" Marion asked before Jo had a chance to analyze whether or not Ted thought her new business was an honest way to make a living.

"Let me do it, Mom," she said with a smile as she stood up. "Whipped cream, Ted?" Then the thought flashed through her mind of one day when she'd been a senior in high school and had stayed home because Brian said he could sneak over to see her. With Marion at work, Jo was alone. Then Brian appeared at the back door with a can of whipped cream. And right there in the kitchen—the very same kitchen—she had stretched out across the linoleum and he had squirted a dollop of cream on her right foot, then licked it off slowly, inch by inch, toe by toe.

Jo snatched the dirty dishes from in front of Ted and

her mother more quickly than she'd intended. Ted's fork dropped onto his seersucker and clattered to the floor.

"Oh," she said, "I'm so sorry. How clumsy of me." She could have said she was overtired, but that would bring up the business again and she didn't want to do that.

Ted stood up and brushed off his jacket. "No harm done. Let me help you with those."

Jo glanced at her mother, who smiled wryly. Jo smiled in return as if to let Marion know that she thought Ted the Butcher was a nice man, and if her mother slept with him, that was fine with her, even though she'd rather not picture that.

Ted carried the dishes to the sink, loosened his tie, and turned back to her mother as he said, "Looks like we have more company, Marion."

The company had turned out to be for neither Marion nor Ted. It was Frank Forbes, looking for Jo.

# 31

As best as he could remember, it had been two
years since Andrew had had sex with a woman,
since he'd felt the soft touch of sweet flesh and
the gentle rise and fall of lean legs wrapped around him
and the warm, welcoming wetness of love.

He didn't know how it had happened that he and Jo
Lyons wound up in the back room of the shop at the same
time with the same needs and same wants on their minds.
He didn't know how, but they made a bed of Sarah's velvet fabric swatches and he told Jo he'd wanted her from
the first day he'd seen her and she said she'd known all
along that he wasn't gay, that no man could look at her
with such longing if he preferred a man.

He said what he would prefer, would be to take off her
clothes, button by button, and if she wouldn't mind, he'd

also prefer to savor each and every part of her awesome body slowly, so slowly, one part at a time.

One throat.

One shoulder.

One nipple that stiffened from the touch of his moist, hungry mouth.

And now, from mere inches above her, he gazed into her naked green eyes. He eyed her sleek body, trying to soak in its beauty so he would remember every curve, every hollow, the wave over her rib cage, the soft angle of her hips. He eyed her, top to bottom, then bent to her pleasure and worked with his tongue.

Quickly, she came, as if she had waited for this moment as long as he had, as if she had yearned for his heat from when she'd first seen him, too.

He toyed with her pulsations a moment longer . . . up, down, around, and . . . in. Then he rose up above her. He glanced down at his penis. Had it ever been so engorged? Had it ever felt so strong, so powerful, so much in command of itself? Never. Not even with Patty.

His strong, powerful, in-control penis then wavered with longing. Andrew smiled. Jo smiled. Then Andrew drew back and began to guide it toward her waiting fervor, toward her fire.

"Daddy?"

Andrew blinked.

"Daddy? Wake up. Mrs. Connor wants to know if we want some rhubarb."

Thank God he'd been on his side when he'd fallen asleep on the hammock in the backyard. Thank God he'd been reading *The Sunday New York Times,* and that it had dropped onto his lap and now concealed the enormous erection strained against his running shorts, which Cassie could not see, but he surely could feel.

"Sure, honey," he said. "Why don't you go help her pick some?"

Cassie raced off and Andrew sighed. He rubbed his eyes and thought about all the yard work he had yet to do, and how Sundays passed too quickly to be spent on a hammock, dreaming of a woman that he could not have.

# 32

Jo's first thought was that something had happened to Lily.

"She's fine," Frank said as he stood on the other side of Marion's screen door. "But I'd like to talk to you about something. If you have a minute."

Marion suggested they go out on the porch. Would Frank like some blueberries, too?

On the way through the kitchen, down the hall, and out onto the screened porch, Jo felt every ounce of the dinner she'd just eaten sit in her stomach like a sudden wad of fear, like the million butterflies that metamorphosed in time for the school play when she'd had the lead, like the lump that she'd felt when she'd finally told her mother she was pregnant and that Brian had left not only West Hope but also the country.

It was, of course, going to be about Brian, because why

else would Frank have come there? Why else would he have tracked her down on a Sunday afternoon? . . .

"It's about Brian," Frank said abruptly when they sat on the faded flower cushions of the wicker chairs.

The blood drained from her head, from her heart.

"R. J. Browne thinks he has found him."

She couldn't breathe. From the moment those words passed from Frank's mouth to her ears, Jo simply forgot her humiliation and pain; she forgot her resolution to move on.

She closed her eyes. "You hired the investigator," she said. She knew she should ask where Brian was now and if he was all right. But Jo wasn't ready to listen.

"Yes. R.J. Browne. You'd told me his name . . . and his business is in Boston . . . it seemed only logical . . ."

Logical. At least someone had remained logical when it came to Brian.

She opened her eyes and looked out to the yard, to the large oak tree where a swing had once swung, where Brian had once pushed her for hours at a time on warm summer days like that one; where they'd eaten fresh peaches and kissed the juice from each other's cheeks and laughed because they were teenagers and the gesture felt daring and grown-up and somehow quite sinful.

"Fresh blueberries," came Marion's voice as the screen door banged and she delivered two porcelain bowls filled with ripe berries and a cloud of whipped cream. Jo said "Thank you" and set the bowl down. She could not eat then, maybe never again.

"He's in Montreaux," Frank continued once Marion had left them alone again. "It's a small town in Switzerland. On a lake."

Jo had never been to Switzerland and had no idea why Brian would have gone there. Had he ever mentioned a secret longing to be in Europe? Had it been one of his dreams that she'd failed to take seriously . . . that she'd failed to provide?

"Jo," Frank said slowly, "Brian's not alone."

Her eyelids dropped again, as if shutting off her vision would shut off the world, would shut out the pain that was about to crash down on her once again—*Brian-pain*, she'd come to refer to it; his own special brand of searing, stabbing hurt that had started after college and had never completely left.

"Brian has never liked being alone." She said it matter-of-factly, as if she were referring to a child or a dog.

Frank ate his blueberries most likely out of politeness than out of desire. Of the two brothers, why had Jo been attracted to the bad one, the misfit, the rebel?

"What else did the investigator say?" she asked in flat, monotone syllables.

"Browne went with his friend, a woman named Faye. Apparently Faye engaged Brian's companion in conversation out by the pool. The woman said they were planning to settle in Switzerland, even if it meant becoming expatriates of America, that it would be okay because there was no place like Switzerland on the face of the earth. She said that Brian was into investments and . . ." At that point Frank paused, not that he needed to. Something in the hesitant, anguished tone of his voice had already warned Jo what was coming next. ". . . and that they'd only been married for a few weeks."

The small cry that Jo heard must have come from somewhere else, from a bird who had broken his wing, out in the large oak. But suddenly Frank Forbes leaned close to her and took her hand and asked if she was okay, and Jo knew then that the cry had been hers.

"The bastard," she said. "The hideous bastard." She supposed it was a word she had needed to use to describe Brian Forbes for a very long time. She had needed to admit that he really was a bastard, a self-centered, vile bastard. The blood returned to her head with feverish heat. "That bastard," she said.

Frank lowered his head. "I'm sorry, Jo," he said. "I am so sorry."

They sat for a moment, Jo holding back a string of curses she would have liked to have spewed out in rapid-fire shots. She settled on "bastard"—plain, simple, "bastard."

"Lily said she'll be home," Frank said, "if you'd like to talk, if you need a friend."

Lily. So Frank had told her, as well. Well, Jo supposed, why not? Lily, after all, had chosen the sensible brother, the one who was kind and considerate and loving and everything that Brian was not.

She didn't go to Lily. Instead, Jo went home. In the past she'd have gone to her office, convinced herself there was work to be done, choked back her tears and immersed herself in the computer and all the possibilities that it held for becoming successful, for proving to herself that just because she couldn't pick the right men didn't mean she was a loser at life.

But if she went to the office she'd have to see Lily, and the last thing Jo wanted was anyone hovering. Not Lily or

Sarah or even sweet Andrew if he were there, which he might very well be because Lily might have called him. He had, after all, quickly become a part of their new mismatched family of the hurt and the hurting and the still-hanging-on. Hell, Lily might even call Elaine, who of course would show up because Elaine was on the down side of a relationship, too, even though hers had been by choice.

Jo dragged herself into her apartment, fell onto the couch, and wished she could vomit the roast and the potatoes along with the secretive smiles that had bounced back and forth between Ted and Marion during dinner, like badminton birdies, all light and atwitter. Secretive, lover-smiles that Jo recognized because she'd had them with Brian, hadn't she? She'd had them as late as Mrs. Dotson's Valentine's Day party in the building in Boston when the picture had been taken that she'd given to the police and didn't care if she ever saw again.

It was then Jo realized she hated all men, starting with her father, who had been the first to leave. It did not matter that Jo never knew the real reasons, only those slanted by Marion's reality:

"He's a man, Josephine," Marion had said. "Men sometimes do that."

And so Jo had expected bad behavior from men. Was it any surprise she'd found one to comply?

She pulled her knees to her chest and hugged them against her. She thought about Brian's marriage—had there been a wedding with pearl satin gowns and a symphony harpist and cranberry crème?

The pain in her stomach crawled up to her throat, then leaked from her mouth in another small sound.

"Oh," she cried, as she looked around her apartment and knew that, once again, she was alone, and that, this time, Brian really was gone. No excuses. Not even to her.

She pulled a toss pillow from the end of the couch, clutched it to her cheek, and slowly began to sob for the little girl, Josephine, who'd been abandoned so young, and for little Amanda or Emmett, who had never even had a chance to live.

# 33

She's not in today? When do you expect her?"
Andrew was on the phone trying to get through to
Maxine Bardwell, another name on Jo's list. They'd
been making calls all Monday morning, following up on
the e-mails to the talk-show producers.

Jo had expected at least one response by noon, at least
one curious nibble to her message about Second Chances
and the opportunity to win a second wedding in the picturesque Berkshires. So far, there had been nothing.
Nothing for their business, nothing to take her mind off
Brian and Brian's new bride.

Andrew hung up with an apologetic smile. "Maxine
Bardwell is out of the country until the end of September," he said. "All of their programming is booked until
then."

"Bullshit," Jo said in a sharp show of anger. "This

doesn't make sense, Andrew. Every freaking producer can't be out of the country or on vacation or 'in a meeting and can't be disturbed.' " She knew that Andrew couldn't be expected to agree with any educated knowledge—he was, after all, only an assistant college professor on sabbatical, trying to finish a dissertation so he'd be called "doctor" and make a few bucks more a year.

She stood up and began pacing the showroom. "Maybe we should send the follow-up releases now."

"Not wait until late in the day so they'll get them first thing in the morning?"

"God, Andrew, don't you get it? We've got to drown them in hype. In order for this to work, we have to secure some decent airtime soon. This week. Next week at the latest. Do I have to remind you that the wedding is going to take place with or without a bride and groom?"

Well, that made no more sense than it did to berate poor Andrew, who was only trying his best.

"I'm sorry," she said, running her hands across her hair and wondering how long it would be before she had more than a few minutes' sleep at a time. "Oh, God, Andrew. It's not your fault. But you don't understand how the media business works."

He scanned the list on the desk in front of him. "No," he replied, "I guess I don't."

"It's just that this is our chance. Our one chance to make a big splash and get something started before Lily and Sarah decide to do something better with their lives." Sarah had kept to herself throughout the morning, working at her design table in the back room. Lily apparently was still in her apartment upstairs. Both of them were probably poised, ready to appear if needed, ready to offer a broad shoulder or an understanding heart on the matter of Brian and what he had done.

They all knew now. They all knew about the Boston detective who had found Brian. They all knew about the woman who was Brian's wife.

The phone rang. Jo snapped around. A talk-show producer? Her eyes darted to Andrew. He smiled again. He let the phone ring again, then he lifted the receiver. "Second Chances," he said. "Andrew speaking."

"Oh, hi," he responded to the other end of the line. He looked back at Jo. He shook his head. "What's the matter, Cassie? I'm pretty busy right now."

Jo returned to her desk. She reread the hard copy of the follow-up release, trying to decide if it was a waste of time. Once, she had known how to do this. Once, she'd had the contacts and the reputation and the chutzpah to do this. Once, the largest and more successful firms in Boston and beyond had entrusted their public relations to Jo Lyons and Associates. But now Jo could not seem to do for herself what she'd once made a fortune doing for others. Made a fortune, then lost it, because she'd been so stupid in love.

"I wonder if she has a lot of money," Jo said after Andrew had hung up the phone. He did not have to ask "Who?" because, of course, Andrew knew.

"Frank didn't tell you?"

Jo shook her head.

"Her father is the head of TransGlobal Film Studios."

She paused briefly, then balled up the follow-up release and threw it on the floor. Of course, it made perfect sense. Brian would not have taken up with a woman with less money than Jo. He did not know how to make money, only how to con it. She wondered how long it might take before that woman, too, was as broke as Jo was, or if that might not happen and he would live happily ever after. "Forget it," she said.

*Forget everything*, she thought.

Squeezing her eyes tightly, she wondered if she should go find a leftover Sunday *Boston Globe* and look for a job the way a sane person would do.

The phone rang again. Cassie, no doubt. Or Marion, calling to check on her daughter.

"Yes, we are," Andrew was saying into the phone. "Yes. Yes. That's correct. Let me put you through to Ms. Lyons."

Jo blinked. "You're not going to believe this," Andrew said as he put the caller on hold. "But it's a producer from *The View*. She wants to talk to you about Second Chances and about having someone come on the show."

It had been a long time since Jo had been in the city, since she'd breathed the energy that always made her feel as if everything were possible, as if the world could be hers. It was how she felt then, when she paused for a moment so that the producer would not think Jo had been sitting next to the phone, waiting for the call that had miraculously come.

"Jo Lyons," she said clearly, her voice sounding surprisingly calm, like the woman who had once been in such control, not at all like the woman who had cried herself to sleep last night, hugging her pillow as if it were a teddy bear and she was only six.

"Missy Clofsky from *The View*." The clipped words

insinuated that Jo should know who Missy Clofsky was, which Jo did not. "We read your e-mail and want to know more."

"Certainly," Jo said. "How can I help?" The e-mail had included the teaser followed by the facts, then a brief bio of the three women partners, excluding the part about Elaine who had bowed out.

"It says here you recognized a need for second weddings," the young woman continued. "Is that from experience?"

"No," Jo replied. "It was because of a friend. She was trying to plan a second wedding, but the only consultants she could locate, handled first weddings—the Cinderella-type fantasies. Not for mature audiences." She laughed a light laugh, but Missy Clofsky did not.

"I've been in public relations long enough to recognize a trend," Jo quickly continued. "My partners and I spoke with several women: No one we spoke with was too thrilled with the choices that ordinary consultants offered, from inappropriate gowns to reception venues that cater to youth. We noticed a niche market; we are filling it."

"In Massachusetts?" The accent was Brooklyn. The tone was professional, not derogatory.

"The Berkshires have become a destination not only for culture but also for fun. We have some wonderful, romantic settings. But this does not preclude the possibility that we might expand to other New England locations when word gets around. When our business expands."

"Which is why you want to be featured on *The View*."

"We're filling a need, as I said in the e-mail."

Pause. Damn. Jo hated those pauses, as if Missy

Clofsky were examining her fingernails or tapping her pencil, trying to decide if her bosses would think Second Chances was worthy.

"And you want to give away a wedding."

"A second wedding. Yes. It's all been arranged. The only things missing are the bride and groom. And the guests, of course. We'll need the guests, too."

Her eyes darted to Andrew, who sat, unflinching, as if he were a Greek statue in a pink shirt with blond hair.

"October?" Ms. Clofsky asked.

"The ninth."

The young woman's sigh *whoosh*ed through the phone. "Too soon," she said. "We can't get you on until after the holidays."

"Excuse me?"

"January. It's the best we can do."

"But the date has been set. The arrangements have been made . . ."

"Sorry. How about January fourteenth? We could give you a six-minute slot then."

"Fine," Jo replied, because she'd dealt with New York often enough to know it was best to take what you could get. She could always cancel if they were no longer in business. She could always cancel if she felt the way she did right now, as if the energy she'd once counted on getting from Manhattan had floated down the Hudson and gone into the sea. "But I'm not sure about the sweepstakes. I mean, the wedding we're giving away is scheduled for October ninth."

"Whatever. We'll talk before January." Missy Clofsky hung up without saying good-bye, and Jo looked at Andrew and simply said, "Damn."

# 34

―――――――――――――――♥―――――――――――――――

*L*esson #6: *Oh, what a tangled web we weave . . .*
  Andrew stared at the keyboard a moment, then typed, *Well, if you're a guy, you're probably familiar with the rest of that old saying. It simply means don't play games, at least not with a woman you might care about. If you do, it's certain to greatly reduce your chances of ever having something meaningful with her, because you will feel like such a piece of crap. You will want to confess and you know where that will get you.*

He knew his words were vague, without example, the bane of any decent journalist. But how could he tell his readers what was really on his mind? How could he tell his readers (his *fans*, he supposed, who, according to John Benson, would escalate in numbers with each printed issue) about the latest scheme that he and John concocted, without exposing who Jo and Lily and Sarah and Elaine really were?

*Excuse me*, he thought, *that would be Jacquelin, Olivia, Sadie, and Eileen.*

He slouched in his chair. The answer was, he couldn't tell his readers any of it. He already had revealed that they were four women, four middle-aged old friends who'd gone into business together. He hadn't been explicit. He hadn't said what they did or what kind of business it was. He'd kept the facts to the women and the roller-coaster emotions of their lives.

He hadn't told them about the second-wedding planning, because it could come back to bite him.

And so Andrew could not reveal that he and John Benson had devised a plan to keep the women out of New York, even though it would mean the big break Second Chances needed, even though it could mean the difference between its success and their failure.

He couldn't admit that he and John were keeping the women out of the spotlight, off national television. He couldn't have said that he might have been nervous as hell when a girl called from *The View*, but that John had called earlier and tipped him off.

"The women might be suspicious if no one calls," John had said. "This second-wedding thing really is a good gimmick. But not to worry," he added. "I'll have one of my girls act as a decoy."

Missy Clofsky had been the perfect decoy, but of course, Andrew couldn't tell his readers that, either. He couldn't tell them that she was in no way connected with *The View*, but, in fact, she worked for *Buzz*. He couldn't tell them that while Missy acknowledged to Jo that, indeed, Second Chances was a great concept, she put them off long enough to stall the possibility that they might learn who Andrew really was and what he was really doing:

That he was a liar.

That he was using them.

That the women at Second Chances were guinea pigs whose lives and whose confidences he was sharing with the world, albeit under cover, albeit with the names changed. Albeit in the name of helping men understand the species God called "women."

*Albeit in the name of a gimmick*, he could have written, a gimmick that would make Andrew and John Benson and a few other people big bucks, at the expense of four perfectly nice, unsuspecting women, one of whom he lusted after and just possibly might love.

But Andrew could admit none of those things, because he could not go public. Instead, he reiterated to his readers that being a sneaky, self-centered snake wasn't a great way to get a good night's sleep.

*If you are a guy*, he typed. *With a conscience.*

He paused another moment, then added: *Unless that's an oxymoron.*

# 35

♥

*DON'T*
*Stand on tradition if it's not what you want. No longer*
*close to family? Have your best friend walk you down the*
*aisle. What about your favorite pet? Tie a bow of tulle*
*around Fido's collar . . . he's probably listened to more of*
*your problems than anyone. Let him be part of your joy!*

The next morning they sent the follow-up releases. Jo had decided she'd no longer sleep; her
body seemed averse to the concept of rest and
relaxation, as if something important might happen while
she was dreaming, like the world as she knew it would
end, not that it hadn't already.

So she spent her days working and her nights braced.

Just before noon, the small bell over the door jingled.
Jo turned from her work to see Marion, a smile on her

face and a woven summer purse draped over one wrist. "I've come to take my daughter to lunch," she said.

"Oh. Mom." Jo looked to Andrew for help with an excuse, but he was smiling at Marion and would not look her way. "We're awfully busy today."

"I'll take care of things, Jo," Andrew said. "You go ahead."

She ordered a salad, though she'd rather eat air and say it had been tasty and she was quite full now, thanks.

They'd gone to the Inn de Contessa and were quickly lead to a table because the maître d' recognized Marion from the chamber of commerce.

"I'm sorry about Brian and that woman, his wife," Marion said halfway through her meal. "I'm so sorry you have to go through this, Josephine. But maybe this will help you get him out of your mind once and for all. Maybe you'll find another man while there is still time." She did not elaborate on what there still might be time for. A husband, Jo supposed. A family.

Jo spoke past the lump in her throat. "How long did it take you to get over my father?"

Steering her fork toward a large piece of mango tossed in with her salad, Marion stabbed once, then popped the fruit into her mouth. "Who said I ever got over him?"

It was not the response that Jo had anticipated. "Oh, come on, Mother. Surely you got over him. 'Sam Lyons, the rat bastard,' I once heard you say to Mrs. Kingsley." Jo did not add that she had been twelve and thoroughly shocked because she'd never before heard Marion swear.

"I never claimed that I got over your father," Marion

said. "But I did get on with my life. I picked up some of the pieces and tried to rearrange them in order that I—we—could still have a good life."

She did not add that her "good life" had included hiding Ted the Butcher in the meat locker for so long.

"Oh, Mother," Jo said. "I'm sure I'll be fine. It would help if our business could get off the ground. It would help if I had some sort of distraction."

"You tried that in Boston. All those years."

Jo didn't reply, because her mother was right and Jo knew it and she hated that she did. Then she said, "Well, at least I'm not letting anyone think I feel sorry for myself."

"You wouldn't do that. I raised you never to do that, didn't I?"

It was true. Marion had never showed public signs of self-pity, so Jo had always tried to follow suit. No matter how pathetic she felt.

"But speaking of getting on with life," Marion added, "you're going to give Elaine's wedding away in a sweepstakes?"

"It seemed like a good idea when I had it. But the media isn't jumping on it, so I guess we should forget it."

Marion sighed, chewed a forkful of the pasta special of the day. Slowly, she swallowed, then asked, "What if I used it?"

Jo had never thought Marion was a good jokester. She was a woman who tried often, but with little success.

"I said, 'What if I used it?' " her mother repeated, then set down her fork and sipped her iced tea. "What if I was the bride and Ted was the groom. Would that help you get the publicity you need?"

Jo laughed, because Marion was her mother and because Marion might appreciate it if Jo thought she was funny. "Thanks, Mom, but this is for real. If we're going to showcase second marriages, we honestly have to have one performed. We couldn't stretch the truth about that."

"Yes," Marion said. "I counted on that." She signaled the waitress and asked for more tea.

The fork in Jo's hand slid onto her plate. She stared at her mother. What should she say?

"It's time I made an honest man out of Ted," Marion continued. "I might not be Elaine's size, but I'm sure that wizard of a seamstress could let out a seam or two, maybe add a short jacket to cover up my underarm jiggles."

Jo stared at her mother. "Elaine's gown has long sleeves."

"Well, there you have it, then. And you girls already have your gowns . . . did you say that they're oyster, as well?"

Speechless. Jo Lyons was speechless. "Not oyster," she finally muttered. "Pearl."

"No difference," Marion said with a laugh. She accepted the new glass of iced tea and quickly sipped. "I've always loved The Mount," she said. "If you don't have a photographer already lined up, Ted has a nephew who dabbles in photography."

She was serious. Her mother, the woman who had led Jo to think that marriage was once-in-a-lifetime and that she'd already had hers, was going to get married again, even though she'd never "gotten over" Sam Lyons, the rat bastard.

Marion was going to get married and she was going to save Second Chances.

Jo raised her glass. "We have a photographer," she said with a smile. "But feel free to include the butcher's nephew. The more the merrier, right?"

When she went back to the shop, the door was locked, a BACK AT TWO sign in the window. Jo quickly found her key and slipped inside. There were things to do now, a new angle to take, that Second Chances could help dreams come true, no matter what age.

Her seventy-year-old mother wanted to get married.

Later Jo would deal with the emotional response she supposed she would feel, with the hesitations and expectations of how the changes in Marion's life might or might not affect Jo's.

For now, there was a wedding to plan. A second wedding.

Tossing her purse into the desk drawer, Jo then took off the pink linen bolero she wore over the matching tank dress, a city dress, out of place in West Hope. No matter. It was time to get busy. It was not time to wonder if her mother decided to wed Ted simply to help Jo get over Brian, or simply to help Second Chances get on its pearl satin, dyed-to-match feet.

It was time to think only of work.

As she sat at her desk, Jo noticed that the red light flashed on the phone. A message awaited. With a short laugh, Jo picked up the receiver to clear whomever it was: an eager florist, no doubt, wanting a cut of the action, or Elizabeth Taylor or Liza Minelli or Madonna in search of consultants for their next ceremony.

Or maybe it was Cassie, calling to say "Hello," because

she was a lonely kid with one "pseudo" parent who worked.

*To hear your messages, press one.*

Jo did as she was instructed.

"Is this Second Chances?" It was a young voice, a female voice. Not Elizabeth, not Liza. "We received your e-mail about the wedding sweepstakes and we want to talk to you about being a guest on *Sakes Alive!*"

Jo blinked. She sat up straight.

"This is Melinda Gant," the young voice continued. "I'm the special-assignments editor to Kevin Green." She then left her number "in the two-one-two area code" and asked that someone return her call.

# 36

♥

It was quarter past two when Lily and Sarah and Andrew sauntered into the shop. Andrew's head swam with scores of new data to convey to his fans.

"If I have sex with a man for the first time, I certainly expect flowers the next day." (That from Lily.)

"A phone call would be good enough for me." (Sarah.)

"But it had better be a nice call. That he hadn't stopped thinking of me, or something sappy like that."

That had surprised Andrew, because he hadn't considered that Sarah would go much for "sappy." Then again, he reminded himself as they crossed the threshold into his gay, "Second Chance" world, that was why he was doing this. To inform the readers how *real women* thought, what *real women* wanted, not what men thought they did.

Jo sat at her desk. She looked up at the trio with what Andrew thought was an oddly smug look on her face.

"Well," she said, "have some of us forgotten we have jobs to do?"

"Right," Sarah said and sat down, tossing her long legs over one arm of the navy chair.

"How was your lunch?" Lily asked, as she perched on the other arm of the chair where Sarah sat.

"Interesting."

They looked at one another as if "interesting" was not a word they might have expected in describing a mother-daughter outing.

" 'Interesting'?" Andrew asked, because he thought there must be more to the story and because, as a guy, he was less patient than the women.

"My mother and Ted the Butcher want to use Elaine's wedding so we'll have a portfolio and she'll have a new life."

For a moment no one said anything, then Lily said, "Your mother? Wants to marry the butcher?"

Jo nodded. "It seems they've been keeping company for a number of years. I don't know if she's trying to help us or trying to help them, but Marion Lyons wants 'a second wedding.' "

Andrew resisted the urge to let out a sigh of relief. With Elaine's wedding "taken," there would be no sweepstakes, no risk of exposure, no entanglements with the media. His job was protected, his cover ensured. No one would be hurt, and the wedding would probably provide him with enough material to keep his column going for six months or a year, maybe longer if he wanted to extend his contract. Wouldn't John Benson be happy?

"There's only one tiny wrinkle," Jo said, and Andrew felt the kind of grim, off-balance feeling one feels when someone gives you good news then adds the word "but."

"*Sakes Alive!* called," Jo continued. "They want us next Tuesday. To announce the sweepstakes."

Andrew really wished he hadn't had Chinese food for lunch. He really wished he'd not indulged in the Hunan Pork that, on a good day, gave him indigestion for an hour or two. *Sakes Alive!* was Kevin Green's show. *Sakes Alive!* was the worst-case scenario he thought that he'd avoided. *Sakes Alive!* would be his downfall. And John Benson's, too.

"Oh, Jo," Lily said, leaping from the chair and nearly taking flight. "This is wonderful!"

"I'm glad you agree," Jo said, "because they're especially curious about you. They asked if you were the widow of *the* Reginald Beckwith."

"Oh, gosh," Lily said, "whatever will I wear?"

"We'll need to worry about a few more things than that," Sarah said. "Such as what to say and how to position our business and how to pitch the sweepstakes."

"And I'll get to worry about my mother," Jo added.

"Oh," Lily said. "What about your mother? What will we do?"

"I have no idea. But I doubt that she'd want us to miss an opportunity like this."

"But is it so great?" Andrew stepped in, aware his words would be unwelcomed, but nonetheless spewing them out quickly because he probably only had one chance and not a very good one at that. "How many of you are really familiar with *Sakes Alive!*?"

"I've watched once or twice when Burch had it on," Sarah admitted.

"I monitored parts of it a few times when I had a client appear," Jo said.

"And I've seen the posters in the train stations," Lily said.

Lily, Andrew thought, was such an airhead she was really quite lovable.

But this was not the time to think about anyone being lovable.

"Kevin Green is a slimeball. He makes a farce out of people and what they do for a living. He acts as if he's enthralled, but his sole purpose is ridicule, the no-holds-barred kind of ridicule." It was then Andrew noticed that his mouth had gone dry. Nerves. Hunan Pork. He walked to the water cooler and filled a paper cone cup.

"I doubt that anyone would be a slimeball to us," Sarah said. "Look at us. We're rather harmless, Andrew."

"Are you kidding? My guess is he'll zero in on Lily. Then he'll eat her up. He'll translate Lily's sweetness into naivete . . . the perfect target for Kevin's kind of crap." He supposed he was being overly harsh on Kevin, but, shit, the life he'd come to love was suddenly at stake. "And God only knows what he'll say about Reginald. No," Andrew said, pacing the floor. "I can't allow Lily— or any of you—to be fed to that piranha." He drank another cup of water, then tossed the paper cone in the basket.

Lily stood up. "Well, my darling Andrew, I appreciate your concern. But the truth is, it's not as if you know the man. And, if you knew me better than you do, you'd know that I can take care of myself. Piranha or not. We shall go to New York and we shall do the show and Second Chances will be a success. And what's more, I hate to pull rank, but please remember that you work for us, and I hope you'll agree to escort us to *Sakes Alive!*, because it's going to be your future, too."

Andrew was leaning against the water cooler, which was perhaps why he didn't fall over. Lily wanted him to go to New York? To *Sakes Alive!*? To Kevin Green?

"As for me," Lily said with her trademark flourish, "I really must get upstairs and decide what I shall wear. Between now and Tuesday is hardly enough time to think about pulling together a new outfit with proper accessories." She danced from the room on her own Lily-cloud, leaving all eyes on Andrew, who of course had no clue what in the hell he was going to do.

# 37

DO
*Expect the unexpected.*

Had she already made a note of that?

The day had gone from bad to good to great, Jo thought as she left the shop that night. Andrew's behavior had been peculiar, but surely he'd get over it. Jo said she was sure her mother would stay with Cassie if Mrs. Connor weren't available, so he really had no excuse not to go to New York. Maybe he hated the city and that was why he had left, but surely it was a big enough place that his ghosts wouldn't be there to haunt him in Kevin Green's studio.

And they would get the publicity they needed.

And Jo would succeed again.

And somehow her mother would remarry.

And all would be as it would be.

As she drove through town, Jo thought about Elaine. They'd been so busy these past few weeks that they hadn't taken the time to check in with her, to make sure she was okay, to let her know there was no need to feel guilty, especially now. Elaine would be glad to hear their good news.

At the next intersection, Jo took a right and headed to the subdivision where the felt flags of autumn now adorned every house, and red geraniums had given way to pots of orange and purple mums.

"Mom's asleep," one of the girls, Kandie or Karen—Jo was forever confusing the two—told her.

"It's only six-thirty at night," Jo replied as if the girl might be lying. "Is she sick?"

Kandie or Karen let out a laugh. "Not really. She's in the family room."

She walked away from the door, leaving Jo to wonder if she should go in and find Elaine for herself. She tried the handle, it was not locked, so that's what she did.

The vertical blinds in the family room were closed, leaving thin stripes of the day's end of sunlight trying to make themselves known. The television was tuned in to one of those home-shopping stations, but the sound was not up. Elaine sat motionless. She was in a housedress that looked to be quite old.

"Elaine," Jo said, moving close to the couch. "Elaine, it's Jo. Are you okay?"

The lump that sat there blinked, but did not respond. "Elaine?"

The eyelids closed. "Go away," Elaine said. "I want to be alone." She wore no makeup. Her hair was flat on one side as if she'd slept on it and hadn't showered for a while. And worst of all, she smelled like gin.

Jo sat down beside her. She reached for the remote and clicked off the TV. "How long have you been sitting here? When did you last have a decent meal?"

Elaine shook her head. "Leave me alone. I'm fine."

"No you're not," Jo replied. "You're depressed. And you're drunk."

Elaine half-opened her eyes, then closed them again.

"And it's stifling in here." Jo went to the sliding glass doors, snapped the blinds, and opened the door onto the deck. She wouldn't have expected Elaine was the type to self-destruct over the decline of a relationship. Self-destruct over Martha Stewart's demise, perhaps. But not over a man.

Then again, she reminded herself, we all do strange things in the name love.

She moved back to the couch. "Get up," she commanded. "You've felt sorry for yourself long enough."

The eyes moved again. "What?"

"You heard me," Jo said. "I'm going to the kitchen to put on a pot of coffee. And you are going to get up and wash your face and brush your teeth and comb your hair. It's time to pull yourself together." It was easy to recognize depression in others once you'd been through it yourself.

———

"Is this how you've spent your days since you broke up with Martin?" Jo asked once Elaine had cleaned up and changed her clothes. Jo had made Elaine a sandwich and they sat on the patio, Jo watching her friend reluctantly eat, her thoughts churning with what she and the others could do. *There must be something*, she thought, *some way to help*.

Elaine shrugged. "Martin cried when I told him I couldn't marry him. Then he left my house without saying a word. He never asked me why, which I suppose was just as well. It's so hard to explain."

Jo felt she should offer some sound advice on men, but she, of course, knew none. She shifted awkwardly on the white plastic chair.

"I hurt Martin terribly; now I've disappointed my friends, too," Elaine continued. "After all you've done for me."

Jo leaned forward. "No you haven't, Lainey." She waited until Elaine seemed to have calmed down. Then she told her about the sweepstakes and the guest spot on *Sakes Alive!* She told her Second Chances would have national exposure more quickly than any of them could have hoped.

Elaine watched. Elaine listened.

Then Jo told her about Marion and Ted.

"So because of you, a long-awaited marriage is going to happen, and maybe our business will take off after all. Even though we're all distressed for you, your decision hasn't exactly turned out to be a disappointment for us. A silver lining in your cloud, I suppose."

Elaine considered Jo's words a moment, then said, "Especially for your mother." Then she added a slow half-smile. "Ted the Butcher? Well, of course, everyone suspected that for years."

Jo did not say everyone except her. She patted Elaine's hand. "You see, there's still hope of true love for the rest of us."

"Lily has never had a problem finding true love."

"Looks like she's found it again. She and Frank Forbes seem to spend a lot of time together. As for me, I think I'll have my hands full running the business."

And then Jo knew how they could help Elaine.

"Come work with us, Lainey," she said quickly. "With all the business that will be coming our way, we sure could use your help."

Elaine chewed quietly, swallowed, then looked out to the backyard. "Sorry," she said. "I'm afraid I'm like Lily. No visible experience."

"Of course you've had experience. You've volunteered at the library for how many years?"

"And I taught second grade for two years, and was a waitress in my father's restaurant when I was a kid. None of which qualify me to plan a wedding."

"Well, we're going to need more help. Besides, you're the one who got us into this! Please, be part of our adventure. It will be just like the old days." Her plea sounded a little bit short of emotional blackmail, but if it would keep Elaine away from getting sucked into a vortex of self-pity, what was a little blackmail among the best of friends?

# 38

Cassie was upstairs doing her homework. ("Sixth grade is awful, Dad! You wouldn't believe what I have to do before tomorrow!")

Andrew cleaned up the kitchen, bemused at the stereotypical thought that if he truly were gay, he perhaps would have done a much more thorough job.

He hung up his dishtowel and retreated to the hammock, aware that the number of evenings were slipping away when he'd be able to do this before the first frost. Or before his scheme unraveled and he was run out of town.

He'd put in an emergency call to John Benson: something had gone wrong. Somehow their protection had slipped through the media cracks and Kevin Green had learned about Second Chances.

Someone, somewhere, had not risen to John Benson's payola. Someone, somewhere, had betrayed the betrayer.

Andrew's cell phone lay lifeless on his stomach, awaiting his boss's thoughts about his fate.

Maybe he should quit his job at Second Chances first. Maybe he should admit in his column that getting too close to too many women at the same time had been a mistake; perhaps he should concentrate on fleshing women out, one female at a time. Which meant the local dating service (ugh!) or, God forbid, the Internet. He supposed he could always look around the supermarket, the laundromat, the bookstore—places he knew women had been told were good haunts in which to meet men, though men preferred the darkness of bars and the coolness of beer and its subsequent self-confidence that was then able to spring so eloquently from their lips.

Then again, if Andrew were so inclined to do those things or go to those places, he'd have done them long before this, long after Patty, long before he was actually trying to make a living by pretending to know what real women wanted.

He'd sent in his last column, which had been filled with the cocksureness of a man, convinced that he and John Benson had outwitted Jo Lyons, convinced that his ruse would go undetected.

Which only proved how little about life Andrew Kennedy knew.

The cell phone rang. Andrew jumped; he nearly fell off the rocking hammock.

"John," he said quickly into the phone. "Man, have we got a problem."

There was a pause for a second, then a voice lightly said, "Andrew? It's Jo. What kind of problem can you possibly have?"

Andrew listened as long as he could stand it to Jo's mono-
logue about Elaine and how Elaine would be at the shop
in the morning and that he should put her to work doing
something, anything. As for Jo, she'd be late—she'd stop
by her mother's and try to find a diplomatic way to break
the news that the wedding would be given to someone
else, someone who could generate more business for
Second Chances, national exposure on a grand, television-
exposure scale. They'd find a way to make it up to Marion,
wouldn't they?

While Andrew tried to think of a plausible answer, Jo
suddenly shrieked. "Television! Maybe we can get *Sakes
Alive!* to televise the wedding! Oh, Andrew, this is so exciting!"

He could have reminded her that that had been done
before, but he supposed Jo would argue that it hadn't
been done for *second* weddings.

With a sigh, he looked at his watch again, certain John
must be trying to get through, unsure of how to activate
call-waiting on this damn phone since he'd rarely needed
it, because whoever called a lowly college professor stuck
somewhere in the mountains?

"I've got to run now," he said, finally wedging a few
words between Jo's litany of big dreams. "Cassie's shouting for me." He quickly disconnected the call, grateful he
had a daughter whom he could use as an excuse. She'd often come in handy for faculty parties, boring dates, and
when he was simply tired but too manly to admit it.

*I hate to run, but I must pick up my daughter at riding
lessons.*

*Sorry I can't stay longer, but I think Cassie is coming down with a cold.*

*I promised I'd help her study for her history exam tomorrow.*

Kids, he thought, and wondered if Patty ever realized all the things she was missing. Then he remembered Patty was no longer childless. She had a son.

He wondered if she would leave her son the way she'd left her daughter.

He tried to distract himself by studying the phone. Just as he located the FLASH/CALL WAIT button, the phone rang again.

"Hello?" he asked, tentatively.

"Andrew?" It was not John. Again, it was a girl.

He sighed. "Yes."

"Andrew, this is Frannie Cassidy. John Benson's assistant."

John's assistant? A kaleidoscope of pictures spun in Andrew's mind. John was sick. John was in an accident. John was dead.

"I was checking Mr. Benson's messages and yours sounded urgent. He's out of the country, didn't you know?"

"He didn't tell me he was going anywhere," Andrew said.

"I guess he kept it a secret, even from me, until they were leaving for the airport. He took Irene on a surprise fortieth anniversary trip to the South Pacific. He is such a romantic, isn't he?"

A romantic? With his wife? Perhaps John had been right, that Andrew should have known better than to give any credence to media gossip. "How can I reach him?" Andrew asked.

"Well, that's why I'm calling. They're on one of those tiny islands that have no communications. Like *Gilligan's Island*, I suppose." She paused. "Forty years. Can you imagine?"

Forty years. No, actually, he couldn't imagine. "When do you think he'll be near a phone again?" He tried not to sound annoyed; it wasn't Ms. Cassidy's fault. But what the hell had John been thinking? He knew the pressure Andrew was under.

"They'll be gone a week. Until next Wednesday."

Wednesday. The day after the *Sakes Alive!* appearance.

Andrew lowered his head, thanked Frannie for calling, then wondered if, having managed to stay married forty damn years, despite the rumors about countless "others," John Benson should be the one writing the column about women.

# 39

♥

---

*DON'T*
*Forget about the kids: yours, his. If they're young, plan a*
*special wedding "activity" that you can do together, such*
*as decorating a practice wedding cake. If they're in the*
*wedding party, practice walking down the aisle together*
*balancing a silly-looking stuffed animal on their heads.*
*Don't forget an on-site baby-sitter. Few people think*
*other people's little children are adorable when they're*
*racing through the church or around the tables at the re-*
*ception.*

As Jo pulled into her mother's driveway the next
morning, she wondered why she hadn't found a
Ted the Butcher in her life, a man who could
commit, a man who wanted to love her for the long haul.

Not that she'd given any man the chance. It was hard

to give a man a chance when the ghost of Brian lingered in the corners of her mind, gnawing at her heart, nudging out her common sense.

The more she thought about it, the more she wanted to scream. Instead, she took a long, deep, yoga breath, shut off the car, and went up onto the back porch of her mother's house.

Through the window of the door, she noticed Marion at the table, a recipe box by her wrist, paper and envelopes surrounding her.

Jo smiled and let herself in. "Looking for more things to do with blueberries?" Jo asked.

Marion laughed. "No. I'm writing out a guest list for the wedding. You said the reception includes seventy-five guests. Oh, Ted and I have lived in West Hope too long. It's so hard to pare down all the folks we both know!"

*Guilt.* It rushed at Jo with the force of a tsunami, a giant tidal wave guaranteed to wipe out most of civilization situated in its path.

"Mother," she said, the wave wobbling her feet. She sat at the table across from Marion. She folded her hands on the embroidered placemat. "That's why I've come."

"To help with the list? Oh, honey, it's okay. It's fun, actually, to think of all the friends I have. All the friends Ted and I have."

Jo stared at the recipe box. This wouldn't be as easy as she'd hoped. "Mom," she said. "I'm here to talk about the wedding. You don't have to do this. You don't have to do this to help Second Chances."

Marion laughed again. "You think that's why I'm marrying Ted Cappelinni? To help out your business?"

"Well, gee. You've been seeing each other for so long . . ."

"Too long," her mother answered. "For the last decade Ted has tried to get me to marry him. If it hadn't been for you, I wouldn't have the courage. I might at first have considered that it would help out you girls. But now . . ." She looked off into space and smiled a smile of secret joy, as if she were a schoolgirl and had been invited to the prom. "I don't know, Josephine. But I think it's high time I had a chance at happiness, don't you agree?"

Jo would have preferred if she hadn't come at all, if *Sakes Alive!* had never called, if she'd never developed such an obsession to succeed.

Marion put down her pen. "I love Ted Cappelinni. That's why I want to marry him."

"Oh" was all that Jo could say. What else? How could she say, "Gee, Mom, I hate to burst your bubble, but the wedding has been called off," or "Mother, I know you'll understand when I say we're going to give away the wedding to someone who will give us better publicity."

"Honey," Marion said as she patted Jo's hand. "I can't thank you enough. I'd forgotten what it was to be so excited. And at my age! Imagine!"

No, Jo couldn't imagine.

So instead of telling Marion the truth about the wedding, Jo kissed her mother's forehead and said she was glad things were going to work out, and that she'd just stopped by to say "Hello" on her way to work. Then she left the house and drove directly to the shop, wondering what the heck she would do now and what she would say to the others.

"I'll find a way to pay for it myself," she said to Lily and Sarah and to Elaine, who had showed up that morning though she seemed distracted and was a little pale.

"That's preposterous," Lily said. "We'll work something out."

"No, Lily. It's bad enough you're fronting this whole operation. I won't have you pay for my mother's wedding, as well."

"I said, we'll work something out," Lily repeated, with an edge to her voice that Jo had never heard. "In the meantime, we need to discuss our wardrobes for *Sakes Alive!* I simply have *nothing* in my closet. Sarah, I want you to create something special for me. Something that says 'successful' and 'fanciful' and a little flirtatious. Frank says I'm adorable when I'm flirtatious."

A twitch, a twinge, a tweak of hurt alighted on Jo's heart, then, thank God, flitted away.

"By Tuesday?" Sarah asked. "I design jewelry, Lily, not clothes, for godssake."

"Well, get over it. And while you're at it, I'll need it for Monday, not Tuesday. We have to be certain that it's absolutely divine. And we mustn't clash!" she added. "Let's choose our colors carefully and not look as if we live out in the boondocks."

Andrew smiled, which was the most animation he had shown since Jo had arrived. Jo shook her head, marveling at the transformation in Lily from helpless child to a woman who had taken charge. Maybe having money afforded one an inner core of strength. Maybe that was why Jo was feeling so indecisive and insignificant and insecure these days.

It would be a different wedding, not Elaine's, but a wedding, nonetheless. Marion and Ted would have Elaine's wedding, and Second Chances would have the beginnings of a portfolio of pictures for the future.

There also would be a second wedding for the sweepstakes, a thirty-thousand-dollar wedding in the Berkshires that they would give away. The time and place would be the bride and groom's choice. The contract would give Second Chances unlimited rights to take, use, and reproduce the photos as they desired, with discretion, naturally.

"Cheaper than national advertising," Jo had commented.

Of course, legally, if the winner preferred the cash to the goods, they'd have to pay up. But the exposure would be worth the risk.

It all looked good on paper.

Which was why Jo did not know why she felt apprehensive Tuesday morning when the white limo arrived at the secretaries' building just after dawn to begin the three-hour trek south to Manhattan.

"We must hire a limo," Lily had insisted. "Arrival is everything."

Jo had protested. "The studio is on the forty-fifth floor. No one will see us."

"We can't be sure of that, can we?" Lily had said and had gotten her way because it was her money, after all.

Still, Jo had worried. How long would it be before Lily became tired of footing the bill?

Andrew had tried to get out of going. He claimed he needed to get busy researching locations and availabilities, for receptions and the like, for the sweepstakes wedding.

Lily would have no part of that.

Then he said the fact was Cassie had a competition Tuesday after school and he hated the thought that he would not be in the bleachers.

Lily said she'd pay the riding school to change the date.

In the end, Andrew just said no, that he hated New York City and that the thought of going brought on an anxiety attack.

Finally, Lily told him he had to go or she would fire him, and how anxious would that make him? In part she'd been being playful, but Andrew took the hint.

So by the time the limo arrived at the secretaries' building, inside sat eager Lily, calm-as-always; Sarah, slightly more animated; Elaine; and an unhappy-looking Andrew. Slipping in beside Andrew, Jo smiled and said, "Good morning." As the long car snaked down the narrow driveway, she wondered if the others eagerly awaited their fifteen minutes of second-wedding fame, and if they should say a group prayer that Kevin Green wouldn't make them look as foolish as Andrew said he would.

The limo made a pit stop. He knew if he had coffee it would give him indigestion, and that was the last thing Andrew needed. The women went inside to use the ladies' room. He took a swig from a bottle of Evian and in his mind reviewed the words he'd typed last night.

*Lesson #7: Don't lie to a woman. If it doesn't come back to bite you in the ass, you'll spend your time poised, waiting for it to bite.*

He then explained that, despite his efforts to thwart

what he referred to as "a daunting business move," the women were insistent, their new venture having risen to become the most important thing in life, their self-confidence teeming with testosterone, as if they were in control and they very damn well knew it.

As if they were—shit—as if they were men.

Of course, he couldn't add that he feared it would change once they met Kevin Green.

Surveying the inside of the limo, the rows of tiny white lights along the baseboard, the thick clear drinking glasses in their holders along the sides, the remnants of the stale, nasty scent of cigarette smoke clawing at the red velour-covered side walls, Andrew glanced at his watch. In an hour and ten minutes they would be in Manhattan. Between now and then he needed to devise a plan that would save his ass until the final credits rolled.

Until this awful nightmare, hopefully, had passed.

# 40

W hat made you want to go into business, Ms. Beckwith? Aren't you wealthy enough?"

"Money isn't everything, Mr. Green," Lily said with her sweet smile. She looked pretty in the pale pink chemise that Sarah had crafted and which was set off by Sarah's silver jewelry and her own pink diamonds. She was sitting next to Kevin. On her right were Jo, Sarah, then Elaine. Andrew was downstairs, watching the show from the bar across the street.

His exoneration had come more easily than he'd expected: "I can't ride in the glass elevator," he'd pleaded as he pointed to the bank of five glass elevators, wrinkled a worried brow, and pretended to hyperventilate three or four short breaths. "Open spaces give me vertigo."

They'd been standing in the lobby of the building where *Sakes Alive!* was to be taped. Lily had been exasperated, but finally waved Andrew off. "Oh, for goodness sake, Andrew, don't come with us, then. Leave him be, girls," she said, marching toward the elevators. "We don't want to delay the show."

So there he sat, on a comfortable barstool, drinking coffee that he finally allowed himself to drink, watching the minisideshow with his heart standing in repose, prepared to pounce on quick command into his waiting throat.

"After my dear Reginald died," Lily was saying, "I needed something productive to do. I wanted to contribute to society. And I wanted to be with my friends."

"Yes, well, I suppose you've spent enough time on the society pages to believe that weddings are, as you say, 'productive.' "

"Oh, my, yes. Especially second weddings. Forty-six percent of all weddings today include at least one partner who has been married before."

Andrew smiled at the way Lily slipped in the forty-six-percent fact that Jo had fed her in the limo. If Lily didn't make it in the second-wedding business, she could hit the talk-show circuit.

With continued poise, Lily said, "It's so reassuring to know that the world no longer expects anyone not to make a mistake, don't you think?"

Kevin tented his fingertips together. He leveled his eyes on Lily. "I guess you're the expert, Ms. Beckwith. You've made several mistakes, haven't you?"

Argh.

Jo coughed. Sarah grimaced. Elaine looked directly into the TV monitor. Across the street, Andrew gripped his coffee mug and braced himself for the sarcasm that was sure to come.

"I've had two divorces, Mr. Green," Lily said. "Poor Reginald died."

"Oh, that's right. Poor Reginald Beckwith. What was he worth, about two hundred million?"

She smiled again. "No."

Andrew was amazed at Lily's composure, at the way she was holding her own against the antagonistic host.

"But I haven't come to New York to talk about my deceased husband," Lily blurted out before he could interrupt with another foolish question. "I've come to talk about second weddings, second chances at love. My friends and I are very excited about our new business in the Berkshires."

"Tell us about your friends. Are they elite widows like you?"

The camera zoomed in on Jo. God, Andrew thought, she really was gorgeous, sophisticated yet homespun. "We were roommates way back when, in college," Lily continued. "This is Jo; she's very smart. And Sarah." The camera panned. "Sarah's highly creative. And Elaine, who you might say was the reason we all came together." Elaine made a tiny wave toward the monitor, having apparently taken the last step out of her depression on national TV. "And, of course, there's Andrew," Lily quickly added, and the camera cut back to her. "He's our handsome, sensitive receptionist, who keeps us all together."

" 'Andrew'?" Green asked, and Andrew froze as stiff as Atlas in the skating rink at Rockefeller Plaza. "You have a male receptionist? Isn't that a sort of switcheroo?"

"Absolutely. But Andrew offers a male perspective on

weddings geared to the more mature woman, the bride who is looking for quality and elegance. Her needs, after all, are different from today's young brides."

"And did Andrew the Receptionist accompany you today?"

Lily nodded. "He's outside. He has acute anxiety problems in the city." It was her turn to look squarely into the camera. "Sorry, Andrew, honey. I hope you're watching, though."

Oh yes, he was watching. The coffee rumbled in his gut.

"How many of your 'brides' wear white?" Kevin Green suddenly interjected with an abrasive chuckle. Sadly, the small studio audience laughed along with him.

Lily smoothed the lap of her pink chemise and did not answer.

"Oh," Green said. "I guess that's a sensitive area." Chuckle, chuckle.

Andrew no longer cared what Green was saying to the women. He was only grateful that the subject had been deflected away from him.

"What about attorneys?" Green suddenly fired questions as if he were a courtroom lawyer. "Do you keep one on retainer for prenups and quickee divorces? Is that part of your second-wedding package?"

Before Lily had a chance to speak, Green added, "Speaking of which, did you and poor Reginald have a prenuptial agreement? He was how old? A hundred and eleven?"

Lily stood up. "If you invited us here today because you enjoy mocking people, Mr. Green, I suggest you find another victim."

Andrew held his breath, hoping Lily could hang in long enough to talk about the sweepstakes. Until she at least repeated the name of Second Chances and said it was in West Hope.

It was too late. Lily stalked off the set, her head held high, her expression unscathed. And Kevin Green faced the camera wearing a smile of victory, misplaced though it might be. The others sat in their chairs, Elaine staring once again into the monitor.

Across the street, Andrew wilted on the barstool with surprising disappointment.

On the way back to West Hope, Lily got quite drunk.

Unknown to the others, she'd stocked the limo with champagne bottles for their supposed victory, for a toast to their success.

Now she drank in silence, as they crawled toward the New York Thruway. "We should have listened to Andrew. We should never have come."

"It's as much my fault as anything," Jo said. "I know Kevin Green's reputation. I guess I got carried away by the thought of the great exposure."

"It's no one's fault," Sarah said. "The guy's a jerk."

"What happened?" Elaine kept asking, because she said she'd been so startled she was there, that she'd tuned out every word.

"Nothing," Sarah said, nursing a glass of carrot juice that she'd brought from home. "He wasn't very nice, that's all."

Andrew didn't say a word. He simply looked out to the spiderweb of bridges and the clog of concrete high-rises and wondered why he hadn't been man enough to have stopped it.

*Man enough*, he thought with a sardonic chuckle. *There's one for the column.*

"Well," Elaine said, "maybe we'll have some calls.

Lily took a long swig from the dark Dom Perignon bottle, then tipped back her head and began to laugh. "Andrew, you old poop, you tried to warn us, didn't you?"

"Lily . . ." he began, but she interrupted.

"It's okay, darling. Really it is. You're smarter than the rest of us, but we're older, so that's what really counts."

They looked from one to another, as if to decipher what she meant.

" 'Older'?" Jo asked.

Lily laughed again. "Older friends. You know. But I guess what really matters is that now we're all friends and we're in this together and I think, no matter what, this is one great hoot."

After a moment's pause, the others laughed, as well.

"Like when your boob fell out into that guy's hand during *Swan Lake*?" Elaine asked.

"Or when we flew off to Minnesota looking for the Olympic hockey players?"

They nodded and laughed some more. Then Lily passed around the bottle and they opened up another, and Andrew thought it was very cool that women could have friendships filled with laughter when their entire futures had just gone down the television tube.

"Here's to Andrew," Lily said and raised a bottle high. "Our poopy, wonderful new friend."

They toasted Andrew and all agreed that, yes, like so many other times together, this was one great hoot.

# 41

♥

He was off the hook, but didn't feel relieved. Instead, he felt like crap, like the bottom of Big Bailey's stall before it was hosed out and fresh hay had been delivered.

As soon as the limo driver dropped him off at home, Andrew changed from his lavender shirt into a plain, old faded denim one. He removed the black-corded silver chime ball that dangled from the neck (his own) that he might have strangled if he could have figured out a way. He peeled off his too-tight jeans and put on the ones that fit: the ones that were a little worn at the knees and were baggy in the ass.

He changed everything except the copper bracelet. Hell, he could use a little magic for his chakras.

Without looking in the mirror, Andrew knew he was himself again.

Driving into town, he didn't have to remind himself that he'd almost blown everything. Despite that the women had a "hoot" of a good time, Andrew had almost hurt them. If Lily had spilled anything more revealing about Andrew, if Kevin Green hadn't had his swelled head so far up his butt that he hadn't seen through the warnings John Benson had sent out, Andrew might have witnessed the demise of Second Chances.

It would, of course, have been his fault for his deceit, his fault for trying to make a fast, underhanded buck.

*Sensitive man, my ass*, he thought.

What made him think he was any better than Kevin Green? Andrew, too, had only been looking out for himself, real *man* that he was. Real ass that he was.

He turned onto Main Street, knowing that the time had come. It didn't matter that he'd like to bed down with Jo the instant he had a chance. It didn't matter that he was more attracted to Jo than he'd been attracted to any woman since Patty. It was time to confess his sins. It was time to confess that he was not a professor working on his doctorate, but a columnist in search of dirt. It was time to confess that he was not a gay receptionist, but a very straight man who had no clue what he was doing except that he had jeopardized the futures of four very nice women who'd done nothing to deserve this.

*Lesson #8*, he thought. *When you've screwed up, take it like a man.*

Jo tried to convince herself it had been worth a try, that they were no further behind than they'd been before *Sakes Alive!* had called. At least Marion's wedding wouldn't cost Lily any more than she'd already spent; at least Jo wouldn't have to feel guilty about that.

Still, she was disappointed.

Even though her mother and Ted were getting married, even though Second Chances would end up with a portfolio, Jo was disappointed that her idea hadn't worked, that they wouldn't have publicity on a grand scale after all. She hadn't wanted to be back where they'd been a week ago, back to wondering if this business would take off or fall flat on Lily's lightly Botoxed face.

Lily, of course, had Frank Forbes now, if she chose to root herself in West Hope. Though it was difficult to believe that West Hope could keep Lily entertained for long.

Sarah could go back to making jewelry and wait—or not—for another dream.

But what about Elaine? Would she retreat to her family room indefinitely? Would she marry Martin after all, because she was so upset that she'd hurt him?

It was less depressing to think about the futures of the others than to speculate on her own.

When they pulled into the driveway at the secretaries' building, Jo said, "I think I'll stay home for the rest of the day. I'll see you at the shop tomorrow." She gave her best attempt at a sincere smile. "We'll conjure up our next marketing strategy then, okay?"

Lily stirred from her nap, smiled, took a pull on the empty Dom Perignon, then went back to sleep.

The limo stopped, Jo said good-bye, and walked toward the elevator with prideful, undefeated-looking steps in case Lily awoke again and noticed.

But once in the elevator, Jo let her shoulders drop, her

jaw sag. She kicked off her city shoes and tucked them in her bag.

She could conjure all she wanted, but Jo knew there was a good chance that Second Chances wasn't going to work. Maybe if at least one of them had a background in wedding planning, maybe if one of them had a clue about the business, it might be easier. But facts were facts. Best to cut their losses before the dream got out of hand and they wound up not being friends.

Sweeping the tired shock of hair from her even more tired forehead, Jo let herself into her apartment. If she'd been a minute more tired, she might have missed seeing the piece of paper on the tile floor.

She laughed. She picked up the note.

*Sorry it's taken so long to get back to you,* the note read, *but I have a job, too. I'm a private airline pilot for Global Paper.*

Jo was surprised. Global Paper, she knew, had three or four manufacturing plants still operating in the Berkshires. Global Paper was where her grandfather had once worked, where a good percentage of West Hope residents still were employed. She tried to remember where the corporate headquarters were—Brussels, Stockholm?

*I'm only here part-time, the other part I'm in Brussels.*

Ah, she thought. Brussels.

*But I'd love to have lunch if you're free. How about Friday?*

She set the note on the counter. Well, at least he had a job. He probably also had a woman in Brussels. Why wouldn't he? He was not a bad-looking man, from what she could remember. He probably made a decent salary. So why was he living in such a mediocre building? Did he have a nicer place in Belgium? Did a woman take care of it . . . take care of him?

She groaned out loud and collapsed onto the couch. She was more tired than she'd realized, if she were obsessing about a man she did not know.

Yet suddenly Jo smiled. Should she risk having lunch? What would be the harm? She could, at least, learn if he was "otherwise involved" before her imagination boarded a Sabena plane and headed six hours (or was it seven?) to the east.

Maybe tomorrow she'd get the opinions of her friends. That's what friends were for, weren't they?

Maybe she'd even ask Andrew. After all, he was a man, wasn't he?

Then she remembered that tomorrow she had something far more important to discuss with the others. Whether or not to close the shop and the business or to keep deluding themselves.

# 42

♥

When Andrew got to the shop, no one was there except for Lily, who was passed out on a chair. Shit. How could he confess if no one was there to hear? Especially the one who made him ache below the waist no matter if he wore the tight jeans or the loose?

He helped Lily upstairs to her apartment. If she noticed he had changed his clothes—his *look*—she did not mention it.

Returning to his laptop, Andrew shot off an e-mail to John Benson. "I know you're coming home tomorrow," he wrote. "Please call ASAP."

At six o'clock Andrew locked the doors and went home to Cassie.

"I'm not going to work for John Benson anymore," he told his daughter over the meatloaf that she'd made, and made damn well for an eleven-year-old. Andrew chewed the mashed potatoes that had been his contribution, because Cassie said he knew how to make them without lumps.

"Does that mean you're no longer gay?"

He laughed. He drank his milk. "Honey, I have a confession to make. I wanted the extra money so we could go to Australia."

Cassie set down her fork and frowned. "Why would we do that?"

He leveled his eyes on her turquoise ones. "Well. To see your mother."

Her freckled nose wrinkled like the linen "poets" shirt he'd worn one day to Second Chances. "Yuck," she said.

His eyebrows shot up to the ceiling of the wood-beamed, cozy kitchen. " 'Yuck'?"

Cassie picked up her fork again, played with her green peas, gluing them to her mashed potatoes and creating polka-dotted piles. "Dad," she said, "why would we want to see her?"

"I thought you would. It's been so long. Besides, you have a brother now."

"Dad, if Mom wants to see me, she knows where I am. It's okay, really it is." Her small shoulders gave a very grown-up shrug. "Sometimes it hurts me when Mom forgets my birthday. But it's no big deal, Dad. It's her loss, you know."

"But . . ."

"If you want to go to Australia because *you* want to see her . . . well, gee, do I really have to go, too?"

He wished that Cassie was saying one thing and meaning quite another. He wished that she were holding back the denial of her childhood, that the truth was that she'd been so traumatized by her mother leaving, that she didn't realize how much she longed to see her. He wished Dr. Phil would take one look at Cassie and say, "Someday this repression will hurt even more deeply."

But that wasn't happening. Even without Dr. Phil, Andrew knew his daughter was saying exactly what she felt. "Yuck," had been her word, and "yuck" was what she meant.

"It's not that I don't love her," Cassie continued. "But I need to be in school, Dad. I like school this year."

"I was thinking we could go over Christmas vacation," Andrew said.

" 'Christmas'? In Australia? But it's summer there then. How can we have Christmas without snow?"

Well, Andrew supposed she had a point. "I just thought it would be nice," he said. "I've felt bad that since I changed jobs and we moved up here that we haven't had the extra money to take the trip."

Cassie put on her baseball cap that was never far from sight. "Dad," she said, "is that the only reason you're writing that column for John Benson? So we could visit Mom?"

What Cassie didn't ask was if he was writing the column so *he*, not *she*, could visit Mom, so he could see Patty again. "Well," Andrew said, "I started writing it for the money. And, yes, so we could go to Australia. But then it became fun. And now . . ."

"And now you're afraid you're going to get caught."

" 'Caught'?"

"You're afraid the women will find out you're straight. That you've been writing the column behind their backs."

"Well, John Benson says the readers love it. Maybe I'm actually helping men understand women."

"Right," Cassie replied with a smile and squished another pea. "Dad, the kids at school were talking about *Sakes Alive!* today. This is a small town. Everyone knew the women from Second Chances were on the show. And that Kevin Green was a total jerk."

Andrew stood up and carried his plate to the sink. "Cassie," he said, because his daughter was so much more mature than he wanted to believe, "I think I've sabotaged their business, though I never meant to." He supposed he could elaborate, but what was the point? Besides, Cassie had reminded him more than once that she was only eleven. "Anyway," he added, "now I think I really like one of the women. And I don't know what to do."

"Jo?" Cassie asked.

"Well. Yes."

His daughter laughed. "Then I suppose you have to find some way to unsabotage their business. Tell her you're not gay. Ask her out for dinner. Then forget about Australia. Geez, Dad," Cassie said with a sigh, "sometimes things are really pretty simple."


Andrew stayed up most of the night.

Forget about Jo, forget about his pride. The most important thing, he knew, was trying to find some way to salvage the business. Maybe the rest would fall into place once he'd paid his penance.

Then, an hour before his alarm would have awakened him if he'd been able to sleep, that too-infrequent light-bulb went off over Andrew's too-thick head. Cassie had been right; sometimes things were really pretty simple.

When John Benson called early in the morning, Andrew outlined his plan.

# 43

***DO***
***Remember this is just a wedding, and while it is impor-***
***tant, don't sacrifice your sanity for the sake of the "per-***
***fect" preparation. Remember all the chaos of the first***
***time around? Strive to make this different, more truly***
***filled with peace and joy.***

We need to talk," Jo said. "All of us." Her eyes
scanned the back room. "Is Lily here? Is
Elaine?"

"I'm here," Lily called from the stairs to her apartment.

Andrew said Elaine had phoned that morning and said
she had to run an errand. She hadn't come in yet.

It was a couple of minutes before they were seated on
the various stools and chairs in Sarah's back room.

"We could wait for Elaine, but it doesn't really matter," Jo said. "We've tried our best, but I think we should face that this business isn't going to work. Yesterday was the last straw."

They moved this way and that on the chairs and the stools. Then Sarah asked, "Why? Because some ass of a TV personality made us look like a bunch of frustrated, middle-aged spinsters?"

No one responded. Who wanted to admit that, among other things, that had happened?

"I have a headache," Lily whined as she massaged her temples. "Do we have to do this now?"

"We do," Jo said. "We have to stop deluding ourselves. We have to face it—except for that *ass*, Kevin Green, no one else wanted us on their show. The media apparently thinks the concept is absurd, unworthy of promoting." It's what she would have told a client if she felt the odds of failure had surpassed the potential to succeed.

"If Elaine hadn't broken her engagement," Sarah said, "things would have gone according to plan."

It was odd that Sarah had become the greatest defender. Sarah the Freethinker. "No," Jo replied. "I got carried away. I'm the one who thought there was a real market for second weddings. I guess I needed to think there was the possibility of a second chance . . . for love." She nearly choked on her tears as she said the last word. God, why was she embarrassed?

"Wait," Andrew said, "there are a few important things that you don't know."

But Lily shushed him. "Nothing is more important than what I'm about to say. I haven't exactly been truthful with you all."

Andrew blinked.

Jo blinked.

Sarah didn't move.

"Right now," Lily continued, her voice dropping a few octaves, "I'd love say, 'Hey kids, everything will be fine because I have unlimited funds from dear, dead Reginald.' " She dropped her gaze and added, "But that's not the way it is."

They all stayed silent, staring at Lily.

"The truth is," she continued, "we've nearly spent all of my allowance from the inheritance. Unfortunately, Reginald left his beastly sister in charge of dispersing my money to me. There's plenty left, but I can't get to it without going through her. Without begging her." She sighed an out-of-character sigh. She rubbed her temples again. "I had so hoped to stretch my allowance by investing in our little business. I was hoping to thumb my nose at Reginald's sister. But the truth is, unless we get some kind of income soon, I'll be out of ready cash, so we'll be bankrupt anyway."

Eyes moved around the room, not knowing where to land.

"Oh, Lily," Jo said at last. "Honey. I thought you had enough to fund us for a year."

"At first I thought I did. But you know me. I've never been good at doing the math. And besides, why would I want to alarm any of you? This is the most fun I've had in years."

Fun? Yes, it had been fun. It wasn't as if Second Chances had been a lifelong dream for any of them. It wasn't as if their lives depended on it. It had only been a spontaneous idea, another hoot. It had only started because Elaine had picked out such a tacky second-wedding dress.

They could go back to being once-a-year friends, couldn't they?

"Well," Jo said, "I, for one, have nothing better to do right now. And the rent's paid until November. My mother really wants to have a wedding and there would be no refunds at this late date. Maybe I'll stick it out. For a while, anyway."

"I don't need a paycheck," Sarah said. "I can't let Marion and Ted get married without my golden linden leaves."

Jo saw small tears begin to slide down Lily's always-happy face. "I love you guys," she said. "I'm really sorry."

"Me, too," Andrew interrupted, "because the picture's not as bleak as everyone seems to think."

Just then, the small bell over the showroom door tinkled.

"I'll get it," Sarah said. "Hey, maybe it's our first real client. Maybe it's Lassie or the Bionic Bride who's come to rescue us."

They exchanged quiet smiles.

Sarah disappeared. When she returned, she wore a scowl. "Jo?" she asked. "There's a man here to see you."

"A man?" Jo wondered. *The noteman?* No, she thought, getting up from the stool. It couldn't be him. "Excuse me," she said as she stepped from the back room out into the light, and into the nightmare that once had been a dream.

# 44

"Brian," she said because there he was and what else could she say? Could she tell him about the crushing sensation in her chest or the heat that burned her cheeks? "Brian," she said again.

He looked so much older. There was gray in his hair and gray in his skin and his blue eyes seemed pale and their shimmer was gone. How could he look so much older when it had been only months since that last night at the pub, since he'd calmly left the table and walked out of her life?

"Jo," Brian said. "Oh, Jo, can you ever forgive me?"

If he'd used different words she might not have hesitated. But those were the same words he'd asked the night he'd found her in Boston after all those years, the night when she'd been foolish enough to take him back.

"Where's the woman?" she asked, remaining in the

same place where her feet had rooted when she recognized his frame and his much older face. "Your wife, I believe?" She wondered why—and when—her feelings had swung to anger. No love. Only anger.

He shifted on one foot. "Frank told me that you knew," he said. "Or should I say, Frank's *investigator* told me when he found me in Switzerland." His tone was oddly accusing, as if his brother had dared to interrupt his life.

"So where is your wife? Did her money run out, too?"

He closed his pale eyes. "I don't blame you for that. Will you ever understand how ashamed I was of losing everything you had?"

*He's looking for sympathy*, she realized. *"Feel sorry for me, baby."* She stood up straight. "You weren't ashamed, Brian. You were angry it was gone."

He shifted again, onto the other foot. "I married her again so I could pay you back."

" 'Again'?" Jo asked. "You married her *again*?"

The world stopped breathing then, awaiting the resolution of two former lovers: the deceiver and the deceived.

He closed his eyes. "What did you think I'd been doing all those years? Did you think I never had a . . . woman?"

She felt a slow burn now, a feeling she was unaccustomed to in Brian's presence. *Brian-pain*, she realized. Bastard.

She raised her head. "And did you think I never had a man?"

He sighed. "Jo, please. My first marriage to her hadn't worked. I thought about you too much."

"Really?" Jo asked. "Or did it stop working because she stopped giving you cash?"

"You have no idea," he said, "what it was like to always be second-best. Not as rich or successful as other people. Just like when I was a kid. Not as clever as my brother. Not as obedient. Not as good."

"Stop blaming Frank for your failures, Brian. For once in your life, stand up and be a man."

"I am," he said. "I'm here, aren't I?"

Then his brother came through the front door. "He's only here because his wife told him to leave when she learned the truth," Frank said. "Admit it, Brian. You came back because you figured Jo was the one woman you could count on. The one woman you could use."

Brian could not, did not, speak.

And Jo's anger turned to pity for the man who, even as a boy, when the game became too stressful, simply packed up and ran. The realization almost made her feel sorry for his wife. Almost, not completely.

And then Jo said, "Brian, your charm won't work on me this time." She took another breath. "Twice," she said. "You left me twice. Once with a baby. Once with . . . nothing." She shook her head as if to reassure herself. "You won't have the chance again."

In the numbing death of love that followed, Andrew entered the showroom and sat down at the desk; Sarah moved into the doorway and leaned against the wall, arms folded, quiet.

Then the front door opened again. Lily came in, stood next to Frank. She must have gone out the back exit and come through the antiques shop.

Jo's friends had Brian surrounded: This time, he wouldn't get away.

Best of all, Jo knew that she no longer was alone.

And all Brian said was, " 'A baby'? There was a baby?"

"You're way too late," Jo said. "Too late for a lot of things." It sadly occurred to her that if there had been a child—an Amanda or an Emmett—Brian might have used her or him to try and stop Jo from doing what she did next.

She took a long, slow breath of strength gathered from the presence of her friends. Then Jo reached down, picked up the telephone receiver, and dialed the West Hope Police.

Embezzlement.

It would not be difficult to prove, according to the police who listened to Jo's story. It would, however, be tough to get her money back. Especially if Brian were in jail, doing ten to fifteen years.

The money didn't matter, Jo said. She no longer cared.

On the way from the police station back to Second Chances, Andrew suggested lunch at the luncheonette two doors down.

"I never wanted to press charges in Boston," Jo said, staring at her uneaten grilled-cheese sandwich.

"He did it to you; he did it to others," Andrew said, which turned out to be true. Frank's detective had found three other woman Brian had scammed in the years between Montreal and Boston, the years that Brian had been loving others while Jo had been working to succeed.

"It must have been difficult to face the truth about your brother," Sarah said to Frank.

Across the table, Frank chewed his tuna sandwich and didn't say a word.

"Frank had covered up for Brian for years and years," Lily explained. "Going back to when you were kids, right, honey?" She nudged Frank, who only nodded. "He was finally sick of it," she said. "He was sick of Brian hurting other people, hurting Jo."

So, Jo thought, Frank apparently had known much more about his brother than he'd been willing to divulge. Jo could hardly blame him. Brian had probably used his charm on Frank, as well, charmed him into thinking he was responsible for the detours in Brian's life. Frank had, after all, been the older brother. The one who had been clever, obedient, good.

Jo shook her head. "How could I have been so stupid?"

"Love," the women said simultaneously.

The men, however, had no comment.

"I used to feel so smart," Jo said. "No matter what was happening around me, I always felt that I was smart enough to make things work."

"You are," Sarah said. "We all are."

"Speak for yourself," Lily added, which made Jo laugh and that felt good.

"Hey, kids," came a voice from the coffee-shop doorway. It was Elaine. "Mrs. Kingsley at the bookstore told me you were in here. Forget about your lunches. I have news."

"As do we," Andrew said, but she waved him off.

"We have an event to plan," she said excitedly. "A woman is on the phone. She and her husband want a different kind of second wedding, a lavish affair in order to renew their vows. You won't believe this, but she said 'the sky's the limit.' " Her cheeks became pinker as she quickly talked.

"She's on the phone?" Jo asked. "Now? Over at the shop?" Silverware rattled. Chairs clattered. They all stood up. Andrew pulled some wrinkled bills from his pocket, while the women scrambled for the door.

"She really means it," Elaine chattered as they hustled from the place. "She's from New York and she has lots of money. Her husband is some kind of media mogul. Her name is Irene Benson. Her husband's name is John."

# EPILOGUE

**DO**
*Enjoy your day!*

Marion's wedding went off without a West Hope wrinkle, which was pretty surprising considering that the women of Second Chances were also immersed in planning a New Year's Eve extravaganza, two hundred New York wedding guests (small but tasteful, *elegantly* tasteful, Mrs. Benson had requested) to be held "somewhere in the Berkshires." The event would infuse a cache of money into the second-wedding business: The women were in charge of everything from arranging the ceremony to securing food and entertainment for the guests, and hotel rooms for everyone, including the inevitable swarm of paparazzi who'd attend.

Marion's wedding, however, was first. It was a sparkling

Indian Summer day. Sarah's linden tree leaves glimmered in the bronze sunlight; Lily's hand-calligraphied cards that noted the donation to The Mount were excitedly received; Elaine was a bridesmaid, not a bride, in a matching pearl gown made at the last minute by the grumbling but dependable woman from Chestnut Hill.

Jo stood up for her mother, still emoting disbelief that Marion no longer was a woman on her own.

Just before they walked down the gold-carpeted aisle, Marion said to Jo, "So, it's a happy ending after all."

Jo did not quite understand, but Elaine nodded. "Thanks to your idea, Marion," she said.

Marion then smiled. "Should I tell her or should you?"

And there among the linden trees, before the second-wedding vows were said, Marion Lyons told her daughter that Elaine's wedding had been a setup.

" 'A setup'?" Jo asked. "What on earth do you mean?"

It was simple, really, Elaine said. Oh, she had wanted to marry Martin, at least, she'd thought she did. But once again, she planned to marry at the town hall. She had not even thought about a formal second wedding. Until the night she'd announced her engagement at a library meeting.

"We need to talk," Marion had said, so they'd gone out for coffee after the meeting. And they had talked.

"I'd give anything to have Jo home again," Marion had said. "I don't know what's happened in Boston, but I think she's having a tough time. If you asked her to be a bridesmaid, maybe she'd remember that West Hope isn't hopeless after all."

And how could Elaine ask Jo without Lily, without Sarah?

So the scheme was planned, Jo took the bait, and she came home.

"No harm done?" Marion asked and kissed her daughter on the cheek as the processional began.

And Jo just laughed and said no, no harm had been done at all.

After the ceremony, Jo and Andrew stood under the tent, sharing apple slices and cheddar cheese. She told him that, as a wedding gift to his bride, Ted had bought one of those new condos over by Tanglewood. Marion pretended she didn't need all the closet space, but seemed to revel in the thought of central air-conditioning.

"But now my mother wants me to move into her old house," Jo said to Andrew now. "I told her no, I never dreamed I'd come back to West Hope. I sure don't want to move into that place."

"There are worse things," Andrew replied. He looked handsome in his pearl-colored tuxedo.

Jo supposed he was right. She could be Brian, now in jail, awaiting trial and a sentence and heavy restitution once he was released. Not that Jo expected any money. But at least he had been stopped, if only for a while. And at least her heart had, at last, caught up with her head. The Brian-pain was gone; Jo was ready to move on.

"I'm afraid we've kept you so busy," Jo said to Andrew now, "that you've had little time for your dissertation."

Andrew laughed. "Life's too short to spend it working."

"I think you said that to me once," Jo said with a broad smile. "And you might not believe this, but I listened. And now, I have a date."

Andrew sipped his champagne, and looked off toward the wedding guests. "With a man?"

"Yes, silly," Jo replied. "With a man. A man who lives in my building. He's from Brussels."

"Brussels, as in Belgium?"

Jo slowly nodded, her gaze following Andrew's toward Marion and Ted, the happy couple.

"And you have a date?"

"Yes. Tomorrow. A real-live date. Who knows what it will lead to."

"Right," Andrew replied and sipped again. "Who knows anything."

As the sun began to dip behind the mountains, a big, round harvest moon rose in the autumn sky. Dinner had been served, the tables had been cleared, and the air was filled with dance music from the small orchestra.

Andrew found Cassie by the gift table, examining the white-and-gold-wrapped boxes and the yards of ribbons and bows. He watched her for a moment: She looked so grown-up in the cranberry dress Jo had helped her find, her hair in curls atop her head, accented by a crown of Sarah's golden linden leaves.

"May I have this dance?" he asked, and Cassie turned to him and smiled.

"So," she said, as he took her in his arms and eased her onto the dance floor. "You didn't tell her, did you?"

She meant, of course, that Andrew had not told Jo that he wasn't gay, that the whole thing had been a ruse.

He shook his head. "I can't, honey. I almost told them

the day Jo said that they should close the business. But that would have been selfish again; I only would have done it so I'd have a chance with Jo."

"What stopped you?"

"Lily. When she said she had no more money, I saw how they pulled together. It's what real friends do. Besides, I knew when the women heard about John and Irene's wedding everything would change. The media will be all over it; it will put Second Chances on the wedding-planning map. I don't want to blow that with headlines about how the former Andrew David had been a big, fat jerk." He didn't add that between now and then, he could only pray that Jo wouldn't fall for this new man from Brussels. It was, indeed, his penance, reparation for his lies.

"Plus, now you won't feel guilty for spilling all their secrets in the magazine."

"Not their secrets, honey. Just the things that make them real women, not shallow fakes."

She seemed to think about that. Then she said, "Will you tell them after John and Irene's wedding?"

"Yes, honey." It was a promise he'd made to himself, a self-imposed deadline that would determine his future after that.

"Well," Cassie said and stood on her tiptoes to kiss Andrew on the cheek, "at least you saved their business. I love you, Dad. But sometimes it's not easy to figure out what makes men tick."

Andrew tickled Cassie on her side, then twirled her around, savoring the mellow sounds of music mixed with the magic of her laughter. Then he realized he had gone through the entire day without thinking about Patty, so he guessed life could be good.

*Lesson #9*, he thought. *Nothing ever stays the same. Which is why sometimes—if we're lucky—we get second chances.*

# ABOUT THE AUTHOR

JEAN STONE lives in western Massachusetts in the foothills of the Berkshires. ONCE UPON A BRIDE—the first in a series about the women of Second Chances—is her eleventh novel from Bantam Books. A former advertising copywriter, she is a graduate of Skidmore College, Saratoga Springs, New York. For more information on the author and her books, visit her web site at www. jeanstone.net.

AND LOOK FOR JEAN STONE'S
NEXT DELIGHTFUL NOVEL FEATURING THE
WOMEN OF SECOND CHANCES . . .

# TWICE UPON
# A WEDDING
by
# JEAN STONE

READ ON FOR A PREVIEW. . .

# JEAN STONE

AUTHOR OF *ONCE UPON A BRIDE*

# Twice Upon a Wedding

For these best friends,
once is never enough....

BANTAM BOOKS

# Twice Upon a Wedding
## April 2005

It was one of those smiles.

It was secretive, mischievous, almost happily naughty.

It was not the sort of smile Andrew would have expected of Elaine. Especially on the day she should have been married. Especially as she wore the gown of a bridesmaid, not a bride, and stood on the top of a grassy slope, overlooking the magnificent grounds of a magnificent estate, watching a wedding reception that should have been hers.

He crossed the lawn and moved next to her. She stood apart from her friends—Lily, Sarah, and Jo—yet was dressed like them in a Vera Wang gown of oyster and pearl. On Lily the dress looked like sassy haute couture; on Sarah, mysteriously earthy and sensuous; on Jo, heart-thumpingly gorgeous. On Elaine, it simply looked like a nice dress, more palatable than the clash of colors she often wore, more fashionable than the stretch pants and big shirts of the car-pooling, PTO-president Mom.

Elaine turned to Andrew, her smile unflinching. He knew that the past weeks had been tough, that she'd risked her future security, her children's happiness, and the success of her best friends' new business when she'd broken her engagement to Martin because "I just have to," she'd said.

"Lainey," he asked, "how are you doing?"

She tipped her head toward the crowd, her lacquered brown hair rigid in its French twist, as she'd called it ("An *up-do*," Lily had corrected). "Fine," Elaine said, "or at least I will be."

"When this wedding is over?" It was the celebration of Jo's mother's new marriage, this one to Ted, the West Hope, Massachusetts, town butcher. It was also the debut event for Lily, Sarah, Jo, and Elaine, once college roommates, now partners in Second Chances, second-wedding planners for second-time brides.

Elaine looped her arm through Andrew's and stood a bit taller. "I'm tired of being ordinary, Andrew. I'm tired of having a predictable life."

He kept his eyes on her. She didn't waver. "There's nothing wrong with being predictable,

Lainey," Andrew said, because so many times he'd longed for just that.

"But my kids are practically grown and I'm unattached. I'm forty-three years old and I want excitement. I want pizzazz."

*Pizzazz* was an old-fashioned, Elaine kind of term, like *French twist*, Andrew supposed. "Well," he replied, because despite months of working to untangle the puzzle, he remained quite clueless about how a woman's mind worked.

Elaine paid no attention to his hesitation. She merely nodded with seeming resolve. "What I want is a makeover. Inside and out."

"A makeover?" His laugh seemed too quick, even to him. "You're going on TV? A reality show?"

But Elaine didn't laugh in return. She took a deep breath, touched her hand to her heart, and said, "The only reality is going to happen right here. Elaine McNulty Thomas is finally going to be like someone else."

Andrew fell silent. Then his eyes followed hers toward Lily, Sarah, and Jo, who stood twenty feet, yet light-years, away. "You want to be like one of them?"

Elaine shook her head. "I want to be like them all."

Andrew slowly smiled. He felt new material building on the gossip horizon, juicy new fodder for the magazine column he secretly wrote. "That would be a tall order for anyone."

Elaine nodded yes. "But I'm going to do it," she said. "What's more, I'll do it in time for the Benson wedding on New Year's Eve."

Andrew's right eyebrow cocked. "In less than twelve weeks?"

Her gaze still didn't waver. "I can do it. I will."

He patted her hand. "I'll tell you what, Lainey. If you succeed in your quest, I give you the first dance at the Bensons' reception."

"And if I don't?"

He smiled and looked back toward Lily, Sarah, and Jo. "Something tells me you will." There was no need to add that he had a goal of his own set for New Year's Eve, if he could just hold out that long.


She was born in Saratoga Springs, New York, where the elite once went for mineral baths and the horses still ran in August. Elaine's father owned a restaurant—*the* restaurant, McNulty's—where reservations were required in season unless you were a Blakely or a Swanson, in which case your table was available any night at any time.

Elaine had been happy to wait on all of them, to remember their names and take their fussy orders and practically curtsy, because that was her job and her fat tips ultimately sent her to Winston College, where she'd been the first in her family to earn a degree.

It hadn't been a bad life.

When she'd been fifteen or sixteen she'd tried to emulate the ladies who wore subtle, chic dresses and stately, wide-brimmed hats, not plain, unimportant clothes like her mother's had been. But once racing season ended, Elaine's mother convinced her she looked out of place. It had been Elaine's last girlhood attempt to *spiff,* her father called it, to *buff,* her kids would have said.

"To look *ele-ghhhant,*" would have been Lily's term.

Lily, of course, could have been any of the thoroughbred ladies. She'd always known what to wear and what to do to look perfect all the time.

But the truth was, Elaine had always felt more comfortable, more *Elaine,* in the bright colors and splash that her mother said were too gaudy but Elaine thought were simply cheerful. Once out of the house, once she was an "adult," Elaine had dressed as she had pleased.

So, maybe she'd been wrong.

She stared at her bedroom ceiling now, eyes wide open despite the fact that it was two a.m. She thought about Lily: she would ask her to serve as her fashion and beauty coordinator. Because no matter what Elaine wanted to believe, what the magazine articles touted, or what the Ph.D.'s said on *Oprah*, Elaine suspected that a makeover must begin on the outside, not on the in.

"How you look is who you'll be." It was a line Lily used often, but it could have come from any of the ladies at the Saratoga restaurant thirty years ago.

She rolled onto her side and snapped on the bedside lamp, her adrenaline softly pumping with anticipation, just enough to prevent sleep, her thoughts awhirl with what changes she'd make and where on earth she would start.

She thought about the chic dresses and the wide-brimmed hats, Lily's kind of clothes. Then she thought about her walk-in closet packed with polyester in every color of the rainbow and some colors in between. She thought about the high-heeled ladies of Saratoga, and about her sensible sneakers and square-heeled pumps lined up according to shades of spring green and magenta and goldenrod for summer.

Tasteless, she sensed, but could not help herself.

She thought about the red patent leathers that matched the red-and-mandarin-striped dress she'd worn last Easter. Lily would have been horrified. It didn't matter that Martin had liked the outfit; she wouldn't think of Martin right now. Or Lloyd, either, damn him.

*Out with the old*, her adrenaline commanded. *You'll dance with Andrew on New Year's Eve, and you'll be the belle of the Benson ball.*

Bolstered by the voices of her imagination, Elaine flung back the comforter. There was only one place to begin this romp, and it was directly across the room.

One polyester, two polyesters. She yanked them from their hangers and dumped them onto the floor. With every yank and every clatter of every hanger, she felt absolved somehow, unburdened, free.

"*Out, out, damn spot!*" she shouted at a purple polka-dotted shirt that she'd worn with purple pants.

"*Off with your head!*" That to a bright pink hoodie that her son said made her look like Peter Rabbit in drag.

She stopped when she reached the royal blue suit that she'd worn for her justice-of-the-peace wedding to Lloyd over twenty-years before. She stared at the tiny pinholes where her corsage had been: three tiny white roses, tied with a pink ribbon. She'd worn a hat, though they'd long since gone out of style. It was a small red pillbox with matching red netting that scooped across her forehead and was torn years later when her daughters were playing dress-up.

She wondered why the suit still hung there, as if the wedding had been yesterday, as if Lloyd had never left her.

The wedding hadn't been like Marion and Ted's.

It hadn't been like the one Elaine and Martin would have had today if she hadn't broken the engagement because she'd realized in time that Martin was merely a Band-Aid, that even kind, kindly Martin could not ease the pain deep in her heart. She simply hadn't dared to let herself love him enough.

Her marriage to Lloyd had not been elaborate. It had been a simple town hall ceremony, with only Lloyd's brother, Russell, and his sister, Celia, as witnesses. Elaine's parents hadn't come down from Saratoga, because she hadn't told them. They thought she was in the middle of her final exams. They didn't know that she and Lloyd were getting married because they didn't know she was pregnant.

She reached inside the suit jacket and touched the waistband of the skirt. She remembered it had been too tight that day—her belly had swelled above average.

*Throw it out*, the new voice inside her urged.

Her eyes widened, her mouth dropped open. *"Out!"* she commanded, then pulled the suit off the hanger and hurled it past the closet door.

"Mother! What are you doing?" Karen, her youngest, had always been a light sleeper. Like her mother, she was the one always on alert, waiting to be sure no one in the house needed anything, because serving others was what she gladly did. Karen was just like Elaine in all those selfless, get-you-nothing-but-headaches and nowhere-but-miserable ways.

"Sorry, honey," Elaine said. "Did I wake you?"

"Wake me? Of course you woke me. Who are you shouting at?" Her head rotated around the haphazard piles of polyester. "Good grief. What *are* you doing?"

"I'm starting my new life." Elaine stopped her purge for a moment. Karen was sixteen, the last child at home: Kandie and Kory were at college. Karen was also the most like Elaine, dressed now in a flannel nightgown and knee socks, her face shiny with night cream from the supermarket health and beauty aids section because it was more economical than the department store kind. Karen had watched Elaine shop economically long before Elaine's checkbook was reduced to a modest alimony: the girl now hoarded babysitting money the way Elaine hoarded coupons and re-used plastic baggies.

Karen stooped down and retrieved the purple polka dots. "But Mom, you love this shirt." She clutched it to her breast as if it were her firstborn.

Elaine laughed. "You're right, honey, I did. And I loved your father once, too." As soon as she'd said those words, she wished she could take them back. She wished she could rewind the moment and erase the sting now visible on her daughter's face.

"I hate it when you're mean to Daddy," Karen said.

Elaine sighed. She returned to her hangers,

some of the fun now gone from her energy burst. "I'm not mean to your father, honey. I'm sorry I said that. It's just that my clothes are out of style and so am I. It's time for a change."

Karen disregarded her mother's apology and continued to rummage another pile. "Your wedding suit," she said. "You're throwing out your wedding suit?" Elaine might have chosen to toss the family jewels for the pain in her daughter's voice.

"Honey . . ." she began.

Karen's eyes narrowed. "Are you trying to be like her?" She did not have to elaborate on whom she meant by *her*. *Her* was Beatrix—Trix—as Lloyd had called her, a county judge, who happened to be pretty and smart and rich, and who happened to have stolen Lloyd from Elaine.

And married him.

And left him after a year and eight months, right after Elaine and Martin got engaged.

"No," Elaine said. "I'm not trying to be her." Elaine didn't know if Karen would think that was a good or a bad thing; the issue was simply too sensitive to ask. The divorce, after all, had been hardest on Karen. Kandie, who was as much like Lloyd as Karen was like Elaine, had not hidden her approval of the new Mrs. Thomas. Then again, Kandie and Elaine hadn't gotten along well since the girl had turned twelve. Kory, Elaine's son, had tried to stay in the middle, not wanting estrangement from his mom or his dad. Karen, who'd been only thirteen the night Lloyd walked out, still believed her parents would get back together, still tried to encourage Elaine to wait for him.

Especially after Elaine broke up with Martin, and the second Mrs. Thomas broke up with Lloyd.

Especially now that it looked like Elaine might have a chance with her ex-husband, as if she wanted one.

"Life changes," Elaine said quietly. "Sometimes we need to move on."

Karen threw the suit back on the floor and quickly left the room.

Of course, she slammed the door.

WJB

July 30,
singing at New Lusk

2700 North Mulberry
Barn on fire